D1245674

Lady Wynwood's Spies series

Recommended reading order

The Spinster's Christmas (prequel)

The Gentleman Thief (prequel novella)

Lady Wynwood's Spies, volume 1: Archer

Lady Wynwood's Spies, volume 2: Berserker

Lady Wynwood's Spies, volume 3: Aggressor

Lady Wynwood's Spies, volume 4: Betrayer

Lady Wynwood's Spies, volume 5: Prisoner

Lady Wynwood's Spies, volume 6: Martyr

Lady Wynwood's Spies, volume 7: Spinster (coming soon)

Standalone novels

Prelude for a Lord

The Gentleman's Quest

Devotional

Who I Want to Be

Lady Wynwood's Spies, volume 3: Aggressor

A Christian Regency Romantic Adventure serial novel

Camille Elliot

Camy Tang
P.O. Box 23143
San Jose, CA 95153-3143
www.camilleelliot.com

Publisher's Note: This is a work of fiction. Names, characters, places,
and incidents are a product of the author's imagination. Locales and
public names are sometimes used for atmospheric purposes. Any
resemblance to actual people, living or dead, or to businesses,
companies, events, institutions, or locales is completely coincidental.

Lady Wynwood's Spies, volume 3: Aggressor/ Camille Elliot. — 1st
ed.

eBook: ISBN-13: 978-1-942225-25-6
Print book: ISBN-13: 978-1-942225-26-3

I am crucified with Christ: nevertheless I live; yet not I, but Christ liveth in me: and the life which I now live in the flesh I live by the faith of the Son of God, who loved me, and gave himself for me.

Galatians 2:20

"And ye shall know the truth, and the truth shall make you free."

John 8:32

Chapter One

Michael Coulton-Jones knew he ought to be profoundly relieved to be breathing, to be in his right mind, to not be injured or crippled or maimed. But at this moment, after waking in a dark, windowless room that held only a cot and the faint smell of moldy potatoes, all he could think of, the sole need that consumed his thoughts, was the dire straits of his bladder.

He sat slowly, sensing that he had been asleep a long while, an unnatural sleep rather than a convalescing rest. His limbs were stiff, but not sore. His head was fuzzy, but not in pain.

What had happened to him? He remembered ...

Silas's meaty fists, slamming into his face, his torso. He clearly remembered the moment one of his ribs had cracked, the pain radiating out like a spiderweb on fire.

He had been hauled down the stairs of the brothel and tied to another chair as he struggled. The ropes had not been as tight as others he had escaped from. If he had time, he could wriggle free. The door leading outside was only a few feet away from him.

And then ... what had happened?

He sat up, his head feeling a bit light and disconnected from his body, but his torso ... no pain. Not even a phantom of pain from the injured rib. How long had he been asleep? He looked down at his arms and legs, but they seemed the same as he remembered. He had not been like unconscious patients who woke months later.

The wall was close enough for him to reach out and touch it, to use it to help him to stand. His overfull bladder groaned in pain at the movement, and he gritted his teeth. His legs were rather sore, reminding him of when he had been recovering from a sword wound. This tightness in his muscles was similar to how he had felt weeks—no, months after the injury. He now noticed a similar dull ache in the muscles of his back, his shoulder.

He straightened, but did not feel dizziness. He would have attempted to stretch if it wouldn't have made his bladder burst.

He gingerly stepped in his stocking feet to the wall beyond the foot of the cot, where the outline of the door was just visible in the gloom. He reached for the latch, and there was none. He pushed, but it wouldn't budge.

He pushed again, with the same result. He was locked in.

Was he still captive? But someone had dressed him in nightclothes made of fine white lawn, a gentleman's garment, and there were fine knitted stockings on his feet, although no shoes. He doubted captors like Silas and that other man would bother with his comfort or his recovery.

The thought of the other man, pale-eyed and cold of expression, made nausea rise in his stomach. He remembered the taste of blood in his mouth, but not his own. Bitterness, then a numbness on his tongue.

He had drunk the Root.

But he didn't remember what had happened after that.

He had been aware of the muffled voices of servants, which perhaps explained the dark room—he was in a storeroom, maybe next to the kitchen. The voices were strangely clear, despite coming through the thick walls.

And then he heard a bell-like voice he recognized.

Isabella.

He couldn't quite hear her words, but he would know her

voice anywhere, no matter how she disguised it. They had played that game as children, he, Richard, and Ugly, one of them hiding behind a bush or tree and trying to guess who had spoken. Ironically, Richard's gift for obscuring his voice had trounced Michael and his sister more often than not.

He began to pound on the door.

And all the voices abruptly stopped.

Surely they knew he was here. They had placed him here, had taken the effort to lock the door from the outside. Why the shocked silence?

He pounded harder, more insistently. He began hopping from foot to foot, trying to squeeze his pelvis and keep his lower regions from exploding.

He wasn't certain how he knew, but people approached the locked door. He heard the whisper of their booted footsteps, their hastened breathing. He even clearly heard a shaking whisper, "What should we do?"

He could immediately tell that it was his sister who had said it, no matter how low and soft.

"Let me out!"

Someone stepped closer to the door, and he could smell Isabella's faint lily of the valley perfume, but she still did not speak, although she must have heard him.

"Let me out! I can hear you breathing!"

"Michael?" Isabella breathed. "Is it you?"

What a strange question. Who else would it be? "Ugly, I'm going to burst if I don't use the privy."

There was a gasp, then a muffled laugh. The gasp was perhaps his mother—that didn't surprise him—but strangely, the laugh didn't sound like his sister.

But then he didn't have time to analyze the laughter because someone was turning a key in a heavy iron padlock. Metal clanked, and the door rattled, and then swung open.

He met three startled pairs of eyes. His sister's glass-green, but then also Lady Wynwood's wide eyes of dark gold, and Miss Sauber's mirthful ones the color of sea-foam.

Oh, good Lord.

It was at that moment that he realized he wasn't in his mother's house.

Michael couldn't look anyone in the eye after returning from the privy in the small paved back area of the house, which he belatedly realized belonged to Lady Wynwood. What surprised him was how wary the servants were as they escorted him upstairs to a guest bedroom, as though he were a rabid dog they were trying not to antagonize.

It was a distinctly unpleasant feeling, that somehow these people *feared* him.

The footman who drew his bath for him was a bit older than himself, with slightly spiky red-brown hair that reminded him of Richard, his brother. The footman's dark brown eyes appeared to be watching Michael closely. But after a few minutes, the footman had apparently seen something in his face or come to a decision, and thereafter did not act any more gingerly than a servant helping a man who had been unconscious for several days.

Or was it weeks? He didn't know. And not knowing was an empty chasm in the pit of his stomach.

"How long was I unconscious?" he asked the footman.

"Seven days, sir," the man answered readily, without a trace of the discomfort that his mother's servants would have displayed at such a strange question.

Upon reflection, he should have known it was not very long, but he'd had an irrational fear that he had lost weeks of time.

The bath was very hot, and it relaxed muscles he hadn't realized he had tensed because of the strange situation. But he did not linger long. Despite the excruciatingly embarrassing moment outside the storeroom door, he still desired to see the women and discover what had happened to him.

And why he'd been *locked in a room.*

The reason why drifted in his conscious mind in threads, the threads he remembered of the dream he'd had before waking. But perhaps out of denial, he didn't pull at those threads.

Not yet, not just yet.

However, he had to wait for his clothing to arrive. The footman dressed him in the late Lord Wynwood's dressing gown and slippers, informing him, "We have sent to your rooms at the Albany for your clothing, sir."

"But my rooms are locked, and I have no manservant," Michael said.

The footman paused, then said, "It will not be a problem, sir."

"Anyone will be unable to enter unless they alert the house manager. It would not do to communicate the fact that I am absent from my rooms."

The man's mouth worked open and closed, and he seemed to be struggling to answer.

"Out with it, man," Michael said.

"Clara can pick locks, sir," the footman finally said.

"Er ... who?"

"Clara, our scullery maid. Lady Aymer gave permission for her to, er, use her skills on your room door."

"Your maid can *pick locks?*"

"She had a colorful childhood," the footman said with a blank face.

He then remembered a rumor he'd heard once about Lady Wynwood's household. Her servants were never improper, but the rumor had been that they were from decidedly unconventional—perhaps even scandalous—backgrounds.

So Michael let the matter go.

And as the footman had said, it was not a problem, because

his clothing arrived a mere half an hour later. By then, he had long since wolfed down the tray of food that had been brought to him and had been clawing at the (very nicely papered) walls in his impatience to learn what had happened to him. He eagerly donned more respectable clothing. At last, he would get some answers.

Except that he wouldn't, at least not right away. As soon as the footman had opened the bedroom door, Miss Gardinier appeared and entered. Before he could question her for her improper behavior, she had latched onto his arm and forcibly shoved him into a chair near the fireplace.

"Miss Gardinier?" he asked at the same time the footman said, "Miss?"

"You have been very ill, Mr. Coulton-Jones," she said as she rather scandalously tested each of his limbs. "If I had been here when they opened the storeroom door, I would have examined you sooner."

No, he was rather glad she hadn't, or he might have piddled all over the floor.

"Do you feel dizzy? Weak? In pain?" she asked.

However, at the time she asked, she was examining the inside of his mouth and he couldn't immediately answer.

"Wa-wa," he grunted.

"Excuse me?" Gray eyes blinked at him.

He pulled his jaw away from her surprisingly strong fingers and said, "I feel quite well."

Actually, he felt unusually well. He hadn't noticed before, but now that he was more aware of his body, he realized that the aches from old injuries were missing—the slight twinge he'd always felt in his shoulder from the knife wound he'd acquired on one of his earliest missions, the stiffness from the elbow he had dislocated on yet another mission, the hip that had never quite felt the same after the explosion on the smuggler's ship that had tossed him and Sep into the Channel.

There was something clinical and yet inquisitive about Miss Gardinier's gaze, and so he told her about the missing pains.

But her reaction was strange. She turned pale and bit her lip, then said, "You were given the Root."

He had known. Of course he had known, for what else could be that memory of blood and bitterness in his mouth? And yet, having her tell him was somehow like a surprise.

But at that moment, swift movement at the open bedroom door was accompanied by a strident voice saying, *"Keriah!"*

Miss Gardinier looked distinctly guilty as she rose and faced Lady Wynwood, whose lips were pressed so firmly that they had disappeared in her stormy face.

"Calvin came to Lissa's house and told me that Mr. Coulton-Jones was awake." Miss Gardinier was obviously attempting to sound reasonable as she said, "Of course I'd rush here to ascertain that he was well, after what has happened to him."

"What *has* happened to me?" Michael demanded.

Lady Wynwood fixed Miss Gardinier with a steely eye. "You may have indeed had Mr. Coulton-Jones's health in mind, but that does not excuse this highly improper behavior."

She had had a physician's detachment as she had examined him, but it had still been rather embarrassing, so he didn't bother to speak up in her defense.

Lady Wynwood turned to Michael. "I apologize, Mr. Coulton-Jones. Won't you please join us in the drawing room?"

"Mr. Drydale—" he began.

"Is present. As is tea."

He'd eaten everything on the tray, but he was still rather famished, so he followed with alacrity.

When he entered the drawing room, he was again attacked— er, approached, but this time by his sister. She reached up and placed her hands on either side of his face, staring into his eyes. It seemed a long time since she'd done that, and he saw the ghost of his brother in her eyes, exactly the same shape and color as Richard's.

"Hullo, Ugly."

The nickname brought a sheen to her eyes, but she blinked it away and released his face, then sent a hard right cross to his shoulder. "You are so infuriating, Smelly."

"Why?"

"Would you really like me to list all the ways?"

"Not really."

"Just so."

He was surprised to find his childhood friend Thorne was also present, but even more surprised by the wariness on his face as he came up to Michael. "How do you feel?" he asked cautiously.

"I am well," Michael answered in an equally cautious tone.

Thorne simply nodded, but didn't quite look like he believed him.

Miss Gardinier had entered the room behind him, and she now said to Lady Wynwood, "My lady, we should have Dr. Shokes examine him."

He would much prefer Dr. Shokes over another examination from Miss Gardinier, even though he was fairly certain she knew what she was about.

Lady Wynwood looked to Mr. Drydale, who had approached behind Michael's sister, but his brows drew together. "I still haven't heard from Dr. Shokes, so we have no method of contacting him."

No method of contact? What about his brother's apothecary shop?

Before he could ask, Lady Wynwood said, "Aya suggested my household doctor, Dr. Heddetch."

Mr. Drydale seemed to be considering it. "Do you trust him?"

"He has been our doctor since before Wynwood died, and he is friends with many of the servants, but I can't say I personally know him well. Aya is closer to him than I."

Then Mr. Drydale shook his head. "I don't want to bring in

more civilians. We can't go into detail about Mr. Coulton-Jones's illness, and after Mr. Shokes ..."

The room grew quiet, until Michael finally demanded, "Will someone explain what has happened?" He could also see a tea tray on the table beyond Mr. Drydale and he was starving.

Everyone was seated except for Miss Sauber, who had risen to her feet when Michael entered the room but had not approached him. It made him unaccountably miffed, until she gave him a plate heaped with piping hot scones slathered with butter, while limiting Thorne to only one.

However, she wouldn't meet his eye, and he wanted her to do so. Perhaps it was simply his dream affecting him, making him yearn for more of her attention. He began to wonder what could have happened to change their relationship while he was asleep. In the days before ... *whatever* had happened, he had been growing closer to her, despite his reason telling him to stay far away from her. Now that he had his wish, he felt disappointed.

Mr. Drydale did not make him wait long. As Lady Wynwood and Miss Sauber served tea, he asked Michael, "What do you remember?"

"I was captured by Silas and a pale-eyed man. They beat me, and then ..." He swallowed, his throat suddenly dry. "... they gave me the Root, I think."

"And after that?" Mr. Drydale asked.

He shook his head. "I don't remember." That may not be entirely true. He remembered rage and darkness, and he remembered sea-foam green eyes and light. Or was that simply his dream?

And so Mr. Drydale told him what had happened. How Sep had gone looking for him with Lady Wynwood's pageboy, how Michael had become a monster.

He knew it had been forced upon him. He knew he hadn't been in his right mind. And yet he was appalled. It felt as though he had ripped open a seam in his soul and seen ugliness and putrid darkness, and it all belonged to him and were a part of him.

"Did I ..." His throat felt raw. "Did anyone ...?"

It was Lady Wynwood who seemed to understand what he was asking. "Unlike when Mr. Dunmark became a crazed madman, no one was badly injured, and no one was killed."

He closed his eyes in relief. He didn't understand why—he had killed before, on missions, sometimes in self-defense, but sometimes not. It was never an easy task, but he performed his duty, a soldier for the Foreign Office.

And yet he was profoundly glad he had not killed any innocents on English soil. It would have weighed too heavily upon him. Because of Richard.

Mr. Drydale also explained how they'd herded him back to the burned factory, and suddenly the sea-foam green eyes in his dream, and the lights, made sense to him. It seemed rather silly now, to have been so moved by those images. And yet, now, *he* was the one who couldn't look at Miss Sauber.

"We were able to render you unconscious with the sedative made by Phoebe and Miss Gardinier," Mr. Drydale said. "In order to dose you, we, er ..."

"I shot you with arrows laced with sedative," Miss Sauber said calmly.

So the mysterious angel in his dream had shot him. *Again.* Any lingering doubts as to how she felt about him were firmly laid to rest. Women did not dispassionately shoot arrows at men they might be fond of.

"Arrows?" He looked down at his arms and legs. "I have no injuries."

Miss Gardinier glanced at Lady Wynwood before answering, "They had closed by the time we brought you here."

"It is fortunate that Miss Gardinier has received some training from her surgeon uncle," Mr. Drydale added.

"I am fortunate to be alive at all." He had not intended to say it, such raw and emotional words, but they flew from his mouth. "I know that the crazed man several weeks ago collapsed because his body could not withstand the stress of his anger and strength. And Mr. Dunmark ran blindly into a horse and was trampled." He had known, even while guarding the two young women in the apothecary stillroom, that it had been fortunate that the ones who had found the Root had been Miss Sauber and Miss Gardinier, who were more interested in creating a sedative than recreating the elixir. "If you had not been there to help me—if there had not been the sedative to put me to sleep—I would be dead. I owe all of you my life, and I am grateful."

Isabella was sitting in the chair next to him, and her hand reached over to twine with his. "I am grateful, as well."

He looked around, suddenly noticing ... "Where is Sep?"

Mr. Drydale explained about searching for Sep, finding him at the church only to lose him again, and then tracing him to the stable.

He was shocked that Isabella had revealed to them her secret. She had kept that secret for close to six years now on orders from a supervisor she would not disclose even to Michael, even though her brother had been the agent sent to protect her on her first crucial mission. However, he now suspected that she worked for the secretive department the Ramparts, since Mr. Drydale had been the one to contact her when needing help to find Sep.

When he heard about Mr. Shokes, he then understood Mr. Drydale's reluctance to use Lady Wynwood's doctor. But he also found himself taut with worry. "Do you know if Mr. Shokes told Jack about Miss Sauber and Miss Gardinier?"

Mr. Drydale had a grim look as he shook his head. "However, Mr. Rosmont and, er, Prince have been shadowing the two young ladies, and there doesn't appear to be anyone watching or following them."

At Isabella's confirming nod, he relaxed. Aside from Sep, his sister was one of the few people he knew who could utterly disappear into a crowd. If she could not see anyone who might be a threat to the young women, then he could be confident they were safe.

But Mr. Shokes's betrayal forcibly reminded him of the danger threatening them. He again experienced the nausea he had felt when he discovered Richard had been killed because of what he'd been investigating.

But he also could not repay the young women's actions with the insistence that they did not belong here. Because it was only through their work than he and Sep were now alive.

"Septimus is chafing in bed, but his knee is still swollen. I only left to attend to Easter Sunday services this morning."

"Easter Sunday?" He thought back and realized that yes, if he had been asleep for seven days, then ...

"Ironic that you would wake today, of all days, Smelly," Isabella said to him.

If he had a better relationship with God, he might have thought it was a sign, or a mark of spiritual favor.

"But you were asleep considerably longer than three days," Isabella added.

"I don't feel as though I've been asleep for so long," he said slowly. In fact, now that he had eaten, he felt more energized and strong than he could remember feeling in years.

He reached for his teaspoon. "My lady, I apologize. I shall buy you a new one." He grasped each end *and bent it.*

There was only stunned silence in the room.

He laid the bent spoon down gingerly. His hand looked as it always had. He felt nearly the same as usual. And yet he was not the same, not anymore.

Or rather ... for a little while, at least, he would not be the same.

"Sir," he said to Mr. Drydale, "you told me what Dr. Shokes

said to Miss Sauber and Miss Gardinier about a man who had been given the Root, but hadn't had another dose."

Isabella had also apparently heard it, because she bit her lip and squeezed his hand.

"We might be able to ... reproduce the Root," Miss Gardinier said in a small voice.

"We may have a clue as to the location of Jack's greenhouse," Miss Sauber said. "But ... the pale-eyed man mentioned that the current batch of plants may have caused the Root to be tainted."

"Tainted?"

"It turns men into Berserkers—what Jack called them—rather than simply giving them strength. It was what happened to Nick. However, Mr. Shokes collapsed first before becoming a Berserker later."

"If we can find some of the plants Jack uses," Miss Gardinier said, "we could ... *maybe* reproduce the Root. But it may not work."

"I do not wish to take the Root again," Michael said firmly. "And especially not if I will become a monster again."

"But ..." Isabella's hand gripped his so tightly he felt his bones creak. "But Michael ... that man who hadn't taken another dose of the Root died. *You'll die.*"

"I know, Ugly."

He had rarely seen her cry. She didn't like to show weakness to anyone, but she also didn't cry in front of him or Richard because she didn't want to worry them. So now, as her eyes swam in her stoic face, she rose and hurried out of the room. Thorne hurried after her.

He knew he had hurt her. But the rage and darkness had frightened him more than any of the dangers he'd faced in France, and he did not want to face that again. And something buried deep inside of him, something he thought he'd lost, clamored that it would be wrong for them to try to create the

Root, that it would be wrong for him to take the Root again.

There was a strained, awkward silence, but then Lady Wynwood said in a quiet voice, "Phoebe, I should like to speak to Mr. Coulton-Jones in private for a few minutes."

She and Miss Gardinier both rose, giving polite curtsies, and left the room, followed by Mr. Drydale after a nod in his direction.

Miss Sauber hadn't looked at him, and while a part of him knew that it would be best not to become close to anyone now, he had wanted to look into her eyes and see how she felt about all of this. And yet, perhaps it was better that he didn't know. Perhaps she felt nothing. She had shot him, after all.

He did not pretend to feel indifferent, but he said to Lady Wynwood, "You needn't be concerned about me, my lady. I have faced death before."

"Not perhaps in this way," she said with equanimity.

"Not exactly," he admitted, "but I was always willing to face death when I went out on missions." He would not be reprimanded by the Foreign Office for admitting to going on missions, not now.

"Was death ever as much of a certainty as now?"

He wanted to say that his death was not a certainty, that they knew nothing about what would happen to him because no one had ever become a Berserker and lived. But he was not in the habit of lying to himself like that. And he had to admit to himself that somehow, this situation seemed worse.

Perhaps it was because of *her*. Not that he would have allowed himself to surrender to his attraction to her. He would have fought it, just as he fought it all the years previous during the few times he saw her at social functions.

He could tell that the pull toward her was even stronger than before, perhaps because she had helped to save his life. Perhaps because she was very similar to his sister in that she knew what he had done for the Foreign Office and not only accepted it, but was involved in it. But it would have been even more necessary that he not act on his feelings, because they were too dark and bleak to allow anyone to get close.

He didn't realize that he hadn't answered Lady Wynwood until she said quietly, "I will not tell you what to believe, but I believe God will save you."

"I know you are very devout, but I would not have thought you'd request a miracle from the Almighty."

"The Almighty performs miracles every day. We often don't see them. God was watching over you—over all of us—when He led Phoebe to find the Root sample, when He gave Keriah wisdom to create the sedative. He guided Phoebe's arrows, even the one on Hampstead Heath."

"I can admit that it was an extraordinary coincidence that those particular ladies—a botanist who is friends with a chemist —found the Root only a few days before I was forced to take it, and that they have the moral character not to be tempted by it like Mr. Shokes had been," Michael said. "But to be honest, I don't know why God would bother with me, after ... all I've done."

She did not pry or ask what he meant by that, but she simply said, "And yet, you are here, alive."

"For now."

She gave a sad smile at his reply. "I believe God will save you," she repeated. "However, I also hope you will settle in yourself how you feel about God and what you believe about death."

He nodded, but didn't answer her.

He knew that he must get his affairs in order, that there were many little things he must see to. But right now, he simply felt numb and alone. Lady Wynwood believed God would save him, but couldn't share that belief.

He didn't believe in miracles, and certainly not for someone like himself.

Chapter Two

The man she was beginning to care about would die soon. Which made it very hard for Phoebe to focus on treacle buns.

Strange as it might be, the treacle buns may hold even more importance than the man, in the grand scheme of things. But as she took the carriage toward Miss Tolberton's home for a visit, all Phoebe could see was Mr. Coulton-Jones's bleak face as he declared he would prefer to die rather than take the Root.

She understood him. She even felt she would choose the same, if the alternative was to become a mindless beast. But she could not so easily accept it, and the emotions had become a tempest of wind and waves and lightning and hail inside of her.

She did not want him to die.

It wasn't as though she had had hopes. She was not so foolish, not after four unsuccessful Seasons. She was too ineligible and he was supremely uninterested. So why did she feel so empty now, as though she had lost something precious?

If she could, she would do something to save him, certainly. It frustrated her that there was nothing she could do.

But essentially, he was nothing to her and she was nothing to him. It would be wisest and most logical for her to take an emotional step back, to allow him to connect with his family, to not form new bonds with him. Or rather, to not strengthen the bonds that had begun to form. Hadn't she learned her lesson about forming emotional ties that could be severed and cause her pain and anguish? Mr. Coulton-Jones was not like her father, and it would not be by his wish, but he would still sever his ties.

She was ashamed of herself because she hadn't been able to look at him in her aunt's drawing room. The knowledge of what he was going through had felt like a flood washing over her head, and she hadn't wanted him to see that in her eyes, nor to have her emotions gush out and embarrass him. And herself.

She visibly started when the carriage stopped in front of Miss Tolberton's house, and Clara, sitting across from her, asked, "Miss? Is something wrong?"

It took an effort of will to draw her mind from maudlin thoughts of Mr. Coulton-Jones. "I am well."

They descended from the carriage and rapped on the door, where a butler let them in with alacrity. "Miss Tolberton is expecting me," Phoebe told him as he took her pelisse and bonnet.

"Of course, Miss Sauber."

Earlier last week, Miss Tolberton had made her promised call upon Phoebe at the time she and Aunt Laura and Keriah had been visiting Mr. Ackett for the first time, so Phoebe had sent a note 'round asking when would be convenient for her to return the visit.

After Clara had been dispatched to the kitchens to wait, the butler led Phoebe through the house. She had been here several times before, mostly during evening parties that the Tolbertons hosted during the Season, and twice for intimate luncheons among the set of friends with whom Miss Tolberton played archery.

The house was small but very richly furnished, which tended to make Phoebe nervous that she would accidentally brush against a vase and knock it to pieces. There were copious portraits of ancient Tolbertons staring down their noses at visitors, and while the drawing room was newly refurbished with the latest fashionable pieces, other areas in the house were crammed with old family heirloom furniture, heavy and dark and smelling like spiders.

Miss Tolberton and her father were like their house—both small and richly dressed. Miss Tolberton was always at the first stare of fashion, while her father was conservative and a cold representative of his ancient lineage.

Phoebe met Mr. Tolberton at the landing on the grand staircase, and she gave a respectful curtsy.

"Miss Sauber, is it?" An irritated crease formed between his brows when he had to crane his neck to look up at her. "I imagine that lately, your father is quite distressed."

Her face was placid as she replied, "We are seeking a quick resolution, sir."

"Ah, good, good. It is always best to be reconciled as soon as possible."

He had misunderstood the word she used, but she did not correct him. "I am come to call at the request of your daughter."

Another crease formed between his eyebrows, but this time it was not directed at her. However, he only said, "I see. Enjoy your visit."

"Thank you, sir." She gave him another curtsy.

To her surprise, the butler guided her not to the drawing room but up another floor to Miss Tolberton's bedroom. It was a large, spacious apartment decorated in peach with emerald-green accents, a rather bold color combination, which somehow did not quite match the sweet, delicate personality of the woman herself.

Miss Tolberton was dressed in a long-sleeved morning gown of pale apple green, with lace lavishly trimming the sleeves and collar. Her fine golden-brown hair had been swept up in a casual knot, and it had a hint of red from the sunlight streaming through the windows.

She greeted Phoebe with a wide smile that brought out her dimples, then instructed the butler, "I am not at home to any other callers."

"Very good, miss." He bowed and closed the door as he left.

She led Phoebe to the settees in front of the blush-tinged fireplace where a lavish tea had been laid. "I hope you do not mind that we may have a comfortable coze here. I feel as though we are drawn closer to one another through our shared harrowing experience." She gave a little laugh.

It was unusual to see her in high spirits. She was never a gloomy personality, but she was often quietly sweet in company with the other guests at archery tournaments or at evening parties. Just as Phoebe had seen another side of her with her charity organization at the church, here was a Miss Tolberton further unfettered from the strictures of polite society.

"I have been eagerly awaiting your call." She began pouring tea for them. "I realized that I did not know your preferences, so I asked Cook to make all manner of good things for us to enjoy."

"I am overwhelmed by your kindness. Everything looks quite delicious."

As Miss Tolberton handed Phoebe her teacup, the long sleeve of her frilly morning gown rose a few inches and exposed her wrist. There was an ugly purple bruise circling it, in the shape of a man's fingers.

Miss Tolberton did not notice at first, until she followed Phoebe's gaze. Her face paled and she tugged the lace to hide the bruise.

It had not been there during the Layton sisters' archery party, when Miss Tolberton had laced up the leather gauntlets she wore when shooting. Neither had it been present at the church, when she had removed her gloves in order to serve treacle buns to Phoebe, Keriah, and Mrs. Laidlaw.

In a slightly over-bright voice, Miss Tolberton said, "How strange it is that I find myself more interested in knowing you now that we have experienced something quite shocking and exciting together. I do hope it is not scandalous of me to say so."

"Of course not. I feel the same. It was quite a distressing occurrence. I was surprised to see you at first, but it was rather comforting to have an acquaintance there."

Miss Tolberton's expression grew troubled. "Was your servant able to speak to Mr. Brimley?"

"He was quite clever. Instead of speaking to him, he followed him to a stable, then returned to tell us."

"Oh! That is very clever, for I had doubted Mr. Brimley would have spoken to your servant at all. Did you find Mr. Ackett?"

"Yes, we returned to the stable later and found him there, injured but alive." Phoebe hesitated, but then decided that Miss Tolberton was likely to hear the story—or a version of it—eventually through her work in the Long Glades, so she might as well confess all. "However, we also found Mr. Shokes, the apothecary, in the stable, and he was dead."

Miss Tolberton gasped. "How terrible! Dr. Shokes was very close to his brother, if I recall. And Miss Gardinier appears to be quite close to the family."

"Did you know the apothecary very well?"

"No, I am afraid not, although some of the other women from the Society of the Benevolent Voice in the Wilderness for the Rescue of Souls Lost in the Darkness of Heathenism have spoken very highly of Dr. Shokes."

Phoebe sipped her tea, which was very hot and strong. "I had no knowledge of your charitable works before, Miss Tolberton. You have kept your good deeds quite hidden."

"I believe good deeds ought to be hidden, but I must also admit ..." She sighed as she served Phoebe an orange sponge biscuit. "I was apprehensive about how people like Miss Farrimond might react if they knew I associated with people in such a low area."

"I don't believe you should care much about what people like Miss Farrimond think of you," Phoebe said tartly.

Miss Tolberton gave a wide smile that was a tiny bit wicked. "That is exactly what I would have expected you to say, Miss Sauber."

"Why, thank you. You mentioned that you visit the women in the area? What do you speak to them about?"

Miss Tolberton's face was neutral as she said, "We are to speak against the wickedness of their ways and entreat them to turn toward the righteousness of God and the church."

Phoebe wasn't certain how to respond to that, so she sipped her tea. It sounded ... rather judgmental and proud.

Miss Tolberton sighed. "But I prefer gossiping with them."

Phoebe snorted her tea.

"Oh! Miss Sauber, are you all right?" Miss Tolberton handed her a cloth napkin.

Phoebe dabbed at her face and a few drops that had fallen onto her dress. "What sort of gossip?"

"Oh, nothing mean-spirited. I like to hear what their neighbors are doing, whose husband found employment, whose child had a birthday, who fell ill. I have become quite familiar with many of the families in that area, which was why I recognized Mr. Brimley."

"It was fortunate for us that you did. I hope you were not scolded by Mrs. Laidlaw."

Miss Tolberton absently stirred her tea. "The ladies in the group are all quite nice. But I am not as interested in spreading their religious message so much as meeting and interacting with the people in the Long Glades and providing needed supplies."

"What manner of supplies?"

"Oh, when we visit a family. I usually leave a basket with

things like blankets, clothing, perhaps some cuts of meat, and always a nice, bright bunch of flowers. I find that cheers the women up immensely."

"Flowers? Are you able to buy flowers in the Long Glades?"

"Goodness, no. I enjoy growing flowers in my greenhouse."

Phoebe was startled. "Miss Tolberton, you are interested in gardening?"

"Oh, yes. I especially enjoy growing poppies. I have extensive experience with the different varietals."

"I enjoy growing roses, myself."

"You do?" Miss Tolberton's eyes shone. "Why, Miss Sauber, we have known each other for over four years, and yet this is the first I have heard of our shared interests, aside from archery."

Phoebe said sheepishly, "I am afraid I am rather focused when it comes to archery, and think of little else when I attend a tournament. And I have usually been so tense when attending balls and parties that my conversation skills are lacking."

"Do you have a greenhouse?"

Phoebe hesitated. "It is on my father's estate."

Miss Tolberton had doubtless heard the rumors about Phoebe and her father, the same as Mr. Tolberton, and she politely replied, "I use a greenhouse on a small property outside of London which my father bought several years ago. I drive out there nearly every day."

"How lovely! I am never so happy as when I am elbow-deep in potting soil."

The two young women laughed together.

"Do you belong to any botanical societies?" Miss Tolberton asked.

"Oh, several. I attend their meetings when I am in town for the Season."

"You will think me cow-hearted, but I have not had the courage to attend association meetings alone."

"It can be very intimidating. Shall I send you a note when next I will attend a meeting?" Phoebe asked.

"Oh, yes, please!"

They delved into a discussion on types of fertilizer for different flowers, until Phoebe realized that she must leave soon and she had not yet acquired the information she had specifically come to get. "By the way, Miss Tolberton, I quite enjoyed the treacle buns you brought to the church. Where did you buy them?"

"The treacle buns? Yes, they were quite delicious, were they not? I get them from a little bakery on the far edge of the Long Glades, on Elm Street. Strangely, it doesn't have a name, although the residents call it Finlay's Bakery, after the owner."

"On Elm Street, you said? Is it nearby the church?"

"Oh, no, it is quite far, but it is on my way to the church. The bakery is near ..." Miss Tolberton wrinkled her nose. "It is near a candlemaker's, which is known to sell good candles at inexpensive prices, but the smell is rather ... pungent."

"I shall ask my servants, perhaps."

"Oh, yes, do not go there alone, Miss Sauber. It is not a *very* bad area, but it is not an area for proper young ladies."

And Phoebe was oh, so proper.

"Speaking of that," Miss Tolberton said with consternation in her blue eyes, "might I ask you not to tell anyone in our archery circle about my work with the Society of the Benevolent Voice in the Wilderness for the Rescue of Souls Lost in the Darkness of Heathenism? I don't wish to announce to anyone about my charity work, for it would seem too much like bragging while pretending to be humble."

Phoebe was amazed at Miss Tolberton's sensitivity. "Of course, if that is your wish. But I personally feel that your work is quite admirable."

"I thank you." Miss Tolberton smiled. "Shall I see you at Miss Farrimond's archery party next week?"

Phoebe felt an uncomfortable wriggling sensation in her breastbone. "I had not known about it. I probably have not been invited."

"Not invited? That is outside of enough!" To her surprise, Miss Tolberton's eyes blazed with fury. "Simply because you are staying with your aunt? It is hardly scandalous. Miss Farrimond can be so petty."

Phoebe tried to be generous. "It may not be in her control. Her father may desire to cull favor with mine, or with my father's fiancée."

Miss Tolberton's eyes softened. "I noticed that odious Mr. Vernon cheated at the Layton sisters' archery party when he mentioned your father's engagement in the moment before you shot your last arrow. I hope you will forgive me, but you seemed quite upset about it." She asked shyly, "Are you resigned to your father's remarriage, or is it causing problems for you? I don't wish to pry, but I would like to offer help if I can."

"That is quite kind of you. My father did not tell me until the morning of the archery party, so I was still in shock over the news."

"But that would mean … Mr. Vernon heard the news before you did? Before his own daughter?" Miss Tolberton's expression was indignant. "I also saw the events at Miss Farrimond's party, with your father and his fiancée. I was looking for you later in the evening when I heard you had left the party early. I don't understand why your father would treat you thus. Is there truly nothing I can do for you?"

Phoebe was touched by her concern. "My father wishes to send me to Bath to care for an elderly aunt and doesn't wish me to remain in town for the Season." Especially since he had already stolen her dowry. She damped down the surge of anger and continued, "I am endeavoring to convince my father to allow me to stay."

"But if you are staying with your aunt, Lady Wynwood, why

should he be affected if you stayed in town? Is the elderly aunt in dire need?"

"I don't believe so ..." Although she wouldn't put it past her father to say that Grand-Aunt Bethia was quite ill and Phoebe was being selfish in refusing to attend to her.

"Even if your aunt isn't in need, your father might put it about in society that she is, which would paint you as an uncaring and ungrateful daughter, Miss Sauber," Miss Tolberton said, as though she had read Phoebe's mind. "This is quite untenable!" Her dark pink lips pulled into a pout, and she looked like an angry kitten.

"I appreciate your kindheartedness on my behalf, Miss Tolberton." But in reality, what could be done?

Miss Tolberton seemed to realize that, also. Her expression became hard. "It is quite unfair that men have such control over women, regardless of their wishes, and even sometimes their best interests." She rubbed her wrist, apparently unconsciously. "My father was displeased with me because I made up an excuse in order to refuse an invitation to dance with Mr. Adderly last night."

Just the mention of his name made Phoebe's shoulders tense. Mr. Adderly had an unsavory reputation for stealing kisses— and perhaps more—from young women in dark corners whether they wished it or not. Luckily, Phoebe was much taller than he and so he had never asked her to dance. But he often manipulated his dance partners into walking with him in the garden or along an empty corridor in the house.

"Perhaps your father does not know of Mr. Adderly's reputation?" she asked weakly.

Miss Tolberton's eyes grew flat and hard. "He does, but he does not care, because I am not his daughter. I am his pet."

Phoebe understood that scorn. She felt it herself every time she remembered her forged signature on the funds transfer documents that stole her dowry.

And yet they were both helpless. It was as Miss Tolberton had said—men had control over women, regardless of their wishes.

"Is there nowhere you may go to escape from him?"

Miss Tolberton's expression grew soft, resigned. "No. Miss Sauber, I envy you. For if I had an aunt living in London, I would move out, also."

Phoebe would never have expected beautiful, petite and feminine Miss Tolberton to ever say that to her.

Miss Tolberton saw her discomfort and distress. She smiled to try to soothe it away. "Goodness, I have become maudlin. Pray, forgive me."

"There is nothing to forgive."

"My only excuse is that I have come to feel so close to you, Miss Sauber."

"It is a shame that we have known each other for four years and yet have never had occasion to speak so candidly with each other." While she valued Keriah's friendship, it had sometimes been lonely for her to have no one amongst their social acquaintance who shared her love of gardening. Phoebe felt she was such a boring person, and she had no one with which to share the few topics of conversation she most enjoyed. Yet if she had made more of an effort to reach out to those around her, she might have found Miss Tolberton's hidden depths long before today.

Miss Tolberton smiled. "We can make up for lost time by becoming quite good friends from now on, shall we?"

Phoebe found herself returning that infectious smile. "I should like that very much."

Miss Tolberton stood at a window and inched aside the curtain. Down below, Miss Sauber's carriage pulled away from her home and left with a clatter of wheels.

She did not know what to make of Miss Sauber.

On the day she'd seen Miss Sauber at the church, she had arrived early to find two women speaking to the rector most urgently. She recognized them as two of the more talkative gossips in the area, Mrs. Seymore and Mrs. Ellis. "Did you hear of it?" Mrs. Seymore was asking the rector, but when she saw Miss Tolberton, she immediately hurried to her. "Did you arrive alone, Miss Tolberton? The streets might be dangerous today."

"Nonsense, Sarah," Mrs. Ellis said to her friend. "It happened last night."

"What happened?" Miss Tolberton asked.

"A man—"

"He must have been drunk," Mrs. Ellis interjected.

Mrs. Seymore glared at her friend. "I was getting to that. A drunk named Archipelago Constipation went absolutely mad."

Miss Tolberton thought privately that if she had a name like that, she'd go mad, too.

"No, it wasn't him," Mrs. Ellis said impatiently. "He was the one *before* this one."

"Oh, you're right. We don't know this one's name."

Miss Tolberton was completely turned around and dizzy trying to follow their conversation. She looked to the rector, who sighed and said, "Mrs. Seymore, Mrs. Ellis, you are confusing Miss Tolberton."

"Oh, I apologize, dear," Mrs. Seymore said. "We'll start from the beginning again. Last night some unknown man went completely mad."

"A drunk," Mrs. Ellis repeated. "He destroyed property and injured a score of people."

"He may have been drunk," Mrs. Seymore said, "but it seems strange, doesn't it? That Mr. Constipation man was supposedly drunk, but he was the same way."

"He destroyed property?" Miss Tolberton asked.

"Smashed up doors and windows," Mrs. Seymore said.

Miss Tolberton's breath caught in her throat. She remembered hearing about the other man—although she hadn't known his name—who had displayed remarkable strength as he ravaged carts and attacked people. He had eventually been trampled by a horse. And there had been another man just like him last night?

"But then those people showed up," Mrs. Ellis said, apparently irritated that her friend was taking too long to tell the story. "And they seemed to be trying to lead him away."

"Foolish thing to do," Mrs. Seymore said. "The man was dangerous, I tell you."

"If they hadn't, he might have hurt more people," Mrs. Ellis said. "I wonder who they were?"

"Where did they lead him?" Miss Tolberton asked.

"One of those burned factories on Harding Lane," Mrs. Seymore said.

Mrs. Ellis leaned in close and lowered her voice. "And then the strangest thing happened. That crazed man just *disappeared*."

"Now, Mrs. Ellis, you mustn't spread rumors," the rector chided her.

"It's true! My cousin lives nearby and she heard the ruckus, and then suddenly the sounds stopped. And when people got the courage to come out to see, the factory was empty."

The rector looked worried. At the time, Miss Tolberton hadn't known about Mr. Ackett lying injured in the basement. He had likely been concerned that his injured guest had something to do with the crazed man.

She had arrived early and had time to spare, so Miss Tolberton had made an excuse to leave. A few streets over, she found a hackney to carry her to Harding Lane so she could see the factory for herself. And outside, on the street, she had found it.

A broken arrow. Finely made, like the ones she used herself at her archery tournaments. What was even more curious was that she recognized the fletching, although she couldn't place it at first.

She returned to Brannon Church. Mrs. Seymore and Mrs. Ellis were long gone, but she was shocked to see Lady Nola descending into the basement.

Miss Tolberton knew all about Lady Nola. She was primarily a midwife, but she knew much about the human body and was often called upon to physick patients. Lady Nola was rather taciturn, but Miss Tolberton had spoken to her several times and they had once had a short conversation about herbs.

Miss Tolberton followed Lady Nola to the basement, where she'd immediately recognized Mr. Ackett. Lady Nola had warned her not to say anything to anyone, and Miss Tolberton had returned upstairs in a state of shock.

Then several minutes later, those men had arrived and taken Mr. Ackett away, and in following them out of the church, she'd seen Mr. Brimley accompanying them. And then she'd suddenly seen Miss Sauber, of all people!

Miss Sauber was one amongst her archery friends whom she would never have imagined to see in an area like that one. Miss Sauber was not snobbish, certainly—not like Miss Farrimond—but she had seemed very comfortable in her world of polite society and not the sort to venture out of it.

And as soon as she saw Miss Sauber, she remembered where she'd seen that fletching before. It had been Miss Sauber's arrows, which she said she fletched herself.

What had Miss Sauber to do with that man who had gone mad the night before? She remembered Mrs. Seymore and Mrs. Ellis talking about a group of people who led him away to that factory. Why had they done that? And what had they done to the crazed man, the second in several weeks to appear in the Long Glades?

She had also heard rumors about a *third* man, weeks ago, who had been the same—apparently drunk, violently destructive, and impossibly strong. He had killed two men before suddenly collapsing in the middle of a road, dead.

And Mr. Constipation less than a fortnight ago, and then the man she had heard about at the church. Three men with extraordinary strength, extraordinary rage.

And today's visit had been curious. What had made Miss Sauber want to know about treacle buns?

She had considered confessing about finding the arrow, but something had held her back. Even beneath Miss Sauber's normal, friendly, polite face, there had been something ... intent, and implacable. A stone wall that Miss Tolberton had never seen in her eyes before.

And so now, as she watched Miss Sauber's carriage roll away, she resolved to simply wait and watch.

Yes, she would keep a close eye on Miss Sauber.

Chapter Three

It was late in the afternoon, around the time most of fashionable society would be circling in Hyde Park, when Laura heard carriage wheels outside her home. Within minutes, Sol arrived with his houseguest, Mr. Ackett, who was hobbling on crutches.

"Good gracious!" Laura had not expected him so soon after his dreadful evening at Jack's stable. "How did you manage the stairs?"

"Slowly," Mr. Ackett replied.

"Septimus is a stubborn cuss," Sol said acidly. "He insisted upon accompanying me."

They had arranged to meet today, when Laura would be "at-home" to callers. Her neighbors were accustomed to a stream of visitors and would be less likely to remark upon this group, arriving near the end of calling hours so as to avoid any other guests.

Phoebe had adjusted a seat for Mr. Ackett so that he hadn't as far to step before he could sink into a chair near the fire and the tea tray. Keriah, strangely, had simply stood and curtsied to him. For once, Laura couldn't read the girl's face, which was a calm, polite mask.

It was only a minute later that another carriage arrived, and soon Lady Aymer and Mr. Coulton-Jones were shown into the drawing room, accompanied by Mr. Rosmont.

Mr. Coulton-Jones looked very calm, just as he had when he snuck out of Laura's home yesterday. But then she peered more closely at him and realized that rather than calm, he was dazed ... and desolate.

He had insisted on returning to his rented rooms at the Albany as soon as possible, since it was scandalous for him to remain in her household, even though it was a closely guarded secret. He had insisted he felt well, and Keriah hadn't found anything wrong with him—aside from his supernatural strength. Without Dr. Shokes to give his opinion, there had been nothing else they could do for him.

However, he had agreed to have her footman, Fred, accompany him as his manservant for a few days. She had been surprised to hear that he didn't have a manservant, so it was convenient to send Fred, who could alert Laura and Keriah if Mr. Coulton-Jones's health took a sudden turn. His sister had insisted that it would be folly for him to live alone after what had happened, and he couldn't use one of his mother's servants, who would tell his mother about his activities.

Phoebe calmly poured tea for their guests. However, Laura caught Sol's slight frown as he looked at Phoebe, and she knew the girl couldn't quite hide her pain.

Because it was very obvious to Laura that her niece was in pain. She had always suspected that Phoebe had a slight preference for Mr. Coulton-Jones, despite not interacting with him much over the years, and in the few days before his rampage, they had interacted even more. She may have come to care for him more than she even realized herself, and news of his condition would have caused her some inner turmoil.

Or perhaps her pain was related to her worry over her father and what he intended to do. Laura could relate to how helpless and angry Phoebe was feeling, because she spent years under the yoke of a cruel man who only cared about himself. But she also remembered the black winds that had shrouded her head and her heart, and she didn't want Phoebe to have to struggle against that darkness.

By unspoken consent, they all looked to Sol to begin. He had a troubled expression as he looked at Phoebe and Keriah. She knew he was struggling with the necessity of using civilians—and two young women, at that—in this dangerous work, especially in light of what had happened to Mr. Ackett and Mr. Coulton-Jones. And yet they had been invaluable in saving the lives of those two men.

Unusually, Sol hesitated before speaking. Then he sighed and said, "If you were all my usual agents at the Ramparts, I would deliver a sound insult to all of you and then ask for reports of your assignments."

"You can still insult us, Uncle Sol," Phoebe said placidly, although there was a twinkle in her eye.

"I would prefer not to be insulted," Keriah said.

"Why don't we start with reports, then?" Lady Aymer said with a smile. "We'll start, if you approve?" she asked Sol, who nodded.

Mr. Rosmont cleared his throat uncomfortably, with a quick glance at all the women in the room who were not his childhood friends, but then began, "Prince and I searched Mr. Farrimond's house last night. Since Nick and the pale-eyed man were at his party searching for Michael and Mr. Ackett, we expected he would have long destroyed the message that Mr. Ackett saw Silas deliver to the Farrimond servant. But we found it in the smoking room."

"Thank you for telling us where to find it, Miss Sauber," Lady Aymer said with a nod at Phoebe.

"Unfortunately," Mr. Rosmont said, "all the note said was, 'Our business is now concluded.' It was signed only with the symbol."

Sol gave a deep, disappointed sigh. "They cut off ties with

him."

"It seems that way," Lady Aymer said. "Jack's group knew that Mr. Farrimond had been exposed."

"It was likely due to the affair with Allinton." Sol glanced at Phoebe and Keriah. "Did Laura tell you about it?"

Phoebe nodded. "Jack's group likely knew Mr. Farrimond had been compromised the moment he delivered the false parcel."

Sol's face was grim. "We have known since last summer that there was a mole in the Foreign Office. If we had known about Farrimond sooner, we could have questioned him."

"Will you still question him now?" Laura asked.

Sol nodded. "However, there is nothing incriminating in the note to accuse him of treason. He might know more about the group, but I suspect he will simply say he never saw the note in his life and someone must have left it in his house."

"There is the possibility that he knows very little about the group," Laura said. "As we know from the incident with Mr. Allinton, they seem fond of giving messages with instructions, with no contact with the letter writer."

"Speaking of letters," Sol said, "have you found anything else in your letters?"

"Letters?" Lady Aymer asked.

"I have been attempting to piece together a dead man's life," Laura said. "I have been looking through old ledgers and appointment books, and I wrote to my friends to ask them to return letters I wrote to them in the year before Wynwood died. There is a great deal more than I had initially thought, but I am attempting to draw up a list of who among Wynwood's old acquaintance might match the initials from within the pocket watch."

"Any matches?" Sol asked.

"No, but I have not gone through everything yet." A thought occurred to her, and she gave Mr. Ackett a wide smile.

Something in it made him lean away from her, although his

face remained as expressionless as usual.

"Mr. Ackett, might I borrow your services? I can promise you the finest offerings of my chef if you will help me."

The skin around Mr. Ackett's eyes tightened in a grimace, but he bowed to her. She suspected paperwork was not his preferred pastime, but she also suspected that he hated boredom more than paperwork. He would not be running over rooftops any time soon, much as that might pain him to admit.

"Aunt Laura and I have also been searching through the house for other places Uncle Wynwood may have hidden something," Phoebe said.

"Did you recall any other places you might have seen the symbol?" Sol asked her.

Phoebe shook her head. "We have been looking closely in all the rooms where he liked to spend time."

"He hated being disturbed," Laura said, "especially when he sat in the library drinking, so we have searched the library from top to bottom." She winced. "The problem is that I renovated the library right after his death, and nothing unusual was found then." It had been of utmost importance to redo that room, even though they had cleaned away the blood. She never would have thought she would regret that decision.

"There is also the possibility that any of the carpenters who did the renovations destroyed what Lord Wynwood may have hidden," Mr. Coulton-Jones said.

"Or if it was valuable, they could have simply taken it for themselves," Mr. Rosmont added.

"If you like, I might look around," Mr. Ackett said.

Sol said eagerly, "An excellent idea. I know of no one else who can search a house as you can, Septimus."

The young man nodded, but there was a phantom pain in his face. Laura recalled that Sol had told her Mr. Ackett had often been used to secretly infiltrate homes and rooms to search for items, relying on his athleticism to move silently and undetected. Would he ever be able to do so again?

"Please continue to search," Sol told Phoebe and Laura. "Wynwood can't have had only one hiding place."

Laura agreed that it was likely there was at least one, if not more other places Wynwood would have secreted things he wanted to keep from the dangerous group he had associated with. She would be glad to relegate that duty to Mr. Ackett and Phoebe, because she feared she was not searching as diligently as she ought.

She was afraid, deathly afraid of what she would find and how it would make her feel.

It had to be the *library*, of all places. Perhaps at last her past was catching up to her.

"Phoebe, did you speak to your friend about the bakery that sells the treacle buns?" Sol asked.

She nodded. "It's called Finlay's Bakery, although it doesn't have an official name. It's on Elm Street near a popular candlemaker's shop, at the edge of the Long Glades. Calvin and Clara knew of it, although they're not as good friends with the owner as they are with Auntie Ann's Bakery."

Mr. Ackett's mouth quirked up at mention of the kind-hearted shop owner who had helped him to find Michael.

"The bakery is not close to either Brannon Church or the stable where Mr. Ackett was taken," Phoebe continued, "but the twins say that it is near the river."

Sol's eyebrows rose. "Now we need only find a well and perhaps a theater nearby."

"Thorne and I can search the area," Mr. Coulton-Jones said.

"Take the twins with you," Laura suggested, and Mr. Rosmont nodded agreement.

"I'll also join you," Lady Aymer added.

Mr. Coulton-Jones opened his mouth as if to say something, but then wisely heeded the pointed look his sister shot in his direction.

Lady Aymer continued, "Thorne and I have been hanging around the Rusty Lock for the past few days."

It took a moment for Laura to remember that it was the name of the tavern in Jem Town where Jack's men liked to drink together, and where Mr. Ackett and Calvin had overheard where Mr. Coulton-Jones was being held.

"We discovered how Jack knew Mr. Ackett was in Brannon Church," Mr. Rosmont said. "A veiled woman handed a note to Elliot Brimley to give to Jack that had the information about the wounded man. One of the other men saw her, but couldn't see under her veil. Her clothes were plain, but not poor."

"It may be that one of the women from that charity organization told Jack," Lady Aymer said.

"I looked into that organization," Sol said. "They were started many years ago and many people are familiar with them, although not many know what they actually do in the Long Glades. However, I discovered something rather disturbing." He cast an apologetic glance at Phoebe. "On the day you were there, only an hour after you'd left, they found a woman's body outside in the graveyard. Mrs. Pamela Wright."

Phoebe gave a small gasp. "Miss Tolberton mentioned her name. She was supposed to be there and they were wondering at her absence."

"She'd been stabbed through the heart," Sol said.

"That's difficult to do cleanly," Keriah murmured.

"She also had a crumpled veil in her dress pocket," Sol added.

"Did Jack kill her?" Mr. Coulton-Jones asked.

"But why would he do so if she was the woman who told him about Mr. Ackett?" Mr. Rosmont asked.

"Perhaps there was someone else who hadn't wanted her to tell Jack about Mr. Ackett," Lady Aymer said.

The thought of yet another mysterious group with their fingers in the pie made them all pause in grim silence.

"Those are all things to consider," Sol said, "but we ought

not to speculate in too many directions. I don't wish to spend time chasing shadows. We should remain focused. Keriah, you've been making sedative?"

"Yes, although we have been having difficulty in procuring more mandrake root. I've written to my aunt, and I am certain she could find some, but it will take time for it to reach London."

"In the meantime, I've asked some of my friends in the botanical societies to which I belong," Phoebe said.

"We're also experimenting with other roots and fungus," Keriah said, "since the sedative wasn't as effective upon Nick, who was already taking the Root."

"Is there anything else?" Sol looked around at them all. When they remained silent, he said, "We cannot continue to meet out in the open like this. Phoebe and I have managed to clean a usable room in Stapytton House. We'll meet there tomorrow, at the same time, with any new information."

Sol had used his vast resources to very quickly lease the manor house belonging to an impoverished nobleman named Mr. Stapytton, which lay just outside of London. Stapytton House was not very old, but lack of funds had caused it to fall into hopeless disrepair, which had made the leasing arrangements very easy and swift. The roof had been damaged and most of the rooms were unusable from water damage and rot, but it had a small glass conservatory that had once housed a few fruit trees, which was perfect for Phoebe's botanical experiments, and Keriah had been using the stillroom next to the kitchen for her experiments.

"Sol," Laura said, "allow me to pray for us."

He hesitated, but then said, "Please, go ahead."

She bowed her head and gave a short prayer for protection and guidance. She knew Mr. Ackett and Mr. Coulton-Jones would be embarrassed to be singled out, so she prayed for the general healing of each of them, knowing that Sol still carried himself stiffly from his time fighting with Mr. Dunmark, and the men on the Root, and Mr. Shokes.

When she raised her head, she had half-expected derision or at the very least discomfort from Mr. Rosmont, but he had a pensive expression on his face, as though her words had impacted him in some way. She had not prayed anything special, so she wondered what it had been. She somehow felt that God was trying to shake something loose in him, strange as that sounded.

Lord, she silently prayed, *Thou knowest his heart. Please continue to speak to him.*

Since facing her fears and her shame over Mrs. Jadis, she had felt her prayers had more trust behind them. Her emotions still rose up like a boiling pot every so often, but she was able to pray and seek the Lord's peace. Sometimes it worked and the anxiety did not overwhelm her. Other times, she kept praying until she felt more in control of herself.

She and Phoebe walked their visitors to the front door, but as Mr. Coulton-Jones was leaving, there was a bleak expression that crossed her niece's face, which broke Laura's heart.

They turned to climb the staircase back up to the first floor, and she hooked her arm through Phoebe's. "I have been thinking about your situation, my dear, and wondering what can be done."

Her niece stiffened, then sagged. "I don't know what can be done, Aunt Laura. A single young woman has few options."

"Just as Sol has gathered people around him to do what he cannot, we shall do the same," Laura said stoutly. "Never let it be said we were too proud to ask for help."

"Who were you considering?"

"I would like your permission to write to the Cambrook family attorney."

"Not the Glencowe family attorney?"

"He is certainly capable, but Mr. Cossman is younger. He

worked under his father before he passed away, and he can be much more *creative* in his thinking."

Phoebe gave a half-smile. "It is difficult to imagine a creative lawyer. Aren't they all old, stuffy men?"

"Fear not. Mr. Cossman may yet turn into that." They proceeded past the drawing room to the door to the library. "But for now, we shall take advantage of his unconventional way of thinking to see if he may know of a way to recover your dowry."

Phoebe sighed. "I fear that may be a lost cause, Aunt Laura. It is not that I have any marriage prospects—" Her voice caught. "—but I feel ... I feel as though someone has squashed a lovely cake I was intending to eat." She managed a smile as she said it, although there was a trembling at the corner of her mouth.

Laura laughed. "That was quite an interesting way to describe it. But you have no need for your dowry funds if you stay with me, so you may rest easy on that head."

"Will I be able to remain with you?" Phoebe threw herself down on an overstuffed chair in front of the library fireplace. "My father could simply put it about that I am being selfish in not going to help an elderly relation in great need. Even Miss Tolberton realized that my father is likely to attempt that tactic."

"I am ashamed I did not realize before, but that is very possible." Laura sat across from Phoebe. "However, there is an easy solution. I can write to Bethia and ask for you to remain with me instead of going to her in Bath."

"Will she really agree to that? She must have wanted me to come if she is trading her horses and carriage for me." Bitterness flavored her tone.

"I am certain I can offer something Bethia might want. She has always relished bargains—it is a game to her. Very well, let us play."

Phoebe rose and wandered toward the desk, piled high with papers. "Shall I help you? We have a few hours before dinner."

"That would be lovely, thank you. But first I must go upstairs to collect a shawl."

In her bedroom, Laura went to the door to her dressing room, where Aya was mending a torn hem. She was about to rise as Laura entered, but she waved for her to remain seated. "Aya, do you recall where I put the Portuguese dictionary?"

Her maid's dark blue eyes grew troubled. "Are you certain you wish to do this?"

Laura sighed. "I am afraid I must. She is the only person who might know more about Mrs. Jadis."

Aya pressed her lips together briefly, then asked, "Are you prepared for the answers she will give?"

"I must be, mustn't I?" She glanced down and realized her hands were trembling, so she clasped them together. "I must trust in the Lord to sustain me." That kind of trust was difficult for her, but she had been doing many difficult things lately.

"It's in the second drawer." Aya nodded toward a dresser in the corner of the small room.

"Thank you, Aya."

Laura retrieved the dictionary and sat at her dressing table, pulling a sheet of paper and a pen and ink pot from a drawer.

She began the letter, "*Para Senhora ...*"

Chapter Four

The inn was quieter than most, because it had a reputation for discretion, and for customers and innkeeper alike minding their own business. So anyone who had taken a room on the floor would hear the unmistakable sound of a fist hitting flesh, over and over again. But no one would come to investigate. No one would come to his rescue.

They were afraid they would be killed if they did.

The room was too small for the four people inside it. The largest man, a great beast who towered over him, was the one punching his face and his torso. The chair he was tied to was large and heavy, too wide for his slender frame but sturdy enough to keep him steady as the large man beat him. They had only tied the ropes around his chest, and he gripped the chair seat with white-knuckled hands.

One particular blow slid across his sweat-slicked cheek. His head twisted with the right hook, and blood flew into the face of the woman sitting on the bed. It splattered across her freckled skin and tangled in her straight, white-blonde hair.

"*Désolé*," the large man said.

She grimaced and glared at him, but simply wiped her face with a handkerchief.

The fourth person in the room, a short man with swarthy skin and dark, curly hair, looked up from the book he was reading as he leaned against the far wall, out of the way of the larger man's flying fists and close to the lone candle sitting on a washstand. Then he went back to his book.

No, no one would care that they were torturing him. No one would come to save him, either, because no one knew he had been taken.

The woman and the shorter man had approached him in front of a gaming hell, requesting information and privacy, which was not unusual. He'd seen them in the small back room he rented in the gaming hell for that purpose, with his bodyguard outside the room.

The large man had killed his bodyguard easily, and the three of them had carted him away.

He had left himself open, had gotten too arrogant to think no one would touch him. No one in London, maybe. He hadn't considered people from across the Channel.

He didn't want to become involved in the secret dealings Jack's group was up to. Maner simply collected and sold information. He didn't take sides. He didn't act.

Oh, except for his little project. But that had nothing to do with Jack's agreement with the French.

And while Maner had only had suspicions Jack and his cronies were talking to Napoleon's people, now he had solid evidence it was true. Too bad it was too late.

The man paused in his application of his fists to his face, and the woman gave a long, drawn-out sigh.

"Well, Maner?" She had a very faint French accent that was hard to notice if he wasn't listening closely.

He spat blood. He had been aiming at the man's boots, but he missed. "Well, what?" Except that a few teeth were loose and he'd cut his tongue, so it came out sounding more like "Wah, wha?"

She sighed again, but didn't answer. She'd already asked twice before, and was apparently not going to repeat herself again.

It galled him that these people wanted information without paying for it. He hated people like this, bullies who simply took whatever they wanted. They believed they were more important than anyone else, so they were entitled to whatever they desired. Everyone had to bend over backwards for them. Everyone had to give in to their demands.

He could give them the information they wanted, but then that would set a precedence. He couldn't afford to lose his reputation, because it was all he had. It was the only way the physically weak could survive in this cesspool of a city.

So far, they weren't certain he knew the answer they were seeking. If he indicated that he had that information, how would it change what they did to him? Would they make him an offer if that would enable them to get the information with more ease and less effort? Or would they simply keep beating him until he cracked and told them?

His entire business was based on his ability to read people, and he knew, in his gut, that they would keep pounding him. That was the type of people they were. They would never give anything if they could take it instead.

"I don't know where it is."

The woman was short, so she sat comfortably on the low bed. She leaned forward and recrossed her legs. "We have asked around in this city. Everyone says that if there is any information, Maner Hansen will have it. He deals in information. Are you saying there is information that you do not have?"

"There's a lot of information I don't have," he said testily, despite the pain. "I may deal in information, but it doesn't mean I know everything all the time. I'm not omniscient."

The large man's brows drew down in confusion at the English word, and the woman explained to him in French. In reply, the man punched Maner again.

His muscles must take all the blood away from his brain.

He eyed the woman (with his right eye, because his left one was swollen shut). "But I can find out. If you give me an offer."

She rose to her feet and approached him, and the large man stepped back. Her face didn't change from its mildly irritated expression as she slapped him soundly.

The slap burned his skin in a way the punches hadn't.

She had swung so hard that her long sleeve rose on her forearm, and she tugged it back down. "There will be no offer. Give us what we want."

He spat blood again, and this time hit her plain brown skirt.

He wasn't entirely certain how she would react, but in his experience, most women were easy to rile up. If she became angry, she might say something she didn't intend to say. It was a strategy he used often to gain information.

She looked in disgust at her skirt, but then simply nodded at the large man.

Suddenly, thick fingers were grabbing his ear, which was slick with sweat and blood.

"Owowowow ..."

He had barely registered the gleam of the man's knife before the pain swept down the side of his head.

Maner howled, every nerve ending screaming, a ringing and a roaring resounding at the same time. The pain was worse than anything he'd ever felt before. His ears had always been most sensitive to cold, to heat.

And without his ears, he couldn't do business. He couldn't survive.

She waited until his shrieking had softened to panting sobs, then she leaned closer to him. "An information merchant cannot deal in information if he cannot hear the commodity in which he buys and sells. Talk, or he'll take the other one."

"I'll talk, I'll talk," he blubbered.

"Where is Jack's greenhouse?"

"It's the top story of a boarding house in the Long Glades."
She scowled at him. "There are hundreds of—"
"It's near Fenbear's Playhouse," Maner said.
"What street?"
"It doesn't have a name."
She gave a huff of frustration. In French, she said something derogatory about the English city of London.
She motioned to the large man, then said to the shorter one, "Stay here with him."
"I told you what you wanted," Maner said. "Let me go."
She gave him a smile that was not beautiful, but somehow it fit in her pale, oval face. "You might be lying, Maner. If you are, we'll have another discussion when we return."
"What do I do with this?" The large man held up the bloody ear, which had smeared red all over his fist. The purple stone in Maner's earring glittered in the feeble candlelight.
"Bring it with us," she said to the man, but she smiled directly at Maner as her voice grew low and breathy. "I know just where to leave it."
And suddenly, despite the flaming pain in his ear, Maner's entire body felt cold as ice. "No! Don't!" If she did, he would know. *Jack* would know it was Maner. "No!" he screamed even as the woman flung the door open.
But despite his cries, no one would come to his aid. It was why she had chosen this inn, and it was why she was unconcerned as she paused in the doorway to blow Maner a kiss. The large man followed her out and shut the door behind him.
Maner began to quietly whimper, tears running down his nose along with blood and sweat and snot.
The short man barely looked up from his book. He crossed the space and lightly hopped into the small bed, leaning back and continuing to read.
Maner closed his eyes and let his breathing slow. To his

guard, it would seem he had fallen asleep or slipped into unconsciousness.

His rope bonds had loosened when they cut off his ear and he had struggled in his pain. He shifted his arm slowly, silently, bringing it more forward.

They hadn't tied his feet, so he very cautiously repositioned his leg, drawing it closer to the side of the chair, then slowly raising his foot. He watched the guard through his lashes, but the man didn't notice his movements.

He grasped the top edge of his worn, cracked boot and slipped out the naked blade that had been hidden inside the leather.

He lowered his foot as slowly as he'd raised it, then eased his arm back. He was very flexible, and he bent his elbow, moving his hand around to the back of the chair so he could saw at the ropes around his chest. They gave way with more ease than he had expected.

He froze when the man rolled over onto his side, his back to Maner.

Well, that made things a lot easier.

In one swift motion, he rose and took the few steps to the bed, then bent over and slit the man's throat. The smell of blood already filled the room, mingling with the tallow of the candle, but now Maner smelled blood that wasn't his own.

He regretted the mess when he took the man's coat and could feel the warm wetness against his neck, but he had to disguise himself as he left. The man had set a rolled up comforter and a crushed hat on the washstand, so Maner wrapped the scarf around his bleeding head, hissing as the knitted fabric touched his ear, and then hissed again when he drew the hat down low over his forehead.

The dark of the inn's hallways, and then once he was outside, the dark of the London streets hid the blood on his clothes and face. He felt dizzy, but hoped he only looked like a drunk, a common enough sight. He kept his head low so that no one would notice him, so that no one would recognize him.

He had to hide. He had to make plans to leave London—no, he may even need to leave England.

Because he was a dead man.

Chapter Five

Michael was too anxious, and it was because of the woman who was walking next to him as if she hadn't a care in the world.

Miss Sauber was merely acting the part of the wife of a simple clerk. She had her hand tucked into his arm and they were moving down a narrow street that had no name, but which was known to all as the street where Fenbear's Playhouse was located. She appeared to be relaxed, but he saw the flicker of her eyes and knew she was aware of their surroundings. And also aware of how overstrung he was.

She had already shown herself to be capable, even before he was sedated. Yet every part of him objected that she was a civilian and ought not to be here, that she would distract him, and that he had to protect her.

He was being overly cautious. He knew this. After all, it was a busy street in early morning. And yet he couldn't help himself from growing tense whenever someone ventured too close, or a noise startled him.

And it seemed there was more noise than he had ever heard before in these mean streets. Dogs barked, wagon wheels rattled, shutters banged open and shut. He could overhear conversations from people even from yards away, as well as from people inside the houses they passed.

It was the Root. It had made him into a new kind of

creature, after it had made him into the monster.

Miss Sauber leaned closer to him, and he caught the whiff of wildflowers and freshly-cut grass, like towels hung out in the summer sun. She was not wearing perfume, but it was the natural scent that rose from her skin. It filled his senses as it never had before, not when they had danced, not when they had shared a carriage ride to and from the apothecary shop.

Out of the side of her mouth, she murmured, "Stop scowling. You are frightening children away."

He scowled at her.

"No, I will not disappear if you do that hard enough," she replied with equanimity.

In truth, he didn't want her to disappear. He enjoyed having her on his arm, her height putting her face close to his. With other, shorter women—such as his sister, who fooled all the world with her air of fragility—their heads were at the perfect height to stab him in the eye with the feathers on their bonnets.

Miss Sauber had no feathers, and her bonnet was both plain and cheaply made, as befitting her disguise. He had nothing to complain about her attire, no matter how he looked for something—anything—to force her to go home.

He knew why he worried about her—because her involvement reminded him too much of Richard. He knew they were not the same, and yet here she was, with him, searching for a greenhouse that belonged to Apothecary Jack.

What if Jack was there? What if there were men on the Root? Although Thorne and Isabella had blended into the crowd around them, keeping an eye on them, they would not be able to help if something went awry. There was nothing to indicate that anything would go wrong, and yet he still fretted.

His emotions were a stew of feelings inside him, bubbling and simmering. And he didn't know what to do, how he was supposed to feel.

"Where is the playhouse?" she asked.

He nodded toward a building coming up on their left. He, Thorne, and Isabella had scouted out the area around Finlay's Bakery yesterday, quickly ascertaining that there was only one theater in the area, Fenbear's Playhouse. Strangely, it was not very near the bakery, although within a few minutes' walk.

Once they had finally found the theater—made difficult by the nameless street—they had looked around at the buildings, but hadn't been able to determine which might be a greenhouse. So Mr. Drydale had told them to take Phoebe, who would be better able to guess where it might be.

He suddenly caught a scent of lily of the valley, and realized Isabella had passed in front of them, completely unnoticed, a few minutes before. His sensitivity to smell was a distraction and a torture—he thought he must be able to smell every chamber pot that was emptied in the last hour, every rotting rat corpse, every puddle of vomit or urine.

And Miss Sauber's sun-drenched wildflower scent.

Despite the early morning hour, there were clumps of young men outside of Fenbear's Playhouse, talking loudly. From the looks of them, they hadn't yet gone to sleep, and they had imbibed considerable amounts of ale, if the sour tang of their breath was any indication.

Michael moved Miss Sauber away from them, telling himself that his role as a married clerk would have had him doing the same thing. A few revelers looked in their direction, but Michael had applied his makeup carefully to blur his features, and Miss Sauber had done something to make her face look more coarse and plain, so the men quickly looked away from them, uninterested.

Even before they passed the theater, Miss Sauber had been unobtrusively looking around at the buildings. According to Sep, Jack had been friendly enough with the dancing girls at some theater that they chatted with him about the well-water's effects on their figures. So his greenhouse was likely close to the theater and the well, which was down a larger side street only a few yards from the side door to the theater.

Michael and Miss Sauber had started their walk from the far end of the street in front of the playhouse. The tallest building on the street was on one end, and the second tallest on the other end, but Michael had noted that neither building had many windows on their top floors. When they passed the first of the tall buildings, Miss Sauber had shaken her head upon seeing it, so he knew his instincts had been correct.

However, as they passed Fenbear's Playhouse on their left, her hand tightened on his arm as she glanced across the narrow lane toward a building a few houses ahead of them.

The building looked like a boarding house. It was not the tallest on the street, but it was taller than the two buildings on either side of it, with its roof sloping toward the street and dotted by three dormer windows. The floor below the dormer windows had one more window than the floor below it.

And unlike many of the other windows on the street, these windows were sparkling clean.

There were no curtains behind the glass, so they could see inside the room, but with the angle from the street, they only saw the pale grayness of the ceiling. Except that the shade of gray from the attic windows and the windows below were exactly the same.

They continued walking, but Miss Sauber said in a low voice, "The light from the windows of both top floors is the same. I think the attic floor was removed to create one large upper floor. And the rooms seem much brighter than they should have been, especially when compared to the other attic windows in buildings on the street. It makes me suspect he built skylights in the sloping roof facing away from the lane."

"I didn't notice that when we first came to this area yesterday."

"It is only barely noticeable now. It will be more so as the morning progresses, since the skylights are facing the east. But after the sun passes the apex and the day turns to afternoon, the light from the altered upper floor will not be very different from other buildings."

Michael became more alert as they drew near to the front door of the boarding house, but then the tension shot through him like a lightning bolt.

Someone had broken into the front door. Chunks of wood still lay in the street, and the middle plank of the simple plank door had been cracked. The wood around the iron latch was shattered, as was part of the doorframe.

In a slightly breathy voice, Miss Sauber whispered, "There is potting soil in small clumps on the street."

He hadn't noticed the difference, compared to the other piles of refuse, but now he noted the slightly darker color and finer texture of small lumps of soil trailing from the door.

While the street was busy, as might be expected for this time of morning, he now noted that there were small clumps of people gathered in front of the houses around the boarding house and across the lane from it. Occasionally they glanced at the broken door as they chatted with one another comfortably —likely they were neighbors.

"Come on," he said, then headed toward the closest group of people. "I beg your pardon. We were going to that boarding house to inquire of rooms. What has happened?"

"You and your wife best stay away," said an older woman with a long face and large eyes. "It was burglars last night. They swept right inside, knocking down the door even though it had already been locked for the night. We shall all be killed in our beds next!"

"Now, Lucy, no need for hysterics," said another old woman who was shorter and had a round face. She said to Michael and Miss Sauber, "We were right next door, so we heard all the screaming and shouting."

"Mr. Johnson apparently tried to stop them and was attacked," said the long-faded woman. "Poor man, he's got a lump the size of an egg on his head."

"Fool thing to do." An old man standing with them spoke for the first time to Michael and Miss Sauber.

"You can't blame him," the round-faced woman said. "They didn't know the burglars were only after Mr. Ramsy's room."

"Mr. Ramsy?" Miss Sauber asked.

"The renter who has the entire top floor," the long-faced woman said. "The burglars came out of the house with sacks bulging full. One only wonders what he might have had for them to take so much away."

"He works evenings, but he appears to be quite respectable, and is apparently doing well enough," the round-faced woman said. "I always thought it's a wonder he isn't married."

"He doesn't speak much to the neighbors," the old man said.

"*You* don't speak much to the neighbors," the long-faced woman said to her companion.

"Yes, well, Mr. Ramsy is always polite, if rather quiet," the round woman said. "Perhaps because he's self-conscious. He has that rather ugly scar on his cheek."

The mention of the scar made Michael's breathing quicken.

"He would be plain-faced even without it," the long-faced woman said heartlessly.

"He's a nice enough fellow," the old man said. "He always comes home mid-morning with a sack of those treacle buns from Finlay's Bakery, and he's never stingy about sharing."

"You just like it that he always shares with you," the long-faced woman accused him. "That's why you're always out here around the time he comes home."

"Poor man, he doesn't know yet," the round woman said. "He'll arrive soon."

Miss Sauber's hand tightened around his arm at the same time he also realized that they had to move quickly.

She gave them all a sweet smile. "Thank you for telling us. If the burglars were only after the one man, it might be fine for us to see if they've a room open. It might even be cheaper, don't you think?" she asked Michael.

"Let's inquire," he said. He caught the eye of a street urchin who happened to be lounging nearby. The boy slipped away.

"Are you quite sure?" asked the round-faced woman. "It might still be dangerous."

"But you live nearby, don't you?" Miss Sauber asked. "We should like some nice neighbors like yourself."

They nodded to the trio and headed toward the broken door, which opened easily to their touch. Once inside, Miss Sauber hiked up her skirts and took the stairs two at a time, heading toward the top floor.

Michael was startled for a moment, then followed her. He had to admit he didn't make much of an effort not to look at her trim ankles. After all, they were nearly at eye level.

Luckily, they did not meet any of the tenants or the landlord on their mad dash up the stairs.

"Ross and Prince?" she asked as they rounded the landing. She used their code names since they were in public.

"Prince overheard us. They'll keep watch outside."

The top of the stairs opened up to a hallway with two doors, but one was sagging open. Michael laid a hand on Miss Sauber's arm, and he moved ahead of her toward the door, easing it open slowly.

The room beyond was huge, encompassing the entire top floor, with high sloping ceilings dotted on the east side with skylights, just as Miss Sauber had suspected. There was only a hob grate in the corner and several tables set up under the skylights and next to the windows along the west wall. The tables were empty but for piles of dirt and scattered leaves, both fresh and dry.

It was the smell that hit him the hardest as he walked inside.

A flowery scent that he had never smelled before, and yet that he somehow recognized. Just a whiff made him suddenly inhale, drawing that scent deeply into his lungs, as if to fill his entire body with it.

Miss Sauber was unaffected by the smell—or perhaps it would be more accurate to say that she seemed to not be as affected as strongly as he had. She brushed past him into the room, drawing out of her bulging reticule several cloth sacks. "Hurry and help me," she said, moving to one of the tables. "One bag for each table—keep them separated."

She opened the sack and simply swept everything on the table into it, dirt and leaves and roots. Then she bent and scooped dirt and dried leaves from the floor into the same bag.

Michael took another bag and did the same for the table next to it, but his attention was caught by a torn green leaf on the surface. There was a fresh, spicy smell that emanated from the leaf, and he picked it up. The leaf smell was different from the floral scent in the air, and yet somehow similar. And it also evoked that same deep yearning, that same sense of familiarity that drew him. He crushed the leaf to bring out more of the smell, then raised it to his nose.

"No, don't!"

A firm hand on his wrist stopped him. The touch of her glove was rough, but her fingers were strong and supple, circling his wrist. He turned to look into sea-foam green eyes and wanted to drown in them, just as he wanted to drown in this spicy scent from this mysterious plant.

"You don't know what it is, or how it will affect you." Her voice seemed to come from the end of a long tunnel.

Her gaze grew sharper, more concerned. "Lazarus?"

It was the unfamiliar name that shocked him from his dream-like stupor. He had been the one to suggest it at the start of their mission, feeling the irrational need to joke about his rise from the dead when he knew his days were numbered.

"I'm sorry," he mumbled, dropping the leaf only reluctantly. It embarrassed him, his lack of control over himself, or perhaps the fact that she witnessed it.

"You should search the room for anything else," she said in a businesslike tone. "I'll concentrate on collecting samples."

Yes, that would probably be best. A part of his mind was shouting at him that the strange appeal of these plants was unnatural and he should be wary.

He skirted the table, his eyes roving on the empty ones next to the west windows. There were small round water stains in the warped wood, which was scattered with more soil. The pots on this table had been smaller than the ones on the larger tables in the center of the room.

As he drew near to the grate in the corner, he smelled it—a fetid, metallic scent. Old blood. Flesh just starting to rot.

It lay on the floor in the middle of the space between the stove and the nearest table, laid deliberately where it would be seen but not accidentally trampled upon. A human ear, smeared with blood that had dried to a color darker than wine. Something glittered purple under the blood.

He picked it up, and immediately smelled a cloying perfume that brought back memories of Paris.

The ear had been hacked off with a serrated knife, but recently, perhaps only a few hours ago. It held an amethyst earring in the shape of an oval, in a silver setting with a ring of tiny silver beads around it.

He immediately knew whose ear this was.

"What is th—bleargh!" Miss Sauber had drawn close to him but now cringed away.

"Give me a sack."

"I don't have any left. Here." She handed him her reticule.

He dropped it inside, but then realized she would need to carry it. When he hesitated, she held her hand out for it.

"Are you certain?"

She swallowed. "I shall have to be." She took the reticule from him and gingerly draped it around her wrist.

"Are you finished?" He took the sacks from her. "We must hurry."

They raced down the stairs, the sacks slung over his shoulder. As before, no one came out of their rooms to stop them— perhaps sensing that it would be best to be unseen when the mysterious Mr. Ramsy finally returned to his rooms.

At the front door, Miss Sauber paused and nodded toward the sacks. "We mustn't let people see you with those. I'll watch and tell you when to exit."

She opened the front door, leaving it slightly open, and hesitated on the step. The seconds ticked by.

He was about to simply rush out, regardless of who saw him, when she gestured with her hand for him to follow her out. He exited just as a crowd of rowdy men who had been standing in front of Fenbear's Playhouse walked past the door of the boarding house, shielding them from the eyes of the neighbors.

They hurried down the lane in the wake of the rowdy men, but he hadn't gone more than a few steps when he felt a tug at the sacks. He glanced down and caught a flash of glass-green eyes.

He relinquished the bags to the street urchin, and Michael saw a larger man take two of the sacks from the boy before they both melted into the darkness down a narrow alley.

Miss Sauber had apparently also seen the exchange, because she slowed her pace so that the rowdy men outdistanced them and tucked her hand again in the crook of his arm. They passed the trio who had spoken to them earlier but who were now gossiping with two other women. Michael and Miss Sauber gave all five neighbors a friendly nod before walking away.

He was about to release a breath of relief when he suddenly caught a glimpse of a square jaw, a small, rounded ear, and ugly yellow hair under a black hat. It was instinct more than reason that made him tug Miss Sauber behind a blacksmith arguing with a coachman outside his smithy.

A slender figure in a plain brown coat passed by them and the arguing men. He didn't look at them.

Michael had never seen Jack in the flesh, either with or without his makeup. But he recognized this man, with his aquiline nose and high cheekbones, one of them marred by an ugly, bubbling pink scar, which he was even now scratching at.

Michael had only seen that face once, but it was enough for him to remember.

He was the man from Richard's drawing.

Chapter Six

Jack had no makeup on. It was how he hid his greenhouse—no one knew it was Apothecary Jack who was Mr. Ramsy, so no one noticed the plain, scarred man who worked in the evenings and only visited his rented rooms during the day, when the morning light shone through the skylights onto his plants.

The sight of the murderer, walking the street like any other man, caused his jaw to tighten until it was as hard as a rock. His fists clenched, and he could only think about pounding them into Jack's face.

This man had killed his brother. Perhaps not on purpose, perhaps Richard had simply been a casualty of the murders of those two men from the Foreign Office, but Michael didn't think so. Richard's life was nothing to him. Any human life meant nothing to him. He did not deserve to be strolling along and eating a treacle bun as though he were a normal person.

But even as he thought it, Jack suddenly stopped, a half-chewed bun in his mouth. He twisted this way and that, not simply turning his head but his entire torso. He did not look in their direction, but Michael eased them both out of sight.

Was he able to smell anger? Or hear unspoken rage?

Michael closed his eyes and tried to draw deep breaths, but the noxious smells he could now notice burned his nostrils. He tried breathing through his mouth but ended up tasting raw sewage on his tongue.

Then he smelled wildflowers, and sunlight, and felt a soft hand that enfolded his clenched fist.

It was just a gentle touch. He realized that Miss Sauber had released his elbow when he hid them from Jack's searching gaze, but now her fingers grazed his tight knuckles, then his tensed biceps, then his trembling shoulder. Her soft caress soothed him, and wildflowers replaced the rotten smell in his nose, a cooling thread that drew his mind from the ugly anger.

Spreading from the places she had touched, he relaxed his muscles and released his anger. For now.

"I saw ..." His throat was dry and tight.

"I saw him, too."

"He looks like Richard's drawing."

Her face grew still and hard, like stone, and her eyes flickered over his shoulder where Jack had been. "Do you think Prince saw him?"

"Perhaps."

"He could follow him." Her voice had deepened, grown raspy and sharp.

Hope grew in him like a small fire. He took Miss Sauber's hand and laid it again in the crook of his arm and they continued, but he tugged at his right ear in the signal for Isabella to approach him.

It took her a while, but then he saw the urchin leaning against the wall of a building a few steps ahead of them. The boy came up with his hat in hand. "A shilling for me poor sister, sir?"

Michael dug in his pockets for change. "Did you see him? The scarred man."

Isabella's face grew pale even under the smearing of dirt and makeup. "No," she breathed. "He was here?"

"He passed not ten feet from us."

Her lips pressed together. "Sorry. I'll watch the house for

him."

"Be careful. He almost noticed us." Michael flipped a coin into her hat, and they moved on, but not before he caught another whiff of lily of the valley.

Prince never wore perfume when on assignment, so he knew it was simply her. But he was also aware of Miss Sauber's wildflowers as she drifted on his arm, and he began to wonder if Jack would notice that faint fragrance in his greenhouse room.

And if he noticed, would he be able to follow that floral aroma, like a dog? He might be able to track her if the trail was fresh.

He tugged her around a corner down a narrow track between houses, filled with dirt and refuse, which spilled out onto a wider street. He guided them toward several large groups of people, passing through them or closely around them. It was lucky that Isabella had not gone into the house, also, or Jack might have been able to follow her trail.

"What are you doing?" she murmured through her teeth.

"I can ... he could ... he might be able to follow us by scent."

She gave him a sidelong glance. "Best get us a hackney, then."

He managed to hail one along another wide avenue, and it dropped them off at an inn where he'd arranged to stable an unmarked carriage and horse.

Thorne was there ahead of them, and handed them the sacks they'd passed to Isabella. Michael told him about seeing the scarred man, and Thorne's face darkened.

"I'll go back to help Prince," he said. "We'll meet you at the house."

Michael and Miss Sauber drove out of London, but Stapytton House lay barely an hour from the city proper. It had originally been a small hunting lodge that someone had renovated a century or two ago into a home, but the surrounding land was still largely forested, and the cultivated areas had grown wild in short order when the current owner's funds had run low.

They swept up the driveway, which had been just barely cleared of weeds enough for them to drive the carriage. However, he knew from their brief meeting yesterday that the front door was warped and too difficult to open, so he instead drove through the remnants of old flower beds to the side of the house.

He found a space to park the carriage under some oak trees, next to Lady Wynwood's unmarked carriage. He took the sacks of dirt and leaves, and they entered through a side door that led directly into the kitchen. Through a small door, he could see Miss Gardinier in the adjoining stillroom, which was filled with scientific equipment that he might have remembered seeing in Mr. Shokes's apothecary stillroom.

She caught sight of them and greeted them, but didn't move from where she was pouring liquid into a flask sitting over a burner. "Back so soon?"

"When you've reached a good place to stop, we shall tell you what happened," Miss Sauber told her.

"Mr. Drydale is in the conservatory," Miss Gardinier told them, and went back to her flask.

Michael wasn't certain why Mr. Drydale would be in the empty conservatory, until he saw the man looking out through the glass walls at the overgrown garden in back. There was a stiffness to his stance that spoke of things on his mind, but he smiled at the sight of them—with perhaps a touch of relief, as well, and Michael realized he must have worried about them.

"Shall we wait for Keriah to finish?" Miss Sauber suggested. "So that we need not explain twice."

"Where are Mr. Rosmont and Lady Aymer?"

"They are hoping to follow Jack."

Mr. Drydale's eyes grew sharp. "*Jack?*"

"I'm here, I'm here." Keriah hurried into the conservatory. "What about Jack?"

Michael explained about the burglary of the greenhouse.

"Who in the world would dare to steal from Jack?" Mr. Drydale murmured.

Miss Sauber belatedly remembered the gruesome item in her reticule. She handed it to Miss Gardinier, who barely batted an eyelash at the sight of the bloody ear. "Oh. From a man, I believe."

"What's from a man?" Mr. Drydale demanded, then bent to peer into the reticule Miss Gardinier held. He caught a glimpse and grimaced. "I see."

"There's the scent of a French perfume on it," Michael said.

"There is?" Miss Gardinier sniffed at the bag. "I don't smell it." She held the bag toward Miss Sauber, who hurriedly shook her head.

"Perhaps only I could smell it," Michael said. "But I'm certain it's French. I smelled enough women's perfumes in Paris that it's unmistakeable."

"Only *you* could smell it?" Miss Gardinier asked. "What do you mean?"

Yesterday, when reporting what he, Isabella, and Thorne had discovered around Finlay's Bakery, he hadn't told any of them about the cacophony of sound and smells he'd experienced. He wasn't certain why he kept it to himself—perhaps because admitting his new abilities made him feel ... less human. However, now, it was necessary to come clean. "My hearing and sense of smell are stronger than before. The street smelled terrible."

"Even *I* thought the street smelled terrible," Miss Sauber said dryly.

"In the greenhouse, I smelled the plants ..." He recalled the strangely familiar floral scent, the equally familiar spicy scent of the leaf, and the feeling of needing to smell more of it. He shuddered at the weakness he had felt, the utter lack of control over himself. At the time, he hadn't cared, but now, he was repulsed by his weakness. It felt like being enslaved. "I also smelled the perfume on the ear. And outside, I could smell when my sister was nearby." He tried not to flush at the thought of smelling Miss Sauber's wildflowers and sunlight. Because if he mentioned that, of course he would not sound lecherous *at all.*

"And your hearing?" Miss Gardinier's eyes had begun to glow with interest. "What exactly could you hear?"

"Later," Mr. Drydale interrupted. "Mr. Coulton-Jones, continue."

"We didn't have much time, so Miss Sauber took samples of soil and plants from the room, and then we left."

"What kinds of plants were in the room?" Mr. Drydale asked.

"I think there were two types." Miss Sauber took the sacks and upended each one in neat piles on the tables that had been set up in the conservatory.

The smell wafted toward him as soon as she did, with that air of familiarity or remembrance, even though he was certain he'd never smelled it before. It made him dizzy, and he closed his eyes.

Miss Gardinier noticed. "Mr. Coulton-Jones?"

He didn't like being vulnerable, but he also didn't want to keep information from these people who had saved his life, and might do so again. "The smell affects me. It makes me want ... to smell more of it."

"If this is the plant Jack uses to make the Root, then I wonder if it is like a person's dependence upon laudanum," Miss Gardinier murmured. She was studying him carefully, taking his pulse, looking into his eyes. "Your pulse is faster and your eyes are dilated."

"In the greenhouse, you picked up that leaf," Miss Sauber said.

"I felt an overwhelming urge to smell it," Michael said.

"You seem in fine health, otherwise," Miss Gardinier said, "but perhaps it would be best for you to remain a few feet away."

"That's a good idea." He didn't want his feelings, his body to be shackled by whatever that plant was.

Miss Sauber turned back to the dirt and leaf piles, although she moved with more caution now that she knew how it had affected him. The light in the conservatory was excellent for her to sift through the contents.

"I cannot say exactly what the burglars took from the greenhouse," Miss Sauber said as she bent over the table.

"Do you recognize the leaves or roots?" Mr. Drydale asked her.

"No, I've never seen these before." She spread some of the leaves out. "Some are dried and some are fresh, torn when the plants were stolen."

She moved to the second pile, which corresponded to the second of three tables in the greenhouse. "These leaves are similar to that one, but slightly different. However, the soil seems to be the same composition, which might indicate they were both the same plant. Or they could have been two plants that had the same nutritional needs."

She moved to the third pile and her brow furrowed. She picked up a leaf, then sniffed it.

"Miss Sauber!" Michael said at the same time Miss Gardinier yelped.

"I believe this table had lily plants," Miss Sauber said. "I would guess common trumpet lilies."

"Lilies?" Mr. Drydale seemed baffled.

"In the Root sample, we found trace amounts of lily pollen."

"You're right, I had forgotten," Miss Gardinier said.

"Did Jack mix the Root solution in the greenhouse?" Mr. Drydale asked.

"Hmm ..." Miss Gardinier regarded the tables of soil and leaves as Miss Sauber continued looking through them. "I would guess not. I think there would have been more pollen, if that were the case. Likely the lily pollen fell onto the roots that he used to make the solution."

"I will need to borrow your microscope, Keriah." Miss Sauber held out a handful of tiny roots she'd picked from the pile of dirt from the first sack. "I think these are the roots Jack used for the Root."

"Can you grow new plants from any of this?" Mr. Drydale asked.

Miss Sauber hesitated, but her face was not hopeful. "I can try. Some plants will grow from roots alone. It is possible that these will."

"If only the burglars had left a plant or two," Michael said.

"I wonder if Jack had seeds? Of if he has other greenhouses?" Miss Gardinier said.

"He most certainly has another greenhouse," Miss Sauber said. "This one was too small. He also grows poisonous plants that he sells through his business, and there were none of them in that space. He likely has a larger greenhouse near London. But I can tell that this greenhouse, these plants were special. They needed daily care, and he could not entrust them to anyone else."

"According to the neighbors, he arrived every day around mid-morning," Michael said. "We saw him on the street."

"Yes, I had nearly forgotten you mentioned Jack." Mr. Drydale looked both alarmed and angry. "Did he see you?"

"No, although it was a close thing." He explained about Jack's lack of makeup, and the scar, and Richard's drawing. Just the telling made his neck tighten as he recalled Jack's insouciant expression, the way he meandered through the people on the lane. "He would have found out about the burglary in another few minutes, so I asked Isabella to remain in the area and follow him."

"It's quite bold to steal from a man so powerful," Mr. Drydale murmured.

"Someone also killed that woman from the charitable

organization, after she'd told Jack about Mr. Ackett's presence in the church," Miss Sauber said.

"They may not be connected," Michael said slowly. "The murder of that woman was secretive—they left her body in the graveyard, but no trace of who had done it. However, this burglary was brazen, and from the ear, they also don't seem to care that Jack knows they're thumbing their noses at him."

"What do you mean about the ear?" Miss Gardinier asked.

"I know whose it is," Michael said.

Mr. Drydale's eyebrows rose. "How?"

At the same time, Miss Gardinier snapped her fingers. "From the earring."

"What earring?" Mr. Drydale asked, then answered it himself, "Ah, never mind. Who is it?"

"Maner Hansen. I met with him when I was searching for Apothecary Jack, although he was rather tight-lipped. He didn't want to cross Jack, although it was obvious he had information about him."

"How does he know about Jack?" Miss Sauber asked.

"It's his trade, information. If you need to know something, he can sell it to you."

"I've heard of him," Mr. Drydale said. "He has a vast network of people who eavesdrop or sneak into houses, whatever it takes to find out what he needs to know."

"Eavesdrop …" Miss Sauber frowned and stared out the windows of the conservatory as she thought. "When we were searching for Mr. Ackett, Calvin and Clara had me speak to certain men on the street. They were very strange, because they seemed to be only pretending to be doing nothing, but they were very observant of their surroundings. They seemed to be attempting to eavesdrop on certain people who passed them. Or perhaps they had deliberately followed those people in order to listen in on their conversations."

"Yes, that sounds like Maner's people," Michael said. "In a

way, Maner Hansen is an underworld lord himself, like Jack."

"And someone wanted Jack to blame Maner Hansen for the burglary," Miss Sauber said.

"Which probably means he's still alive," Mr. Drydale said. "Where would he be?"

"Whoever tortured him wouldn't want to be with him when Jack finds him," Michael said. "They'd let him go—or he would escape—and he'll go to ground. Finding him will be difficult."

"But he will need someone to take care of his ear for him," Miss Gardinier said. "Where would he go to be patched up?"

Michael shook his head. He had no idea.

"I think I know who to ask," Miss Sauber said slowly.

Mr. Drydale seemed to know who she meant. "Ah, yes, you're right. I should have thought of them."

"Who?" Michael asked.

"The twins," Miss Sauber said. "Calvin and Clara."

Phoebe's aunt gave her the last answer she would have ever expected.

"No, my dear," Aunt Laura said, "I'm afraid I can't let you do that."

Phoebe was momentarily speechless. "I can't speak to the twins?"

Sitting next to her on the sofa in the drawing room, Uncle Sol frowned at her aunt. "Laura, what's the meaning of this?"

"I don't want you speaking to them about Maner Hansen."

Her aunt had that polite-society smile on her face, unperturbed and sweetly gentle, but Phoebe noticed her hands clasped in her lap, the knuckles white.

"Why not?" Phoebe asked.

The polite-society smile cracked, just a little. "He is connected to their mother."

She sucked in a breath.

Phoebe, Keriah, Mr. Coulton-Jones, and Uncle Sol had arrived at her aunt's townhouse only minutes ago. Phoebe hadn't felt comfortable talking to the twins without her aunt's permission, but now it seemed she wouldn't receive it at all.

At that moment, steps echoed as visitors climbed the staircase. The door opened and Graham announced, "Lady Aymer and Mr. Rosmont."

Phoebe traded a bewildered glance with Mr. Coulton-Jones. She had expected Mr. Rosmont and Lady Aymer to have been another hour at least, following Jack.

Lady Aymer was no longer in her urchin boy disguise, but had changed into a simple dress and put her hair up in a tight knot, which she could do without assistance. Mr. Rosmont also had switched from the plain, slightly rumpled workman's outfit he'd been wearing while following Phoebe and Mr. Coulton-Jones to Jack's greenhouse.

Mr. Coulton-Jones rose when they entered the room. "What happened?"

"Is that tea? I'm famished." Lady Aymer sat next to Phoebe on the sofa. "Do pour me a cup, Miss Sauber."

As Phoebe complied, Mr. Rosmont said, "He was only in his greenhouse for a few minutes."

"He threw a terrible tantrum," Lady Aymer added. "Worse than our cousin's children, and they're only five and six years old. We could hear him screaming all the way from the street."

"We tried to follow him when he left," Mr. Rosmont said.

Lady Aymer sipped her tea. "I don't believe he knew he was being followed, but he's incredibly good at disappearing in a crowd."

"I lost him after only three blocks," Mr. Rosmont said.

"I lost him in five," Lady Aymer said. "It could be that he has a method of sneaking away so that he can reapply his stage makeup. After all, he wouldn't want anyone to know that the scarred man is Apothecary Jack."

"We returned to Stapytton House, but since you had left, we reasoned you would be here," Mr. Rosmont said.

"What was in those sacks you took from Jack's greenhouse?" Lady Aymer had already helped herself to two jam tarts.

Mr. Coulton-Jones explained again what had happened while Phoebe snuck looks at Aunt Laura. She hadn't known the twins' mother was alive. Why were they with her aunt and not with their family?

Mr. Rosmont had the same idea as Phoebe. "Calvin and Clara might know who he might turn to in order to be stitched up."

"I will not allow you to speak to them," Aunt Laura said quickly.

The room was silent for nearly a full minute, with various shades of surprise and confusion on everyone's faces except for Aunt Laura.

Phoebe glanced at Uncle Sol, who was frustrated but at the same time concerned. And then she realized what her aunt was doing.

The only reason she would act this way when she knew the circumstances were important was in protection of someone. In this case, the twins. She felt she needed to protect them from Maner Hansen and their mother.

"Aunt Laura." Phoebe's voice was low. "I don't know everything about their backgrounds, and I know you wish to protect them. But this is also important—not only because Maner Hansen is injured, but also because there is too much we don't understand about everything that is happening, everything surrounding Apothecary Jack."

"We already know how dangerous Apothecary Jack is," Uncle Sol added, "and the group he belongs to."

"And ... I believe the twins would want to help, though it might hurt them," Phoebe said.

Her aunt closed her eyes briefly. "Yes, I know it is important.

But despite how helpful they have been to you, they are both only eleven years old."

Phoebe could honestly say that she had forgotten their age, especially since they carried themselves with such a grave manner. But that had been caused by the suffering of their lives before they were saved by Aunt Laura.

Aunt Laura sighed. "But they would want to help, no matter how I would try to protect them. Aya would say that I was smothering them. Very well." She glanced at Uncle Sol. "I will speak to them alone, and only Phoebe may accompany me."

They settled in her aunt's bedchamber, and Aya went to fetch the twins. Aunt Laura's face was the same color as the pearl fireplace. Her hands had begun to look both red and white from their clenching.

"Phoebe." Her aunt's voice was harder than she heard it in a long time. "The twins do not know that it was their mother who put them up for auction."

Her throat tightened so swiftly, she thought she might choke.

"Be careful in what you say to them. Do you understand?"

"Yes, Aunt Laura."

"It is solely for their sakes."

The door opened, and Calvin and Clara entered. When they saw their mistress's face, however, they grew tense.

Aya had also brought some jam tarts and laid it before them on the table in front of the fireplace. Aunt Laura attempted to smile, gave up, and then asked, "Would you like to eat first or afterward?"

"First," said Calvin.

"Afterward," said Clara.

"Why?" Calvin demanded of his sister.

"If I eat first, it might make me feel queasy afterward."

"Oh, good point." Calvin turned to Aunt Laura. "Afterward, please, m'lady."

She managed a small smile at their exchange. "It is not so

very bad, but it might be difficult for you. Phoebe?"

She studied their faces, rounded from good food and yet with still a barrenness in their eyes that had nothing to do with the present, but the past. Yes, she understood her aunt's protectiveness of these two. "I hope this will not upset you, but we think Maner Hanson is badly injured, and we need to find him."

Both Clara and Calvin went white at mention of his name, but that was their only reaction.

She hesitated, then decided to explain everything that had happened today. She felt they should know, since she was asking for their help.

"If he escaped," Clara said, "and was bleeding badly ..." She chewed on her lip. "He'd probably go to Lady Nola."

"Some people believe she has healing powers," Calvin said with a slightly scoffing tone, "but others see her if Dr. Shokes isn't available."

"Where is Lady Nola?" Phoebe asked.

"He won't be at her home by now," Calvin said.

"Lady Nola doesn't let patients stay for longer than an hour. That's the rule. Everyone knows that."

"So if someone is in bad shape, they usually summon her to their house."

"If Maner went to Lady Nola, he would have left already."

Phoebe noticed that Clara used Maner Hansen's first name, not his last. She filed that away as something else she couldn't ask them about. "If there were people after him, where would he go after leaving Lady Nola?"

The twins were silent for a long moment. Clara chewed on her bottom lip while Calvin scowled at the plate of jam tarts.

Finally Calvin muttered, "He's got a secret place."

Clara's leg swung sidewise and kicked him. He transferred his scowl from the plate to his sister, then looked away again.

"Is it a dangerous place?" Phoebe asked.

"No …" Clara said.

When she didn't answer further, Phoebe asked, "How do you know about it?"

However, it was Aunt Laura who answered. "They discovered all sorts of things from living on the streets."

"How do you know he will be there?"

"It's his special place," Calvin said. "No one will find him there except people who know about it."

"Who knows about it?"

Clara hesitated, then said, "Just us."

Phoebe wasn't as skilled as her aunt at spotting lies, but she was fairly certain Clara had lied just now. However, they were also their only hope of finding Maner Hansen. "Can you tell us where it is?"

Both twins bit their bottom lips in exactly the same way. If the situation weren't so dire, it would have seemed comical.

"We'll take Keriah so that she can help patch up Mr. Hansen."

Clara gave a small smile. "No one calls him Mr. Hansen."

"His bodyguards do," Calvin said.

"Not all of them." Clara sobered. "The people who took him would have had to beat his bodyguard."

"We don't know if Maner escaped from them," Phoebe said, "but there's a chance they let him go, since they left the ear— er, earring in the greenhouse so that Jack would go after Maner."

The twins shared a searching look, a silent communication that only they understood. Then Clara said, "We'll take you to him, miss."

"No," Aunt Laura immediately said.

But the twins gave her two identical, mature looks. "It's all right, m'lady." Calvin's voice had a depth and strength that she hadn't heard from him before.

"He'll be surprised to be found," Clara added. "It would be

best if one of us was there."

"Thank you," Phoebe said.

However, she felt her aunt's hand firmly grip her forearm. "Phoebe, I would like you to remain here and not go with them."

She blinked at her aunt. "Not go?" She glanced at the twins, who looked equally confused. "Why not?"

"If the twins must lead us to Maner's hiding place, then it would be safest for him not to *see you.*"

"Yes, miss," Clara agreed.

Phoebe shook her head. "I don't understand."

"Maner knows the twins work for me. If he sees them alone, he may think they are working separately from me, but if he sees you ..."

"He'll know you're involved," Phoebe realized.

"And he may begin to suspect anyone who may be close to me."

Uncle Sol.

Phoebe nodded. "Yes, you are right."

Perhaps not surprisingly, the twins were able to devour the jam tarts at only slightly slower speed than normal.

Phoebe felt as though she'd been running and slammed into a door. Working closely with Mr. Coulton-Jones today had made her feel strong and capable. She had not been afraid, but she had been focused. She had been part of a team. She had been useful. She had had a greater purpose.

And now ... she was staying home.

Even though she understood why, she still felt a bit of disappointment as she watched everyone else prepare to leave. Lady Aymer and Mr. Rosmont had left early in order to change back into their street disguises and meet them at a dock in the Long Glades that Calvin and Clara had told them about. Keriah went upstairs to also change into an older gown that would not look out of place.

While waiting in the front foyer, Uncle Sol approached Aunt Laura. "I don't like not knowing things." It sounded like he was trying to sound gentle and reasonable, but there was a growl of frustration in his voice. "I'm responsible for their safety. I should know any potential dangers."

"You are right," Aunt Laura said gently. "But I can't tell you, Sol."

"Why not?"

She touched his hand briefly, and her face was drawn and sorrowful. "Because it is not my secret that I am keeping."

Chapter Seven

The twins were nervous. And it made Michael nervous, also.

He didn't think they were anxious about the area, although it seemed more sinister than other places he had been.

There weren't many people that could be seen on this narrow, lonely lane near the river. The buildings here were not so high, so the light of early evening colored the dingy houses a burnt orange color.

But his heightened senses could clearly pick out the people who could *not* be seen. Even without the Root, he would have suspected that their presence did not go unnoticed.

Michael was alone with Clara and Calvin, while Isabella loitered several yards away, keeping watch over them. The twins had been less familiar with this particular area in the Long Glades, but it was its distance from Maner Hansen's normal haunts in Jem Town that made it ideal for his hidden hiding-hole, which they knew how to find.

The shadows here seemed darker than most. Michael and the twins instinctively avoided looking in those shadows too closely, to avoid eye contact with anyone who may be lurking there. He was glad he had left Miss Gardinier with Thorne, hidden in a lean-to next to a factory. It was not nearby, but Clara said that it was easy to enter and exit unnoticed.

They were not taking the direct route to Maner's location,

because Michael felt it would be best to determine they were not being followed. It did not appear to be the case, but he could still feel eyes upon him from the cracks of windows and doors, from dark alleyways.

"There are people watching us," he whispered to the twins. "They'll see us find Maner's location."

He didn't imagine it—both twins tensed at the mention of Maner's name.

"It can't be helped," Calvin said, barely moving his lips.

"They'd have seen him enter it, anyway," Clara added.

He didn't know how to feel about what Lady Wynwood had said earlier, about the secret she was obligated to keep. A part of him understood, but another part of him wanted to know so that he could better protect these two children. He knew they had worked diligently to help save both himself and Sep, and he owed them more than simply gratitude. Or perhaps he was being protective of them because they were young, and yet they were part of this strange team of people.

Or perhaps he simply didn't like seeing that hollowness that never went away from their eyes, but which seemed to engulf their faces at this moment, on their way to find Maner Hansen.

The twins did not seem to dislike Maner, nor did they seem to be afraid of him, but something about him made them apprehensive. And so Michael readied himself for anything, determined to protect them if needed.

It was perhaps lucky he did, because he became aware of three men who started following them. He noticed them nearly from the moment they moved from their hiding place behind a building. The men had not been following Michael when they entered this area, but it appeared they had seen him and decided to investigate.

When Michael and the twins first drew close to the river, there had been one man who had followed them, scuttling from shadow to shadow. Then Michael had turned to look directly at him, and he had slunk away.

But he could tell that these men were of a different caliber. They made no effort to hide their figures behind them, and they walked with boldness in an area where most tried to pass by unremarked.

Michael was prepared when two of them caught up to them. The leader was taller even than himself, with a thick neck and a wide barrel of a torso. "Hey, friend. How much for the kids?"

The rage flared like a sudden blue flame, making him clench his fists, and yet his head remained icy cold. "They're not for sale."

"We weren't asking permission." Barrel-man smiled, exposing blackened teeth.

Michael punched him in the mouth.

He had been steeling his fist for the impact of teeth against his knuckles, but he only felt a soft crunch. He didn't pause to wonder at it and kicked out at the torso of the other man, who was leaner and had a scar across his mouth that made him look like he was sneering.

The kick sent sneering-man stumbling backwards several feet before he fell hard on his backside. The blue eyes that stared at him were stung with shock.

Michael immediately turned back to barrel-man, whom he assumed would be a more difficult opponent. However, the big man had toppled backward, not even trying to break his fall with his hands. He was knocked out cold.

Michael looked down at his hand, and instead of the bloody mess he expected from hitting teeth, there were only a few cuts on his knuckles. The cuts were deep, but they had already stopped bleeding, and he hardly felt any pain.

He faced the sneering man, also keeping his eye on the third man who had remained some distance away, partially obscured by a shadowed doorway.

Sneering-man leaped to his feet, the sneer on his mouth now

a reality as he snarled incoherently. He rushed toward him.

But strangely, he seemed to be running slowly. Michael easily blocked his roundhouse swing with one arm, the impact barely a thud against his forearm, and then swung at sneering-man's narrow jaw.

Sneering-man's eyes rolled toward the back of his head, and he also fell to the ground, unconscious.

Michael didn't pause, but turned toward where the third man was standing. However, rather than following the example of his fellows, the man turned and ran away.

The street seemed abnormally quiet as the man's footsteps faded away. He had taken out two men in the space of seconds. They had not been very trained fighters, but he was barely breathing heavily.

The twins' eyes were wide as they stared at him. He had difficulty meeting their gazes and looked down at his knuckles again. The deep cuts had already partially healed into merely shallow cuts.

"Are you two all right?" he asked them.

They nodded. They had no need to ask how he was, because they saw the lack of injury to his hand.

"Stay close to me," he told them unnecessarily, for lack of anything else to say.

"Miss Keriah gave us sedative knives," Calvin said, but then Clara nudged him and gave him a speaking glare.

Mr. Drydale had told him about the knives smeared with sedative paste that they had used, but Miss Gardinier hadn't given Michael a sedative-laced knife. And he realized that the sedative knives weren't to protect them from normal predators.

It was to protect them from *him*.

"Do you have an extra sedative knife?" he asked.

The twins glanced at each other, then Clara produced one and tentatively held it out to him.

He took it. "I will not let anyone harm you," he promised

them, "including myself."

Those identical light brown eyes stared at him a moment, and then Clara smiled at him. It was like dawn breaking in that dark street.

They continued, turning away from the river after another quarter mile and following a dirt track that ran between dingy gray buildings that were perhaps factories or warehouses. Gradually, they gave way to squat homes punctuated by taller boarding houses, all of them with the slightly warped wooden boards typical of structures near water. The air was chill and the ground was soft and damp.

There was suddenly an open spot alongside the track, and they came upon an overgrown graveyard. It was a tiny plot, and tenement houses had been built right up to the edge where the remnants of a wooden fence lay in rotting stakes.

Next to the graveyard stood the ruins of a stone church. It had been small when it had been intact, and the few bits of crumbled walls still standing were not only dingy but also darkly discolored from the fire that must have destroyed it.

They picked their way through weeds and bushes, trying not to stumble on loose pieces of stone that had fallen from the walls or ceiling. Closer to the back of the building, the walls were a little higher, although they only rose about three feet above Michael's head. Dead vines draped the stone, which was covered in splotches of gray-green and gray-brown moss.

They reached the open area in front of the back walls, which might have held an altar and perhaps an ancient stone effigy on the floor, but it was difficult to tell if the mound of broken stone had once been carved or was simply a pile of rock that fell from the ceiling. The walls were thicker here and shielded the faint breezes that slithered through the narrow spaces between the buildings that surrounded the churchyard. The walls had been made of massive blocks that had been carved to look like horizontal panels stacked on top of each other, and while some bits of carving had been broken, the majority of it remained relatively intact.

Calvin didn't hesitate, but dropped to his knees in front of one horizontal stone panel about the length of a coffin, and perhaps as high. Clara joined him, and they grabbed at uneven knobs in the carving, and then pulled sideways

The stone panel moved.

It moved like a heavy wooden plank, or perhaps a bit heavier than that. Michael leaned down to help and realized it was indeed a wooden plank, but covered with a thin layer of stone and plaster—even painted with lichen—so that it looked like the other stone panels of the wall. Even with the handholds, it was difficult to slide, and since it was low to the ground, it was difficult to get enough leverage to move it easily.

After only three feet, the plank would move no more. The opening was just large enough for a man to lie down and slide inside. The area beyond was dark, but he followed the twins as they crawled inside.

He found himself on a very narrow landing, bordered on all sides by stone, but it was high enough for him to stand upright. Then he had to bend down again to slide the board back into place, plunging the landing into darkness. However, he caught a glimpse of stone steps leading down. After the plank was fitted over the opening and his eyes adjusted, he could see the faint outline of a door at the bottom of the stairs, rimmed with feeble light from a candle.

He realized that there had originally been a small door here, leading from the back of the church sanctuary, but it had been covered with panel-shaped stone pieces, blocking the entrance to a small basement room. Someone had chipped through the stone of the bottom panel to reveal the landing, then had replaced the broken panel with the fake one.

He reached to grab Calvin before he headed down, wanting to move ahead of him, but Calvin whispered, "Best if I go first, sir."

"No, it's too dangerous."

"Might be worse if I don't."

He couldn't see more than a vague outline of both children, so he couldn't read their expressions, but they had led him here, and he had to trust them. However, he pushed Clara behind him and followed Calvin closely down the stone steps, sliding out his long knife that he had sheathed in a holder at his lower back.

The boy knocked at the heavy wooden door at the bottom, then pushed it open, saying, "Maner?" The way his voice echoed made Michael guess that the space beyond was small and enclosed.

However, as soon as the door was opened enough to let Calvin step inside, the barrel of a pistol appeared from the left side of the doorframe.

Alarm shot through Michael, but then he realized the pistol was aimed at the space above Calvin's head—at about the height Michael's jaw would have been.

The pistol abruptly dropped down toward Calvin.

Michael tensed, but then the pistol was retracted. From the direction of the gun, a high-pitched man's voice said, "Calvin!" A string of curses followed, then, "Did Sinah send you?"

Calvin tensed at the name, and looked toward his left at the unseen man. Then he shook his head and moved another step into the room.

Michael took advantage and slipped inside, his hand aiming for the pistol. He tugged the weapon out effortlessly, catching the man by surprise.

Maner yelped and swiped at the pistol to reclaim it, but Michael had taken another step inside and slid the knife forward to press against the side of his neck. Maner immediately stilled.

He looked terrible. The last time Michael had seen him, seeking information about Apothecary Jack, Maner Hansen had been dressed in plain but fine clothing, wearing them with an arrogance that spoke of his power and influence through the commodity he traded.

He was now in his shirtsleeves, and his fine linen shirt was dirty and stained with blood from his left shoulder and running down his front and sleeves. His brown hair, which had been neatly styled before, was in spikes that stood out all around his long, narrow head, and matted with blood. A bandage had been wrapped around his head, draped a bit low over his forehead so that it covered his ear, but the blood had already soaked through. His left eye was swollen shut and his right one was sunken, surrounded by bruises all over his face, and his skin was waxy. His body trembled, perhaps with cold, perhaps with shock.

The room beyond was indeed small, holding only a low cot, a small table and chair, and a low case of shelves that held jars of preserved food and water. A single candle burned on the table, and the air was chill and damp. Mold ran in dark waves along the bottom of the stone walls, and Michael could see the dampness on the stones under his feet. The room was thick with the scent of blood and mildew.

But he also became aware of a floral, green scent. The same scent as in the greenhouse, although much fainter.

Maner had no will—or no strength—to fight. He swayed on his feet before leaning against the wall to prop himself up.

"Sit down before you pass out." Michael withdrew the knife from Maner's neck as the twins went to either side of him to help him to sit on the cot. Michael took the chair and sat across from him.

"How'd you get the twins to help you?" Maner panted. "Is her ladyship involved somehow?"

"Don't know who you mean." It had been obvious from the way Maner had reacted upon seeing Calvin that the man knew these children well. It would be logical that he also knew they now worked for Lady Wynwood.

"We heard you were hurt, Maner," Clara said.

"I'm more than hurt, lemon cake," Maner said, his words more raspy than normal. "I'm a dead man."

The nickname surprised him. Maner apparently cared for these children. So why had they been so nervous to see him?

"We brought a nurse who can help you," Michael said.

"So I can be healed up when Jack finds me?"

Michael untied the reticule from the belt that held his knife sheath and passed it to Maner.

His brows knit as he took the bag, tugging open the strings, and he recoiled at what he saw. But then he looked closer, and he exhaled a heavy breath. "You took it from the greenhouse. Thank God." He closed his eyes, bending his head and touching his hand to his brow.

"Clara, get Luke."

The girl headed back up the steps, and he heard her grunting as she slid the panel aside.

"Thanks for this." Maner held up the bag briefly. "But that also means you want something from me."

"Who did this to you?"

Maner hesitated, his eyes darting away.

"You trying to protect them?"

Maner licked his split lip, and winced. "How do I know what you'll do with the information?"

"The twins'll vouch for me."

The bloodshot blue eyes softened when they glanced at Calvin. "Fine," he said. "It isn't like I have a choice. If Jack catches them, they'll tell him that I told them about his greenhouse."

"Tell me what you know, and I'll try to find them first."

Maner grimaced and rubbed at his forehead. He must be in a great deal of pain.

"I don't know much," Maner said. "They're French."

"Already guessed that."

Maner raised a bleary eye toward him. "You did? How?"

"French perfume."

"Ah." He looked surprised. "I didn't notice that."

"How many are there?"

"Five at most, although I only saw three of them. But from what they said to each other, there were at least two more who weren't in the room with me."

"Describe them."

"There's a woman who's obviously the leader. A pocket Venus, the kind who can cozy up to a man and trick him into letting his guard down. The whitest blonde hair I've ever seen, straight and fine, and it wasn't bleached, it was natural."

The description stirred a memory in him. "Did you get a name?"

"No ..." Maner blinked into space for a second. "But I think I know who she is. Brigitte Despréaux, a spy for Napoleon."

"I thought she was only a rumor," Michael said carefully.

"She might be, but I've heard too many stories from different people, and I'm of a mind that she's real. She moves in secret and she's never been caught. She wears different disguises."

"So what made you think it was her?"

"One person who said he met her told me she had a small mole or skin mark on her inner forearm."

Michael tensed. He'd heard that, too.

"When she slapped me," Maner said, "her sleeve rose up and I saw the mole. People don't put makeup on their arms when they wear sleeves because it'll rub off."

"Lots of French people have moles, Maner."

He waved his hand. "Yes, yes. So it might not have been her. But the hair and the mole makes me think it might be."

It also made Michael think it might be her, but he didn't want to give Maner any information about himself through the kinds of information that he knew.

"What about the others?"

"A big, wide man with a painful right jab." Maner gingerly fingered his jaw. "Hair very short, and black as night. And a second man, shorter. He had more olive-toned skin, and long, wavy black hair. He was reading a book by Voltaire. Unfortunately he didn't survive my escape. I took his hat and coat, but left them at Lady Nola's. Oh, so I suppose there are four of them, not five."

"She's not going to be happy you killed him."

"I'm not happy she had her bear of a man cut off my ear," Maner snapped. He then colorfully described her parentage.

"What else do you know about them?"

"I overheard them talking about the Channel crossing—they spoke in French but assumed I didn't speak it." Maner gave a wide, thin smile. "They came over in a smuggler's boat only a few days ago. And if she is Brigitte, they were sent by Napoleon himself, because she doesn't answer to anyone else."

"What did they want from you?"

Maner gave him a pitying look. "Jack's undergarments. His greenhouse, you idiot."

Michael admitted he deserved that. "Did they say why they wanted it?"

"My guess is that they're looking for the serum Jack's group offered to Napoleon."

Michael frowned at Maner. "How'd you know about that?"

Maner gave him a nasty smile. "Because you just told me."

Michael doubted that. Maner had probably heard about it and already knew it was likely true. "How did you find out about it? Unless you have spies in Napoleon's court? If you did, I'd be impressed."

"You know how it goes …" Maner's voice was nonchalant. "I hear things, even from people from France. And it would make sense since Jack is flaunting his Root all over London."

"Did you know what he was growing in the greenhouse?"

Maner licked his lips, then said, "It's called Goldensuit."

It was as though the air, cold as it already was, chilled even further.

"He makes the Root from it," Maner continued, "although no one knows how."

"I've never heard of a plant by that name. What does it look like?"

Maner scowled at him. "How will knowing about the plant help you to find Brigitte and her crew?"

Michael leaned back in the chair. "I don't have to help you at all if you don't cooperate."

"You only want the plants, not the Frenchies," Maner spat. "It doesn't matter to you if Brigitte escapes England or not."

"But just in case she doesn't escape England," Michael drawled, "you need me to find them before Jack does."

Above all else, Maner was a businessman. "How about this," he said. "I'll tell you everything about the plant if you'll find Brigitte and her men and save my hide from Jack."

"When we find her, we'll find the plants anyway."

"But there are things you don't know about the Goldensuit. Things that could kill you."

Michael could tell from the gleam in Maner's right eye (since his left one was swollen shut) that he wasn't lying. "Like what?"

"Did you know the pollen is poisonous?" Maner said. "It's probably why it's so rare. No one in their right mind would grow a plant that could kill you just by breathing around it."

"How do you know it's poisonous?"

"I heard that Jack and any gardeners he hires wear masks when they go into the greenhouse. All his gardeners are his cutthroats on the Root, so they're not likely to betray him. All he has to do is withhold more Root from them to kill them. And the pollen seems to affect them less than normal men." Maner scowled at Michael. "So when you do find the Frenchies, be careful. If you drop down dead from breathing the pollen, it doesn't help me any."

"True," Michael said.

There was a scraping noise coming from the top of the stairs through the door, which they'd left open. Michael rose to his feet and positioned himself to the side of the door while Calvin stood next to Maner.

However, Clara's voice called down the stairs, "It's us."

Soon, Clara entered the room, followed by Miss Gardinier. She was dressed in boy's clothes, but she hadn't the same gift for acting as Miss Sauber, and simply the way she walked made it obvious she was not male.

Maner noticed right away. "Hello, lovely." Even in his pain, he managed to leer.

She gave him a cold stare. "I could be gentle when treating you, or I could not."

The leer vanished. "I have the utmost respect for you, Doctor."

"Do you know where I can find Brigitte, Maner?" Michael asked as Miss Gardinier moved to check his wound.

Maner winced as she undid the bandage around his head. "She took me to the Planters Flat Inn, but she's likely long gone by now."

"You didn't overhear where they might have gone after taking the plants?"

"No, they didn't speak much when in my presence, aside from currying my hide. Easy, Doctor, they broke a rib."

Miss Gardinier had been trying to lean him over more so she could better see his injury, but at his words she raised his shirt to expose a mass of bruises blooming all over his torso. "Two, is my guess," she said.

"You're not giving me much to find them, Maner," Michael said.

"I can't do your job for you, can I?" Maner retorted. "They took the plants somewhere after they left Jack's greenhouse.

Someone was bound to have noticed them."

"None of your egg-gatherers would have seen them?" With the shape Maner was in, he likely hadn't spoken to any of the men he hired to keep watch and gather information for him across London, and Michael was certain Maner would be sure to have men stationed near Jack's greenhouse.

Maner frowned, then glanced up at Calvin and Clara. "Dent Roe and Chas Lenox. I told them to hang about the area, but I didn't tell them about the greenhouse. They might have seen something."

"Where are they?"

"The twins know where to find them."

The twins nodded solemnly.

"You'd better hurry." Maner winced as Miss Gardinier began cleaning his wound. "Those Frenchies won't stick around. If they haven't already arranged it, they'll be trying to find passage on the next smuggler's boat back to France."

Phoebe was sulking. She fully admitted it. It had been difficult to watch almost everyone leave the house without her.

It didn't matter that she logically knew she wouldn't have been of any use in the search to find Maner Hansen. Mr. Rosmont and Mr. Coulton-Jones were trained agents. Lady Aymer was some sort of state secret. The twins had volunteered to go, despite Maner's connection to their mother. Phoebe wasn't entirely certain how they felt about her, and she could only imagine the torment inside of them, and yet they had been brave and had wanted to help.

She wanted to help, too. But unlike Keriah, who had gone in order to provide medical assistance to Maner, who they knew was missing an ear, Phoebe would have simply been deadweight. She was not as skilled in disguise as Mr. Coulton-Jones, or his sister, and the depraved area they were entering would be a danger to any young woman, whether common or gently-bred.

It still didn't quell her disappointment. She scolded herself for being so immature.

And so in company with Uncle Sol, she left London to travel back to Stapytton House. She hid herself in the conservatory, where she played with her roots and her leaves, and sulked.

But perhaps it was the sulking that helped her to come up with a new theory. And after sulking another hour or two, she had to admit that her theory may not be half bad.

She had even reached the point where she suspected her theory might even be brilliant, and that's when everyone returned.

What shocked her the most was the angry flush on Mr. Rosmont's neck, and the way his hands were shaking, even when he stood still. She noticed that Lady Aymer also looked at her childhood friend with concern.

They all gathered in one of the few usable rooms in the house, which happened to be the butler's pantry. The wine had long since been drunk, taken, or broken, and there were only rotting wooden shelves along the stone walls. But after he'd first leased the house, while Keriah was setting up her stillroom, Phoebe, Mr. Havner, and Uncle Sol had donned gardening gloves and removed as much of the wood as possible, throwing them out in a pile in the backyard. There had been a small table in the pantry, but they had removed that, also, since one of the legs had begun to rot, and there were dark stains across the surface, which smelled faintly rotten, and made Phoebe think that the stains were not wine. They replaced the table with a long, rather fancifully carved table from the library, and assembled a mix of different chairs around it.

Phoebe made tea in the kitchen, and served it along with some biscuits that she had brought with her from her aunt's home. Mr. Coulton-Jones, Keriah, and Lady Aymer sat at the table, but Mr. Rosmont paced along one wall, turned, paced along the neighboring wall, then turned around to repeat his trail. Uncle Sol's eyes followed the young man's movements, but he refrained from commenting about his nervous energy.

"Where are the twins?" Phoebe asked.

"We dropped them off at Lady Wynwood's house before coming here," Mr. Coulton-Jones said. He explained about finding Maner Hansen, and the condition he had been in.

Phoebe asked, "Did you find none of the plants in the room with Maner?"

Uncle Sol looked at her as though her question was confusing. "Why would you think he would have plants there?"

"He was injured," she said. "It is well known that the Root causes rapid healing. Silas's ear scarred over in less than a day. Since Maner knew the location of Jack's greenhouse, I wondered if perhaps he stole a plant or two, and attempted to use the plant to heal himself."

The looks of surprise of everyone around the table, including Mr. Rosmont, made Phoebe frown at all of them. "Are you surprised that the idea came from me, or the fact that none of you thought of it?"

Uncle Sol cleared his throat, and Mr. Coulton-Jones and Mr. Rosmont pointedly looked away from her. But Lady Aymer smiled at her and said, "I do believe the trained agents are in shock, Miss Sauber."

"I didn't see any plants," Keriah said.

Mr. Coulton-Jones's brows drew low over his eyes as he stared at the table. Slowly he said, "I think I smelled that plant —the Goldensuit—when we first entered the room under the church."

Mr. Rosmont paused in his pacing. "You did? I smelled nothing but mold."

"It was very faint, and I might not have noticed it if I had not recently smelled it at Jack's greenhouse."

From Maner's clothes, perhaps? Considering how dangerous

Jack was, she wouldn't have expected Maner to risk invading his greenhouse simply out of curiosity. "It was the smell of the plant, and not the Root?"

"I believe it was the plant," Mr. Coulton-Jones said. "I have not come across the Root since waking, but when I was given the Root before, even with simply normal senses, the smell of blood was overpowering. While out on the street, I noticed that strong smells tend to mask more subtle odors."

Phoebe questioned them again about exactly what Maner Hansen had said about the Goldensuit plant, but he had given them very little information.

"From the leaves and roots that I collected from Jack's greenhouse," she said, "I know that this plant is used in the Root elixir, and it seems similar to poppies. This is not much different from what I thought after I first examined the Root sample." She turned to Keriah. "I wrote out my findings and left it on the stillroom table for you."

Keriah nodded her thanks.

"Tomorrow, we must look into the information that Maner Hansen gave to us," Uncle Sol said to all of them.

"I doubt we will find much, but we can go to Planters Flat Inn, which was where the French group took Maner Hansen," Lady Aymer said. "By asking around the area, we might discover where they went after they left the inn."

"We also have the names of two men who work for Maner Hansen," Mr. Rosmont said. He did not stop pacing even as he spoke. "Dent Roe, and Chas Lenox. Since he paid them to keep an eye out for anything that happened in the area, they most certainly would have seen the men who stole Jack's plants."

"We also must try to undermine their attempts to return to France," Uncle Sol said. "How familiar are you with the smugglers in this area?"

Mr. Rosmont shook his head. Lady Aymer thought for a moment, but then she also slowly shook her head. "In my last mission, I purchased passage back to England with smugglers who dropped me off further north. I have not traveled between England and France from any point near London."

"Septimus might have more extensive knowledge of the current smugglers who work the Channel at this time," Uncle Sol said.

"He will be happy to be relieved of paperwork duties," Phoebe said dryly. "Aunt Laura complains that he keeps ruining her blotters."

"Then Mr. Coulton-Jones, Mr. Rosmont, and Lady Aymer—" Uncle Sol began to say, but Phoebe interrupted him.

"Uncle Sol, may I borrow Mr. Coulton-Jones? I have a theory."

His eyebrows rose, but there was nothing dismissive in his face. "What sort of theory?"

"Since Mr. Coulton-Jones said that he could smell the plants, even faintly, when he visited the bolthole, it means that Maner was in contact with the fresh plants at some point. I believe he has his own greenhouse of plants, or he has recently been to one of Jack's."

"*One* of Jack's?" Mr. Rosmont asked. "He has more than the one?"

"I am fairly certain he has more than one," Phoebe said. "I am thinking about this from the perspective of another gardener. Maner said that he knew about the men Jack hired as gardeners, but Jack wouldn't need other men as gardeners in that tiny greenhouse. I believe Maner must know something about another greenhouse that Jack owns, or perhaps even more than one, although he said he didn't."

"How will you find out more?" Uncle Sol leaned forward slightly.

"If Jack added skylights to that one greenhouse, he might have made another one using the same carpenter. He may have used someone recommended by his neighbors or local to that area of London. We can return and ask the neighbors about carpenters."

"Wait a moment," Mr. Coulton-Jones said. "This is where Jack had his greenhouse. He might return."

"It will be daylight," Phoebe said, "and I am merely speaking to the neighbors. I am hopeful we will be able to speak to the same ones we spoke with this morning. They would recognize both myself and Mr. Coulton-Jones."

Uncle Sol frowned. "It is still not a safe area."

"I know it isn't," Phoebe said, "but I won't be alone." She gave a wide smile to Mr. Coulton-Jones, but it must have looked quite fierce, because he leaned away from her with alarm in his eyes.

"As a protector," Phoebe said, "I'll have my own, in the flesh Samson. I couldn't be in better hands, don't you think?"

Chapter Eight

It was early morning again, the same street again, and Michael felt the same nervousness buzzing under his skin. This time, the buzzing was accompanied by an intermittent pain that seemed to almost whisper against his skull, coming and going like careless caresses.

They had returned to the unnamed street that ran in front of Fenbear's Playhouse, only a few houses down from the boarding house where Jack had had his greenhouse. Michael and Miss Sauber were again posing as a young married couple, and she strolled alongside him, her hand tucked into the crook of his elbow.

However, this time she scowled at him. "Darling," she said through gritted teeth, "people are going to think you are itching for a fight."

He focused on relaxing the muscles of his face, and belatedly noticed the tension across his brow. He was embarrassed that he had lost his concentration on his disguise and that the civilian next to him had to point it out.

Except for his sister, he had not worked with any English female agents. He had worked with two female agents on missions on the Continent, and one had been French while the other Italian. He'd had to adjust his mindset and the way he did things, since he was more used to working with men. Like

Isabella, the two female agents had both been skilled, which had been vastly different from the civilian women he had had to help, who had been trusting him to protect them.

But working with Miss Sauber, a civilian, felt as comfortable as having Isabella next to him. She was observant but not obvious about it, and, well ... she smelled nice.

However, he was still agitated because of the recent sighting of Jack, without his makeup, the scar prominently visible on his cheek. The memory still made the anger flare inside him, like a burst of flame from a spitting fireplace, but now accompanying the anger was the awareness of the danger he presented.

He had looked so innocuous, but Michael knew he posed more of a threat than any enemy he had faced in France. And one of the few women whose personality he actually *liked* was walking into danger by his side.

"This is a bad idea," he said.

He knew he had said this several times already, and Miss Sauber simply gave him a tiresome look.

In a halting voice, he admitted, "I feel as though I must look into the face of everyone who passes us, fearing that one of them may be Jack again."

In a low voice, she said, "I, too, have not let down my guard or become careless. I am fully aware of the risks."

Yes, he had had reason to be impressed with her good sense, and he should have known that she would not take the situation lightly. He swallowed. "It's difficult for me..." He couldn't seem to find the words to express his fears and his concern.

But when she looked up at him, she seemed to understand what he wasn't saying. "Then teach me," she said. "Teach me so that you will have one less thing to concern you, one less thing for you to think about, or worry about."

Somehow she knew exactly what to say. It did not ease his apprehension, exactly, but it gave his mind something else to focus upon rather than his incessant scanning of the street, the nervous flittering of his line of sight. He swallowed. She was right. He could teach her. It would not make the situation safer, but it would ease a fraction of his anxiety.

He glanced at her disguise, at her face, and her body language. "Your clothes are well-chosen," he said, "but there are subtleties in the way you move, and the expressions of your face, that can make people's eyes slide off of you."

"Then teach me," she repeated.

"Tell me, how did you decide how to act for your disguise?"

"I observed other women on the street," she answered promptly.

He nodded. It was what he had expected. "You must strive to become the person you are supposed to be, rather than simply copying their actions. It is like the difference between a truly exceptional actor, and a more wooden one. You commit to the disguise completely, ignoring the social rules that have been ingrained in you, overcoming any restraints you might have. You make yourself anew, without those rules, without those restraints."

She blinked as she thought a moment, then she said, "I believe I understand what you are saying."

He didn't think he had explained himself very well, but her movements changed minutely. She leaned more into him, far closer and more sensually than a proper society miss, and more like a newlywed, a woman comfortable with her body and with physical intimacy with her husband. There were also subtle changes in her face, a relaxing of the lines between her brows, at the corners of her mouth. When she glanced up at him, her gaze was warm but casual, a woman at ease with the man next to her, confident in his affection for her.

He was almost shocked at her skill. The feel of her hand on his arm, the accidental brush of her body against him, were completely natural. He was impressed with her, and yet at the same time, the part inside of him that remained the proper Mr.

Coulton-Jones surfaced briefly and sent heat to his cheeks and over the tops of his ears. It took all his mental discipline to force the blush away.

He cleared his throat. "Yes, that is it exactly," was all he said, but he knew she understood.

He recalled the last time they had been on this street, and his worry for her. She was not Isabella, trained and with several years' experience. But he had to do all he could to ensure Miss Sauber was not like Richard.

"It requires all your mental focus to not lose hold of the disguise." He hesitated, then admitted, "Over Christmas, I was posing as a servant but lost control of my disguise for a moment when I caught a cup that was falling. I was nearly discovered if not for another man distracting attention away from me. It was only a moment, but that moment was enough."

She looked up into his eyes, not Miss Sauber but a young wife —*his* young wife, since he was posing as a low-level clerk. "I will not be distracted," she promised him.

They were nearing Jack's boarding house, and she nodded ahead of them. "Look."

As before, there were young men loitering outside of Fenbear's Playhouse, but there were not so many neighbors gossiping near the boarding house as there had been the last time. However, among those neighbors were the three who had told them about "Mr. Ramsy"—two older women, one with a long face and large eyes, while the other was shorter with plump cheeks, and an older man.

Pulling at Michael's arm, Miss Sauber headed toward the trio, wearing a charming smile that he had never seen on her face at the society functions they had attended. "Hello again," she said. It was as though she were more comfortable here among these plain-dressed strangers than she had been with her acquaintances in ballrooms, surrounded by opulence. He wasn't certain if it was her skill at disguise shining so brightly or if she truly were more at ease with these people.

"Oh!" The round-cheeked woman's eyes widened. "You were here yesterday, weren't you?"

"You entered Mr. Ramsy's house just before he arrived." The long-faced woman's expression was alarmed. "He didn't see you, did he?"

"Oh, no," Miss Sauber said blithely, "we left after only a few minutes. He arrived afterward?"

The round-cheeked woman shuddered. "He was terribly upset."

"Could hear his screaming up and down the street," the other woman said.

The old man nodded, his face grave but saying nothing.

"How distressing," Miss Sauber said. "It must be difficult being neighbors."

The round-cheeked woman leaned forward and said in a low voice, "After Mr. Ramsy left, Mr. Dockery went inside to look around." She nudged her elbow in the direction of the old man next to her. "Mr. Ramsy apparently used the room to grow plants."

"How strange. Is that what was stolen?"

Mr. Dockery simply nodded.

"Did you not see his room when you went inside?" the long-faced woman asked, her eyes narrowing.

"Oh, no," Miss Sauber said. "We searched for the landlord, who shooed us out straightaway. Quite rude."

"We were worried about you when we saw Mr. Ramsy return," the round-cheeked woman said.

"That is quite kind of you, and we apologize if we caused you distress. We found a room to let a few streets over."

"So we shall be neighbors, of a sort, after all." The round-cheeked woman smiled. "I am Mrs. Palley, and this is Mr. Dockery and Mrs. Falconer."

"Mr. and Mrs. Jones," Miss Sauber said, as though she had

been introducing herself as such for several months, and not for the first time just now. "We managed to let an attic room, but there is only one small window. Mr. Jones convinced the landlord to waive our rent for a few months if we paid for a skylight to be built."

"How clever of you." Mrs. Palley beamed at Michael.

"Do you know of any carpenters nearby who have built skylights before?" Miss Sauber asked.

Both women turned to Mr. Dockery, who took a moment to think, then said, "Mr. John English, Mr. Samuel Curnick."

"Oh, yes, they are both very respectable," Mrs. Palley said.

Mrs. Falconer sniffed. "I found Mr. English difficult to work with."

"He's simply a bit curt, Lucy," Mrs. Palley chided her friend.

"Where can we find them?" Miss Sauber asked.

Within minutes they were walking away, Miss Sauber waving gaily to the trio, with directions to two carpenters, and Michael hadn't said a single word.

"Was that acceptable, sir?" she asked him as though she were a soldier under his command.

"That was perfect."

She smiled up at him, but she maintained her facade as a young married woman, her smile a bit more warm and her body drawing much closer to him than their normal, proper relationship.

He had to clear his throat before asking, "What made you decide to ask about carpenters?" She had told him her intent before they had arrived on the street, but he hadn't thought to ask her why before now.

"Originally, I tried to find something unique about the soil we collected from the greenhouse," she said. "I hoped there might be fertilizer or additives to the soil that might be special for the plant, because then, Jack would need to find a source for those special additives."

"You thought to look at dirt? I would not have even considered something like that."

"It is simply because you are not a gardener," she said modestly. "But it was a dead end. We could not find anything in the soil that would be any different from typical fertilizer for flowers like poppies and lilies."

He knew that the "we" she mentioned was likely herself and Miss Gardinier.

"I was quite discouraged and wasted too much time trying to find answers in the plant matter we collected. But then I remembered the greenhouse and the fact that the size was a disappointment."

"What do you mean?"

"It was very small. We could estimate the number of pots from the size of the tables and the outlines of the water stains, and we were doubtful that the number of plants in the greenhouse would be enough to make the *medicine* being passed out to *friends*."

So, not enough Goldensuit plants to make the amount of Root elixir circulating amongst Jack's men.

"Also, the tables near the front window had obviously held seedlings. It made me suspect that he grew the seedlings in that greenhouse and then transferred them to a larger greenhouse somewhere else. In which case, he might have used the same carpenter to install skylights in a larger greenhouse elsewhere."

"Why the same carpenter?"

"If I were transferring seedlings to another greenhouse, I would not wish it to be too far away. Also, there had been mention about the issues with the well water, so the other greenhouse is likely not far from the same water source."

Michael had known that Sol Drydale would not involve civilians like Miss Sauber and Miss Gardinier if he did not trust in their abilities, but here again she was proving those abilities. "I don't know that any other gardener would have thought all of that."

"I'm sure they would have," she said. "But I also don't know that Uncle would have trusted any other gardener."

"I am glad he trusted you." He looked down at her hand, tucked into the crook of his arm, and said in a low voice, "I don't know that any other gardener—that any other *archer*—could have saved me. Thank you."

She flushed slightly, but her smile at him was that of a young wife, not Miss Sauber. "You're welcome, darling."

Yes, she had saved him, but for what? He had been given the Root, and his days were numbered.

Lady Wynwood's words had been circling in his head, and he hadn't been able to mute them. He had rarely thought deeply about his mortality, because to worry about death while on a mission would prevent him from doing what needed to be done.

But the biggest question in his mind had been why God would have saved him in that burned factory, why God would have brought this woman, of all the women in London, into his life, into this conflict, when soon he would be dead. All it served to do was make him regret not giving in to his attraction to her.

As he looked into her eyes, he drowned in sea-foam waters, and the words stumbled from his lips before he could stop himself. "I wish ..."

She tilted her head questioningly.

I wish I had spoken to you those times I saw you standing alone against the wall at a soiree.

I wish I had sought you out for the supper dance, to lead you in to supper and talk and laugh with you.

I wish I had not avoided you.

I wish I had not wasted so much time.

"I wish I had danced with you more."

The color of her eyes lightened until they were like jewels, but there was also sadness because she knew, as he did, that there would be no more opportunities for them to dance together.

He cleared his throat. "Don't lose focus," he said gruffly.

She hadn't, really, but his reminder made her turn her face away from him. It felt like removing a warm coat from his body.

Since they were on foot, it took them a little while to find the first carpenter's shop.

"I believe this is it." She nodded toward a low-slung building coming up on their left.

Mr. Curnick's carpentry workshop held a wide set of double doors open to the street, with the sounds of banging and sawing spilling out into the street in a fine mist of sawdust. Inside could be seen two or three men working on various projects, while a balding man stood to the side of the doorway, wiping his hands on a rag.

"Excuse me," Miss Sauber said with a disarming smile, "we're looking for Mr. Curnick."

"You found him," he said. He had barely any hair on his round head, but his face looked young. He had the wide shoulders of a man who worked hard all day at his craft.

"Mr. Dockery recommended you," Miss Sauber said, and the carpenter relaxed slightly at the name. "He said you may have done Mr. Ramsy's skylight."

Mr. Curnick shook his head. "Never did a job for a Mr. Ramsy. Did skylights for Miss Eades and Mr. Stark."

"Would you be willing to give us their direction? We should like to see your work."

He hesitated, studying her, then glancing at Michael. Then he nodded. "Wait a moment," he said, then disappeared inside his shop.

"Why get their directions?" he whispered to her.

"They might still be greenhouses connected to Jack," she whispered back.

Mr. Curnick returned with a scrap of paper with directions written in a careful hand. Miss Sauber thanked him with a smile Michael thought was rather unnecessarily sweet, and they left to find Mr. English's carpentry workshop.

In contrast to Mr. Curnick's shop, Mr. English's shop was considerably more ramshackle. The weathered boards of the front walls were stained and slightly warped, giving a forlorn air to the tall but narrow building. From inside came the sound of a hammer.

When the hammering paused, they knocked on a rickety door with wide gaps between the boards, which looked as though they had suffered fire damage at some point in the past. At the gruff, "Come in!" they entered the shop.

It was a single large room with carpentry tools hung along the walls and scattered across tables. The small windows and back door were thrown open, and the lone carpenter stood near the rear of the room, taking advantage of the light. He didn't look up as they came inside, simply stared down with a frown at the chair he was fixing. After a moment, he stuck a nail in the wood of a leg and hammered it in. Only then did he turn to them.

He had a squint and a sneer to his face, although they hadn't said anything to him to cause him to be displeased. "What do you want?" he said rudely.

With manners like that, Michael wondered that he received any business. He took a step in front of Miss Sauber, sensing that the man would not be pleased to speak to a woman. "Looking for a carpenter to build a skylight. We heard you did one for Mr. Ramsy."

The frown deepened. "Who told you that?"

"Mr. Dockery, down near Fenbear's Playhouse."

Mr. English turned back to the chair. "Didn't do no skylights for Mr. Ramsy. Ye'd best find another carpenter."

"Did skylights for anyone else?"

"Are ye deaf?" Mr. English's voice was louder and sharper than he would have expected, and he scowled at Michael. "I didn't do no skylights. Ye should leave." His hand tightened on the hammer he held.

Michael held out his hands in a placating gesture. "Didn't mean anything by it. We'll leave."

Mr. English's shoulders were too tense, his glare too fierce. Their question should not have caused a reaction like that. Michael only wanted to get Miss Sauber safely away. A brawl with a carpenter would only bring attention, and possibly injury for one or all of them.

They left the darkened workshop. Michael felt Mr. English's angry eyes on his back until the door swung shut behind them.

They walked away, but as they passed the corner of the building, he told her, "Wait here." Then he hurried past the neighboring building and ducked into a narrow alley.

It wasn't an alley, more like a foot-track from the street to the backside of the buildings, but it was relatively free of refuse and trash, and he slipped out onto a dirt path that ran along the backside of the buildings, just wide enough for a dogcart.

He turned toward the back door of Mr. English's carpentry workshop, just in time to see the man exit, settling a hat on his messy brown locks. Mr. English saw him and his eyes widened, not with his previous anger, but with fear.

The carpenter took off at a sprint. Michael ran after him.

The dirt path was hemmed in by the backsides of buildings, but it spilled out onto a busy street. Michael tried to force a burst of speed to catch the man before he reached that street. He at first felt a pain that lanced through the front of his brain, but then was surprised to find his legs responded.

Ah, yes. The Root. He'd nearly forgotten.

He reached out a hand and brushed the back of Mr. English's coat.

Then the carpenter had rushed out onto a wide thoroughfare, not large enough for more than a carriage but thronged with foot traffic. Michael was close enough behind him to follow as he darted between clusters of pedestrians, pushing his way when it was blocked and garnering shouts and curses in his wake.

But as Michael rounded a group of three older women, he slowed. He couldn't see English anywhere.

He continued down the street, scanning the faces and figures. There were no sharp movements to indicate someone fleeing, and English's nondescript hat and brown hair made him blend in with all the other men.

At the crossroad with another wide street, Michael halted. He'd lost him.

He made his way back to Miss Sauber, who had *not* listened to him and had followed him to the backside of the carpentry shop, albeit from a distance. "Are you injured?" she asked as she saw him.

"No."

She sighed. "I apologize."

He stared at her. "Why should you apologize?"

"Since the neighbors hadn't known who Mr. Ramsy is, I had assumed the carpenters were the same." She tilted her chin in the direction Mr. English had fled. "But he obviously knows the true identity of his customer. If we had suspected as such, I'm certain you would have suggested a different method of approaching him."

"The fault does not lie with you. It had not occurred to me, and I am the trained agent."

She squinted at the strip of sky above them. They had started early this morning, but it had taken them several hours to visit both carpenters. "It is not yet too late. Should we go to the addresses of the two people for whom Mr. Curnick built skylights?"

"Let us simply view the outsides of the buildings. After the way we frightened Mr. English, the more prudent approach is probably wisest."

"I doubt either address will be the place we seek, but it is likely that ... *Uncle* would wish us to be thorough."

They exchanged glances, knowing she was referring to Mr. Drydale.

She sighed. "I had hoped to find something about another greenhouse, but I fear this day has been a waste of your time."

True, they had not uncovered any information that seemed useful, but ...

He tucked her hand again in the crook of his arm and looked down at her, catching a faint scent of wildflowers soaked in sunshine.

He couldn't quite say that the day had been a waste of time.

Sol was nursing a cup of coffee he'd inexpertly made at the ancient stove in the Stapytton House kitchen when the sound of a carriage roused him from his morose thoughts. He grasped the pistol on the worn kitchen table before him and walked toward the front foyer so that he could look out the dirty front windows, partially screened by moth-eaten curtains. He relaxed as he spotted Laura's unmarked carriage, driven by Mr. Havner.

He hadn't expected her, especially since it was still early afternoon and as a typical fashionable noblewoman, she might be expected to be shopping or preparing to parade herself in Hyde Park. But he supposed he shouldn't be surprised since Phoebe had left with Mr. Coulton-Jones this morning. Laura had likely been pacing holes in her fine Aubusson carpets all day.

Miss Gardinier poked her head out from the stillroom as he returned to the kitchen.

"It's Laura," he told her.

She eyed his coffee cup. "Shall I make tea?"

"Is your tea better than your cooking?"

She grinned at him. "Infinitely."

Laura entered through the side door and shed her outerwear as she walked into the warm kitchen. She carried a basket, which she set on the table. "Scones from Minnie," she announced.

Miss Gardinier, moving the kettle in the fireplace, brightened. "That will be a relief. I nearly poisoned Mr. Drydale with luncheon."

"You needn't worry, dear, for Sol has a stomach that could eat dirt and not feel ill effects."

"I beg your pardon," he complained, although his lips twisted in a smile. "I have never eaten dirt. I have eaten considerably worse things than dirt."

"Mr. Havner is taking care of the horses and will be in shortly," Laura said as she laid out the contents of the basket.

"You had no social engagements today?" Sol helped her unpack a few cups and plates brought from her home.

"If I did, I would have begged off."

He impulsively reached out to touch the back of her hand as she laid a sealed jar of preserves upon the table. "Phoebe will be safe as can be. She has the strongest man in London with her," he added.

The corner of her mouth quirked upward, but she did not quite smile. She glanced back at Miss Gardinier, who was scooping tea leaves into a pot with her back to them. "It goes against all my rational judgments to have them involved in this. And yet I've involved my servants, and I myself am knee-deep in these foul secrets like a gravedigger."

He frowned at her. "You are not at fault for any of this."

A spasm crossed her face, so swiftly and so subtly that he wouldn't have caught it if he hadn't been looking so closely at her. Then she smoothed her features. "I have made the decisions to involve me and those I care about in these troubles. Perhaps I was not at fault to instigate these things, but I bear responsibility for what I have done with the knowledge. As do we all."

She had spoken quickly to mask her reaction, but he saw that there was still something she was keeping from him. He had suspected it before, but her reaction now fueled his uncertainties.

The part of him that was an agent of the Crown balked at not knowing, at the secrets she was keeping close to her. The knowledge might be vital to the safety of those working for him.

But the other part of him, the man who had seen the pain in her face as she confessed what she had done and said to Mrs. Jadis only hours before her death, shied away from wanting to know. He could not imagine the blows she had been dealt, both physical and emotional, during her marriage to Wynwood, and he knew she must have kept many secrets from her husband simply to survive and to protect her household. The secrets she kept from him would be an extension of that.

Deep inside, he didn't feel he deserved to demand the truth about all her secrets, because despite hazarding a guess as to what kind of monster Wynwood had been, he had done nothing to help her during the years she had suffered. And the confidential orders he had kept from her had only served to deliver emotional blows that must be similar to what she had endured from her husband.

So he didn't ask. After all that had happened, he knew by now that she would tell him when she was ready. She would tell him if it were vitally important.

As he picked up his cold coffee cup, he remembered the thoughts that had kept him occupied before she arrived—his failure to recognize Mrs. Jadis's role in the secret group when he'd first investigated her the year before Wynwood died. It had been a sharp blow to his confidence in his abilities as a team leader and senior agent in the Ramparts. For so long, he had been supremely arrogant to think that he was unusually observant, that he couldn't be fooled. He had been fooled in the worst possible way, because if he hadn't blithely disregarded Mrs. Jadis, if he'd realized she had been involved in something beyond her life as a lord's mistress, he might have known about Jack's mysterious group eleven years ago, rather than only recently.

He'd spoken to his associates at the Ramparts, and put out queries to some select contacts, but as he'd feared, discovering information about a prostitute who had been dead for so many years had proved impossible.

Laura had noticed him frowning at his coffee. "Bad brew?"

That made him smile. "Self-castigation."

"About?"

"Mrs. Jadis."

She grew quiet and a bit tense.

"Did you discover anything?" he asked in a low voice. She had mentioned briefly that she knew a way to find out more about Mrs. Jadis, but she hadn't spoken to him about how she would go about doing that.

She shook her head. "Not yet."

He tried not to seem impatient or intensely curious about how she intended to attain that information, but from the way she looked away from him, he suspected he failed miserably.

"It won't be much longer," she said, although he didn't know what she meant by that.

He supposed he had to trust her. But they had already experienced so much together, it wasn't difficult.

Well, not *too* difficult.

Just as Mr. Havner entered the kitchen, they were surprised by the sound of another carriage—no, that sounded like more than one. He picked up the pistol, which he'd carefully laid upon a shelf far from everyone else and pointing toward the open door to the hallway. He again retraced his steps to the front foyer and the ratty curtains over the windows.

He recognized both Mr. Rosmont and Mr. Coulton-Jones at the reins of two small open carriages. Mr. Rosmont had unearthed an ancient cart from his family estate, which lay only an hour's drive from London, but Sol didn't recognize the cart driven by Mr. Coulton-Jones.

Lady Aymer and Phoebe entered the kitchen only a few minutes after Sol had told Laura and Miss Gardinier to expect more mouths to feed. Phoebe was still dressed in plain clothes, and Lady Aymer was also still in her street urchin's attire, which she had opted to wear for her assignment today with Mr. Rosmont. Sol knew she was short enough to pass as a young boy, but this was the first time he could clearly see her in disguise in the light from the candles. It was not simply her looks that she had changed—she walked and moved like a boy who had grown up on the streets. He understood better why she was often tasked with high-level missions, and why her success rate was also impeccable.

Lady Aymer perked up at the sight of the scones. "Tea? I'm famished." She even sounded like a young boy as she dropped onto a seat at the long table.

When Mr. Rosmont and Mr. Coulton-Jones entered after caring for the horses, Sol noted that they also had not yet shed the costumes they adopted while out on the streets today—and not simply clothes, but like Lady Aymer, they had also not yet shed the mindsets of their disguises. Mr. Rosmont walked like a street bruiser. However, Mr. Coulton-Jones hadn't simply lost his aristocratic posture, there was something indefinable about the way he moved that made him seem exactly as he dressed, like a lowly clerk, perhaps for a merchant. Sol now better understood why the siblings were known for their ability at dissimulation.

Mr. Havner balked at sitting with his employer and the rest of them at the table, until Laura sternly ordered him to do so. She had perhaps had the foresight to instruct her cook to bake for an army, for there seemed no end to the scones and biscuits she unearthed from the basket, accompanied by butter and preserves in crocks covered with waxed paper and tied with twine.

Keriah handed a jar of butter toward Lady Aymer. "My lady, would you like—"

The lady in question froze in the act of licking preserves from her thumb, for all the world like the young boy she appeared to be. Then she laughed. "I forget to leave the role, sometimes. Thank you." She took the jar. "You must call me Isabella. After all, 'Lady Aymer' doesn't lick jam off her fingers. And may I use your first names?"

The two young ladies agreed.

They ate companionably for a few minutes, and Sol was struck by how they reminded him of other teams he had led, and other group meals he had presided over. Although they were a mix of agents and civilians, they interacted with each other comfortably, joking and laughing. How was this any different from the men—and occasional woman—he'd worked with at the Ramparts? Perhaps he could no longer think of Phoebe and Miss Gardinier as civilians. Even Laura was more like a co-leader than a high-born lady who had become involved in these matters.

"All right, you bottomless gullets, can you stop stuffing your faces long enough to give reports?" He would never have spoken thus at a society function, but somehow his usual gruff tone and casual speech seemed more appropriate here, in the dilapidated kitchen of Stapytton House.

"Sol," Laura objected, although her tone indicated she wasn't very serious about it.

Miss Gardinier blinked in surprise, but Phoebe grinned. Or at least, she tried to grin around her mouthful of scone.

Unperturbed, Lady Aymer wiped the crumbs from her mouth with a napkin. "I hope all of you had more luck than we did. Last night, Thorne and I took Mr. Ackett to speak to his smuggler contacts, and thankfully we heard something without needing to travel all the way to the coast. A group of smugglers ferried a Frenchwoman and four men on Tuesday evening to a village just outside of Portsmouth, but on Wednesday morning, someone killed them."

Phoebe frowned. "That's strange. Would Brigitte have a reason for doing so?"

"Possibly," Mr. Rosmont said slowly, "but they'd have needed a compelling reason to want to kill their ride."

"The dead smugglers could have been the victims of some other men they might have crossed," Sol said, "although the timing is suspicious."

"But the other smugglers are still wary," Lady Aymer said. "They don't know why or who, but they all know that the smugglers were killed only hours after unloading the French group."

"The moon is waning," Mr. Rosmont added, "and normally there would be more smugglers' boats crossing the Channel, but many are laying low, unwilling to ferry Brigitte's group and possibly become targets themselves."

"That is a stroke of good fortune," Sol said. "They won't be leaving for another few days. What about the two men Maner mentioned, Dent Roe and Chas Lenox?"

"This morning, Thorne and I went searching, but we only found one of them, Dent Roe," Lady Aymer said. "Luckily, he and Chas Lenox had been at their job of watching the street."

"Were they told specifically to watch that house?" Sol asked.

"No, Maner apparently didn't trust him with that information," Lady Aymer said." But they were in position when Jack's greenhouse was robbed."

"Mr. Roe saw three men and one woman force their way into the boarding house," Mr. Rosmont said. He'd foregone scones and only sipped black tea, which somehow didn't surprise Sol. "They exited only a few minutes later, each carrying bulging sacks. Mr. Roe and Mr. Lenox tried to follow the four, but one of the men noticed Mr. Lenox and came back to beat him up.

Mr. Roe managed to sneak away before they spotted him also, but the last he saw was the man sticking a knife into Mr. Lenox."

The table grew silent as they continued eating. After a few minutes, Sol cleared his throat. "What about the inn where they took Maner?"

"We asked at the inn and in the area surrounding, but found nothing about the French group," Lady Aymer said. "It's not surprising, I suppose, considering their methods. If anyone did know anything, they certainly wouldn't have mentioned it, even by accident."

Sol nodded to Mr. Coulton-Jones and Phoebe. "Did you discover anything regarding the carpenters?"

"We asked Jack's neighbors, who gave the names of two carpenters," Phoebe said. "One hadn't done Jack's skylights, although he gave us the names of two customers who had skylights done—Miss Eades and Mr. Stark."

At the names, Sol noticed Laura's hand jerked as she was raising her teacup to her lips. She placed the cup down carefully.

"The other one insisted he hadn't done any skylights and told us to leave," Mr. Coulton-Jones said. "We did, but I circled around to the backside of his workshop and saw him trying to bolt. I chased him, but lost him in the crowds."

"I hadn't thought that Jack would have told his carpenter his true identity," Phoebe said, "especially since he was renting the room under a false name and he appeared without his makeup every day. But apparently Mr. English knew precisely who his customer had been."

Sol didn't blame them—he had assumed the same, when Phoebe had told him about her plan last night—but he couldn't help feeling disappointed that they hadn't been able to talk to the carpenter at all.

"Too bad you didn't catch him," Mr. Rosmont said to Mr.

Coulton-Jones. "We might have been able to get him to tell you what other properties he worked on for Jack."

"Or he may have had records," Lady Aymer said.

"We went by Miss Eades and Mr. Stark's buildings, even though Mr. Curnick hadn't done Jack's skylights," Phoebe said. "We only did it to be thorough, but we discovered something strange."

"Strange?" Laura's voice was unusually tight.

"Mr. Stark's building was a paper-making workshop," Mr. Coulton-Jones said, "but Miss Eades' address was a ... er ..."

"Gambling hell," Phoebe said baldly, without even a blush to her cheek even though Sol would have thought she had never before even spoken the words before this moment. "And brothel," she added, scandalizing him further.

Mr. Rosmont, Mr. Coulton-Jones, and even Mr. Havner looked uncomfortable at her blunt speaking, but both Laura and Miss Gardinier merely looked interested. "Is Miss Eades the, er, proprietor of the establishment?" Laura asked.

"Mr. Coulton-Jones asked around discreetly," Phoebe said primly, but with a sparkle in her eye.

Mr. Coulton-Jones looked even more uncomfortable, but he answered, "I don't believe so. It is called Hendey's, and the owner is a Mr. Southam, but he appears to work closely with a Mrs. Marsh who perhaps runs the, er, other side of the business."

Sol frowned. "Jack last worked out of a theater, which makes me think he may favor noisy, busy businesses to hide his coming and going."

"I don't believe it has to do with Apothecary Jack," Laura said hesitantly.

All eyes turned toward her. "What makes you think so?" Sol asked.

She didn't answer his question. Instead, she said, "I think the gaming hell is connected to Maner, not to Jack."

Phoebe seemed struck by a thought. "Mr. Coulton-Jones mentioned he could smell the Goldensuit in the room under the church, as though Maner had recently been near the plants. What if he owns his own secret greenhouse?"

"Jack would kill him if he found out," Mr. Coulton-Jones said.

"So he would do all he could to keep that fact a complete secret," Lady Aymer said, "including hiding it from the French group and from us."

Mr. Rosmont glanced out the tiny, cracked kitchen window at the fading light outside. "We could investigate Hendey's tonight. It wasn't an exclusive club?" he asked Mr. Coulton-Jones, who shook his head.

"Who will go?" Laura asked.

"If there is a greenhouse, I should go," Phoebe said.

Laura began rummaging through the basket she had brought, and she pulled out some thick pieces of dark-colored cloth, with sturdy cloth ties sewn to them. "Maner said the plants were poisonous, so Aya and I made these masks for you," Laura said as she passed out the cloths. She hadn't been present when everyone, sans Phoebe, had returned from finding Maner yesterday, but apparently Phoebe had informed her about what they had discovered. Sol was surprised but also impressed that she had thought to make the masks just from hearing that bit of information.

"Thorne and I will go with Miss Sauber," Mr. Coulton-Jones said.

"Prince shall go, as well," Lady Aymer said.

"Please be very, very careful," Laura told them.

"Always," Mr. Coulton-Jones said, although he was only half in jest.

"Jack is unlikely to be there," Mr. Rosmont said.

"True," Laura said, "but if this is connected to Maner, it is probably something he doesn't want Jack to know about. In which case ..." She couldn't help glancing at Phoebe in concern. "... Maner will have taken precautions to protect whatever is there."

Chapter Nine

There was a cool evening breeze that was perhaps stiffer than normal, but Michael welcomed the chill that eased the headache throbbing persistently against his forehead. They approached the brightly lit building housing Hendey's gaming hell, standing out like a lantern on the dirty London street. The sounds of merriment could be heard despite the shut front door and closed glass windows, and the air was thick with the scent of cheap perfume, spilled spirits, and unpleasant bodily fluids that had found their way onto the street.

But undercutting those pungent scents, Michael could detect that low note, a mix of floral and herb, that seemed to thrum deep inside him as he breathed it in. Goldensuit.

When he and Miss Sauber had walked past this gaming hell earlier that afternoon, he had not been able to smell the Goldensuit above the other smells on the street, especially since there had been a cart selling moldy looking onions and garlic nearby. But in the dark of night, the cart was gone and only those seeking entertainment wandered close to Hendey's.

Finely dressed men—and one or two women—entered and exited the front door, causing bursts of laughter, shouts of triumph, and groans of defeat to punctuate the normally quiet air of the street briefly before being shut away. The women who arrived for the gaming tables wore hooded cloaks, while those who arrived to service the gamblers wore considerably less clothing.

When he, Thorne, Isabella, and Miss Sauber had gathered to decide upon their plan for tonight, it had been Isabella who insisted upon Miss Sauber accompanying Michael and Thorne as a high-flier. Both men had immediately objected, but Isabella pointed out in a practical voice that there would be little other options for Miss Sauber to infiltrate the building without causing notice. The female gamblers were too few and the only female servants not in the kitchens were working the floor as companions to the clientele. And above all, since she was the only botanist, Miss Sauber must enter the building with them. Isabella would keep an eye outside in her disguise as Prince.

So now, with Thorne walking on her other side, she walked arm in arm with Michael as they approached the front door of Hendey's. Isabella had contrived a costume for her, one of her own evening gowns that had required frighteningly little alteration. Through the open front of her evening cape, Miss Sauber's bosom looked as though a stiff wind might shake it loose from the gown's low-cut bodice, while the lace ruffle at the hem to hide the shorter skirt offered a glimpse of her ankles with every step.

Michael and Thorne had simply worn finely-tailored but nondescript evening clothes to accompany her, and they blended in with the other men inside. And Miss Sauber, her hair styled with an overabundance of curls and paste jewels, was not out of place at all in the company of the "working women" who wandered amongst the gaming tables.

Michael found himself embarrassed by the excellence of Miss Sauber's performance. "How in the world do you know how to act like … like …"

"A mistress?" Her voice was matter-of-fact, but he didn't miss the hint of humor in her tone. "The ones who accompany their lords to the opera all the time?"

Now he felt even more embarrassed to bring the subject up to her, a genteel young woman who had been expected to ignore the men flaunting their mistresses every week when she attended the theater during the Season. Yet she was quite skilled at copying those fallen women as her guide to her behavior—he would never have expected her to be a proper society miss. However, her excellent acting also made him distinctly uncomfortable as she leaned her body into him, because a part of his mind couldn't forget that this was *Miss Sauber.*

"You are being too ... familiar." His voice was hoarse.

"I thought she was being quite natural," Thorne said obliviously.

"Would you rather I was prim and respectable?" she demanded. She evidently knew he was being unreasonable and wasn't about to allow him to get away with it. "I thought the point was not to be noticed."

The problem, of course, was that Michael noticed her far too much, but he couldn't admit that and look even more immature and unprofessional than he already did.

"People will take note if you're too uncomfortable with her," Thorne added, continuing his streak of unhelpfulness.

"I could always be the other gentleman's mistress instead," she said.

"No," he said immediately.

She finally did lean away from him slightly, in order to regard him with eyes that glowed like jade in the candlelight of the large room. Apparently his quick answer had pleased her, which pleased him in a strange way, too.

Now that he was here and had a chance to consider it, Hendey's was an excellent place for a greenhouse. There were fewer players during the day but it was never entirely empty, and on any given day, there would be different people hanging about, so the greenhouse owner—if it was Maner—could come and go as he pleased. And if he arrived at night, he would be nearly invisible in the crowd.

There were two large rooms in the front of the house, both the size of small ballrooms, filled with various gaming tables, and the low ceilings made the noise both loud and close at the same time. There were mostly men, but scattered amongst them were a few high-society women. A few accompanied gentlemen, but some had arrived alone and were in deep play. Serving drinks or watching the games were scantily-clad women. Occasionally, a gentleman would take his chosen woman up the grand staircase in the front foyer to the upper rooms, which were set aside for private play—of cards and also between the sheets.

As they entered the foyer, a very tall, thin man approached them. His dark wavy hair was a touch longer than was fashionable and was quickly breaking free from its neat styling to give him a wild appearance. His patently false smile seemed to be filled to the brim with long-suffering. "Are you new here, gentlemen? May I assist you in finding a table?" He did not have the self-abasing tones of a servant, but acted more like a very polite house guard. From the scars on his knuckles, Michael would guess he had multiple duties as host of this establishment.

Michael cast his gaze around the rooms as though bored. "Vingt-un, perhaps?" he drawled. He glanced at Thorne as though asking for his preference, and received an impassive nod in return.

"Very good, gentleman. I would be happy to lead you to a table with some open spaces. Will the lady play, as well?"

Michael bit out a harsh laugh and didn't even glance at Miss Sauber. "Not unless I want to lose the entirety of my purse tonight."

A condescending smile hovered on the edges of the man's mouth. "This way, gentlemen." He led them through an open doorway to the room on the left and seated them at a table quite near the doorway. He did not offer Miss Sauber a chair, and Michael did not insist upon it—it would draw attention to the eye as an oddity when they left the table, and he didn't want this man to notice when they snuck away.

"Thank you." Michael slipped the man a coin, which softened the hard planes of his face.

"You are quite welcome, sirs. My name is Dawson. Please do not hesitate to call for me if you need anything. Enjoy your play." He gave a short bow and left them.

After Michael and Thorne had bought chips, Miss Sauber leaned over Michael's shoulder under the pretense of looking at his cards. It was as though he were embraced by her subtle floral scent. He had to blink to focus on what the other players were doing with their hands.

"Why cards?" she whispered, her voice tickling his ear.

"The host is smart and has a good eye for faces," he murmured to her, turning his head slightly toward her face, ensuring that the other players at the table would think he were only saying sweet nothings to his ladybird. "He knew we were newcomers. It would seem strange if we said we were here for a private party and wouldn't need an escort to the room."

"You are so clever, my darling," she said in a slightly louder voice, and he heard the smile in her voice.

Other men at the table gave her appreciative looks that lingered on her figure, so Michael shot them all with frosty glares that should have frozen their nether regions. Next to him, Thorne coughed lightly and gave him a sidelong look.

"What?" he demanded.

"Oh, nothing," Thorne replied as he opted for another card.

For several minutes, Michael lost steadily. Finally, Miss Sauber leaned down over his shoulder again, and he glanced at her. Belatedly he realized she was giving the other players a tantalizing view of her cleavage, exposed by the low-cut gown, and he had to resist the urge to throw his coat over her torso. "What—" His voice was hoarse, and he cleared his throat. "What is it?"

In a low voice only he could hear, she said, "You were right. Mr. Dawson has been watching us." Everything about her—the sensual expression on her face, the subtle tilt of her head, the sinuous way her body moved closer to him, all looked as though she were describing the delights he could anticipate in her bed that evening. It was almost discouraging when she said, "But now he has moved to the other room across the foyer. We can leave soon." She pressed a soft kiss to his cheek, and he felt the slight stickiness of the cosmetics that reddened and fulled her lips against his skin.

The other men at the table gave him baleful looks. He couldn't resist a smirk in reply.

Thorne again coughed, and Michael's smirk disappeared.

When the dealer took Vingt-un, Michael collected his markers and rose to his feet. "Demm'd boring. What do you say to Hazard?" he asked Thorne.

Thorne gave a small shrug, then also collected his markers, and rose to follow Michael.

They left the room and entered the foyer once again, but this time they climbed the large staircase. The first floor was open and U-shaped, lined with doors that were all firmly shut, but they bypassed them all to find another set of stairs leading to the next floor.

The hallways there were again U-shaped. They had far thicker carpets and doors spaced closer together, indicating small bedrooms rather than gambling rooms, and muffled sounds of intimacy could be heard as they passed. Both Michael and Thorne had reddened faces as they attempted to escape the floor as quickly as possible. He was shocked—shocked!—that Miss Sauber merely looked confused, but perhaps she was not fully aware of what she was hearing.

They discovered a narrow set of stairs at the far end of the hallway. Michael led the way up, walking on the soles of his boots so that he would make as little noise as possible on the uncarpeted, creaking boards. Miss Sauber's evening slippers were only a whisper of sound behind him, and Thorne followed just as quietly.

He hadn't noticed it earlier, but he realized his legs felt a little heavier than normal, a little more stiff. He tightened his thigh muscles, clenched the muscles of his stomach. He couldn't afford to be cold and unprepared.

He could smell the Goldensuit several steps before they climbed onto the top floor of the building. They were faced with a short hallway with two doors on the left side, and a lone door in the middle of the wall on the right. If Michael's sense of direction was correct, from the position of the stairs in the layout of the building, the two rooms on the left were small while the one on the right would be one large room. Perfect for a greenhouse.

They crept down the short hallway, and as they passed the two doors on the left, Michael put his ear to the doors. He shook his head to his companions to indicate there were no sounds from within.

They crossed the hallway to the door on the right, and this close, Michael could hear voices inside. They were low and he might not have heard them without the Root in his veins, enhancing his senses.

"Maner," he whispered. "And I think four other people, three men and a woman."

"Masks," Miss Sauber reminded them, and they attached the cloths over their faces. Thorne fussed with his, and his face screwed up in a look of irritation.

"On three," Michael said, drawing a knife from his boot. Thorne had also drawn his knife, but to his surprise, Miss Sauber drew up her skirts and unearthed a slim blade from a strap on her leg.

"What are you doing?" he hissed.

She did not take offense at his tone. "I know how to use it." Her voice was steady, her eyes calm.

What shocked him even more was Thorne's affirming nod.

He didn't have time to argue. He counted down, and then grasped the door latch. It opened easily under his hands, and they burst into the room.

There was one man directly in front of the door with his back to them and one hand holding a bulging sack. A woman standing in front of him shouted, but it was too late. Michael aimed a heavy blow with the butt of his knife to the back of the man's head, and he crumpled, unconscious.

The large attic room had a low, slanting ceiling dotted with skylights, under which stood several tables—all empty save for bits of dirt and dead leaves. The air was dusty with pollen, and the scent of Goldensuit hit him in the face, a sharply throbbing smell that made him want to rip off his mask.

Maner lay on the floor halfway into the large room, curled up as though he'd been trying to protect himself. Above him stood a large, burly man with his leg raised to deliver another kick, but he paused when he saw them. Closer to the door stood Brigitte, a short, buxom woman with straight ice-blonde hair and even more frigid blue eyes, dressed in breeches and a slim-fitting white shirt and coat. Next to her was a third man, slender with a shock of brown hair that stood out from his head and a long scar. All three of them wore cloths tied around their faces, but only the slender man held two more bulging sacks, one in each hand.

Michael could handle himself in a fight, and had been rigorously trained by some veteran agents in the Home Office and on the field. He was skilled enough to hold his own against larger men like Silas when he had to, but a brawl like this was Thorne's element. So he went for the slender man while leaving the larger one for Thorne.

The slender man dropped the two sacks he had been carrying and unearthed a knife in the blink of an eye, slashing at Michael. The man's movements seemed strangely slow, until he realized it was because the Root had enabled him to react faster. Michael dodged easily, waiting for an opening before whipping in with his blade to open a cut on the man's side. He hissed and jumped back, but not fast enough—Michael's knife bit deep into his arm, slicing through muscle. The man howled and dropped his knife, curling his body around his injured arm, his face squeezed tight with pain.

The scent of blood was strong in his nostrils, and it seemed to make his heartbeat pulse harder and faster and deeper, resounding in his ears. The blood mixed with the Goldensuit reminded him of that whiff he caught just before the Root potion was forced upon him. While it had revulsed him before, now it seemed to meld and pair together perfectly in his senses. Blood and Goldensuit, Goldensuit and blood. The combination stood for strength and power, and it felt intoxicating, like the heady fumes from a glass of aged brandy.

A crash distracted him from his opponent, and he turned to see that the large man had grabbed the neck of Thorne's coat and thrown him against the wall. There was a fluttering of cloth, and he realized Thorne's mask had been ripped off.

It was only when the big man abruptly turned toward Miss Sauber that he realized she had engaged in a knife fight with Brigitte—and she had backed the French spy into the corner. In fact, one of Miss Sauber's knife attacks had slipped through the opening of Brigitte's unbuttoned coat and cut through the fabric of her shirt, soaking the edges of the fabric with red.

He was too far away, but he instinctively moved toward Miss Sauber when the big man went for her. She turned from Brigitte in time to duck when the large man's fist swung at her.

Michael brought his attention back to his wounded opponent

in time to bend backward away from an awkward slash of the man's knife, held in his uninjured hand. His knife dropped too low and Michael was able to kick at it, sending it spinning. The impact of his foot with the man's hand dropped his shoulder down and brought his head too far forward. Michael moved with the motion of his kick to close in on the slender man and drive his elbow hard into the man's temple. He staggered backward, the cloth over his mouth slipping.

Michael turned back to Miss Sauber in time to see the big man's fist catch her full across the cheek, sending her spinning to bump into the wall and stumble to the floor. Her mask slipped, but she grabbed her face quickly, keeping it in place.

Suddenly, an unholy howling rose in the air, almost like a wolf, except that the sound was more guttural, ripped from the throat of the animal making it. Michael could hear the rage in the sound, and something in his blood responded, making him want to howl, too.

Then he realized that the sound came from Thorne.

His friend was on his hands and knees only a few feet from Miss Sauber, but while she was tying her mask back on, Thorne's face was unprotected. His mouth was twisted into an open-mouthed snarl, while his eyes were wide, glittering, and unfocused. He screamed again, his hands grabbing at the sides of his face. His maddened expression made Michael's entire body jerk in shock.

Brigitte wasted no time, grabbing two of the sacks on the floor and racing for the open doorway. The big man moved not toward Miss Sauber, but toward the groggy third man whom Michael had knocked out when they first entered the room.

Michael turned his attention back to the slender man, who had paused to stare at Thorne. He hadn't bothered to retie the cloth over his face, and Michael now saw a scar that ran along one jawline. The man was still hunched over and off-balance, so Michael stepped in and kneed his chin. He wobbled and dropped to the ground.

Michael spotted the large man also heading out the door, picking up the last sack on the floor on his way out with his other meaty arm around the torso of the third man.

Without warning, Thorne suddenly came barreling toward Michael. He barely managed to sidestep him, and Thorne stumbled.

After missing Michael, Thorne didn't hesitate, but immediately flung himself at the last Frenchman.

He fell upon the man like a wild beast, baring his teeth and growling. He attacked with his fists, but then he spotted the man's fallen knife and grabbed it. Before Michael could stop him, he stabbed at the man over and over, blood spraying across the walls and floor, falling warm against Michael's cheeks, splashing across his waistcoat and the front of his coat.

Michael grabbed Thorne and heaved, pulling him off of the man. They both fell backward onto the floor, the knife clattering away.

Thorne recovered more quickly, scrambling to a crouch, then launching himself at Michael.

His vision became filled with Thorne's livid, crazed expression, spittle raining on his face as his friend attacked him, his voice coming in grunts and snarls, his hands punching relentlessly. Michael blocked ferocious blows to his head and shoulders, faster than Thorne had ever thrown them. If he hadn't lost the knife, Michael would have been stabbed several times in the space of a couple heartbeats.

The Root seemed to deaden the pain of the punches, and after a few precious moments of surprise, his training reasserted itself. He slipped in a jab directly in Thorne's face, which jerked his head backward. He followed with a solid blow to his torso and tried to fling him off, but Thorne merely rumbled low in his chest and kept pounding his fists toward Michael's face. He blocked a few, but others connected with his chin, his cheek, his temple. Then one hit him directly in the throat, and he choked, his arms ceasing to respond to his frantic brain. His vision darkened around the edges.

Thorne suddenly jerked, and he flung his arm in a backhanded blow that hit Miss Sauber and sent her flying away. She had apparently drawn too close behind them. But the moment allowed Michael to draw a pained breath through his tight throat, and his hands closed around Thorne's wrists.

Thorne struggled for a few moments against him, but then his movements became sluggish and slow. Finally he slumped and fell sideways, unconscious.

Michael scooted backward, and only then did he see the small handle of a knife protruding from Thorne's back. But he had been so powerful, surely that small blade wouldn't have stopped him? He reached for Thorne's throat and felt the dull thud of his pulse, slow but strong.

Miss Sauber was shakily getting to her feet. Her mask was still in place, despite the blow Thorne had delivered to her, but her eyes as they rested on Michael were wary, and he didn't understand why.

"Are you injured?" he asked.

She blinked in surprise. "Are you?"

He rose to his feet, feeling aches in his joints and stabbing pain in his throat, a more throbbing pain in his jaw where Thorne had gotten a solid punch. "I am well."

It was then that he realized he had lost his mask.

He wondered for a wild moment if he ought to try holding his breath, but he was panting too heavily to do that, and he must have been breathing the pollen in the air for several minutes now.

He waited.

And waited.

And didn't feel any different.

Miss Sauber stared at him with wide eyes, expectant, but

after a few minutes, seemed to realize he wasn't going to do anything violent or deranged. "Do you feel well?" she asked again.

"I am well." In fact, as he continued breathing the pollen, he almost felt rested despite the fact he had been in a strenuous fight. The stiffness and sluggishness he had noticed in his muscles had disappeared—his limbs felt hot and liquid, strong. And despite the various pains on his face from Thorne's blows, his headache had also left him.

He stared at the pollen drifting in the air, gleaming a dull gold color in the lamplight, and even the smell seemed rich and decadent to his senses. The enticement to breathe in more of it was stronger now, and it was an effort to find his mask on the floor and tie it back on. The pollen didn't seem to have affected him, but a part of him realized that there was no knowing what would happen to him if he continued to breathe it in.

He then noticed the still body of the man Thorne had stabbed. The blood no longer gushed from his wounds, and his sightless eyes stared at the low ceiling.

Not far away lay another body, and he realized with a start that he'd forgotten about Maner. He had apparently been knocked unconscious from the beating he'd received from the large Frenchman just before they'd entered the greenhouse.

And near Maner, Thorne lay still, his breathing slow and shallow. "What happened?" Michael asked.

"I stabbed him with a knife laced with sedative," Miss Sauber told him.

"The same as ...?" The same as the sedative they'd used on *him*?

She understood, and nodded.

"I don't understand." He looked around at the empty tables. There was very little in the greenhouse besides the tables, a few buckets, and some rusting gardening tools. There was a small empty grate, but the room was warm, perhaps from the heat rising from the rest of the building.

And then there was Thorne, sprawled out on the floor, who had gone mad the moment his mask had been torn off.

He looked into Miss Sauber's eyes, and the same question was mirrored there.

"What in the world happened to him?"

Chapter Ten

Thorne's eyes felt glued together, and he opened them with effort. Light stabbed at him like an icepick into his skull, and he turned his head to the other side, where the dimness was a relief.

What had happened to him? He felt much like he did after a night of staying up too late and drinking too much.

No, it felt different. There was a restlessness ... something more than a restlessness, a tension that twisted in his gut.

He blinked and sat up, then shivered in the chill of the room, which he didn't recognize. The sheets were finely woven and smelled fresh, but the bed itself was merely a thick straw mattress on the floor. Heavy drapes made of rich fabric had been hung at the windows, but the walls were covered in peeling wallpaper, and the clean-swept floor had no carpet. He heard the faint whistling of wind, and realized that it came from the windows. Some warmth came from the fireplace, but the fire had gone out long ago.

He glanced down and realized he was still in the clothes he'd worn to the gaming hell, minus his boots, which he saw propped against the wall, and his coat, which was neatly draped over a plain wooden chair next to the mattress. He reached to pull them both on, then went to the whistling window and swept aside the drapes.

The glass window was closed, but the frame was so warped with water damage that the cold air blew directly into the room through cracks in the wood. Someone had stuffed rags in the largest holes, but it accounted for the brisk temperature.

He scrubbed his hands over his face, feeling fuzzy-headed. Yet there was also that strange agitation that made him ball his hands into fists before releasing them.

Something was wrong with him.

He tried to recall what had happened, but couldn't remember anything besides entering Hendey's, playing cards ... Had they gone upstairs? He seemed to recall doing that. He also remembered a melee, but not how he had come to be involved in it.

And he remembered rage. Thundering, black, roiling rage that had consumed him. All the anger at his father, at his wife ... and himself. He remembered the explosion he'd felt at Timothy ... No, that hadn't been at the gaming hell. That had been ... nearly two years ago.

Echoes of that rage still burned in his gut. It came in waves—one moment he wanted to put his fist through the peeling wallpaper, the next he wanted to clutch his chest and curl up in a ball.

What happened?

He stumbled towards the door, fumbling with the knob before finally wrenching it open. Then he recognized where he was—Stapytton House. He'd probably been installed in the only bedroom not ruined by mold on the ceiling and walls, although the window frame made it equally unlivable.

His full bladder distracted him, and there was no chamber pot in the bedroom, so he headed downstairs to the kitchen. He startled Isabella, who was at the stove.

"Bella ..."

She smiled at him, and unembarrassed, said, "Privy is out the door."

Thorne reflected that he was probably more embarrassed than she was. They had known each other since they were children, but he had been more aware of her as a woman in recent years, despite his efforts not to think of her in that way.

When he re-entered the kitchen, Isabella was removing a bowl from a rickety cabinet. "How do you feel? How are your injuries?"

Injuries? He didn't feel injured at all, even though he had vague memories of trading blows with a large Frenchman. "I feel ..."

He felt angry. Powerful. A mighty Grecian god who would rain thunder on mortals.

He shook away the vision and tried to calm the storm that had begun to brew in his stomach. "Hungry."

"The soup is heated." Isabella ladled some into the bowl, which she set on a tray on the kitchen table.

"You didn't ... cook it, did you?"

She regarded him with narrow eyes, although he'd tried to make his voice sound as neutral as possible. "No, it is from Lady Wynwood's excellent chef."

He stopped himself before sighing in relief.

"But I will have you know," she continued, "that my skills in the kitchen *have* improved since I was ten years old."

"Of course," he said automatically. However, the smell of nutmeg still gave him flashes of gruesome memory about that horrible bout of food sickness when he was fifteen.

"Head down to the butler's pantry to eat before Keriah finishes whatever smelly experiment she is currently busy with." She motioned to the closed stillroom door.

He at first thought he saw a wisp of smoke seeping from under it, but surely he was mistaken.

The only really comfortable room in the house was the butler's pantry, since even the kitchen was quite drafty. A relatively well-preserved library table had been placed there, and he sat with Isabella seated next to him, watching him eat.

"How are you really feeling?" she asked. Her eyes had darkened to ivy green with concern, but her face was calm.

He could never hide from her, this woman whom he trusted most in the world. His mind shied away from that thought even as it formed. "I feel tense. As though I'm waiting for a fight. I feel full of fire and ..." *And rage.* "... and vigor."

"What do you remember from last night?"

"It was last night?"

"It's about noon now."

His jaw clenched. At least he hadn't lost more than a few hours of time. He somehow knew he had slept longer and deeper than a normal night's rest, and he had worried he'd lost days of time. "I think I remember that we found the greenhouse, full of that plant, the ... the ..."

"Goldensuit. Did you smell it?"

The question confused him. "Smell it? I don't believe so. The greenhouse just smelled ... green."

She seemed relieved. "Go on."

"There was a fight." He tried to dredge up what else had happened. He saw confused images. Pain from the blows he'd taken from the large Frenchman. And then the fury.

He began to recollect, bits and snatches of images. "I attacked Michael. And then I killed that Frenchman." He had killed men before, as missions dictated, or in self-defense from an attacker. But he remembered slamming that knife into the body, feeling the warmth of the blood, smelling the coppery tang and wanting to bring forth more, make it gush out all over the floor ...

He shuddered.

Suddenly, soft arms wrapped around him, along with lily of the valley, comforting like a familiar coverlet.

He hadn't realized he was shaking until she held him. She said nothing, simply embracing him for long minutes, until the trembling eased.

She sat back in her seat. "What happened?" He knew what she was really asking—What had made him lose control?

"I don't remember when my mask came off. I was on the floor. I hurt all over." He vividly recalled the pain now, that ache across his back where he'd hit the wall. "And then I felt only wrath, and madness. I don't remember the last time it consumed me like that."

She reached out and grasped his hand, holding it in hers.

He continued, "I remembered my father's insults, and Drusilla's arrogant face when she told me Timothy wasn't mine." His voice faltered. He couldn't confess even to Isabella the hatred he'd felt for Timothy, the boy he'd been forced to raise as his own, who was another man's spawn.

And the fact that in that moment he had felt fury at a child made the shame wash over him, erasing the comfort he'd felt when she held him. He leaned his elbow on the scarred wooden table and covered his eyes with his hand.

She somehow knew he didn't want her to touch him. "You were tense before, Thorne, but it's worse now."

"I was tense?" He dropped his hand to look at her.

"For about a year, now." Her mouth tightened. "Since a month or two after your father died."

He looked away from her. Thoughts of his father only made him resentful, and that was on a good day. On a day like today, when his emotions were on a knife-edge, it would make him boil over.

Steps sounded outside the open door, and then Michael entered. He'd apparently been looking for Thorne, because he smiled. "It almost seems unfair."

The words and smile relaxed Thorne, took his thoughts from the dark places they had been peering into. "What do you mean?"

Michael sat down across from him. "Miss Sauber was

complaining about the bruise on her face and not being able to completely cover it with rice powder, while you look like you haven't done anything more strenuous than go for a walk."

Thorne frowned. "I should be more bruised, too."

"Keriah thinks it was the Goldensuit pollen you breathed in." Isabella glanced at Michael. "Both of you are mysteriously uninjured, despite engaging in a bout of fisticuffs."

"The pollen? I thought only the Root caused quick healing."

"Is there any other way to explain your lack of bruises?" Isabella asked.

"Even the knife wound on your back had healed over by the time I brought you back here last night," Michael added.

"Knife wound?" He stretched his back, and now he thought he might feel a bit of tightness in his upper left back, deep in the muscle. "Did you cut me?"

"Miss Sauber stabbed you," Michael said.

Thorne blinked. "She what?"

Isabella answered, "She had a sedative-laced knife and used it on you before you pummeled your best friend."

He gave a long exhale. "I hadn't known she had one of them with her."

"Phoebe told us she actually had two," Isabella said. "One for a man on the Root, which she used on you, and another for a Berserker. She will be glad you finally awoke. She was fretting over giving you too strong a dose."

"A man on the Root?" He remembered wanting to utterly destroy the Frenchman he had stabbed. When Michael had stopped him, he had wanted to destroy him, too.

He had acted more like a Berserker.

Thorne tried to tell himself that it was the pollen that had drawn out that violent side of himself, but the rage hadn't come from nowhere—it had sprung from his issues with his family, issues he had either denied or had been avoiding.

He looked up at Michael. "I am very sorry."

Michael didn't try to gloss over it—he respected Thorne more than that. "Apology accepted," he said firmly.

"I think I understand, now, what you might have felt when they forced you to drink the Root." Thorne rubbed his face again. "The rage was overwhelming, like a conflagration. I had no control over myself, but ... I also didn't *want* control over myself. I simply wanted to rip apart everything in sight." When pounding at Michael, he suddenly remembered that his face had been unmasked. "I knocked your mask off. But you didn't feel anything?"

Michael's expression became grave. "I didn't feel the same rage as when I was given the Root. Maybe *because* I had been given the Root."

Light footsteps heralded the arrival of Miss Gardinier, who breezed into the butler's pantry with the faint scent of chemicals. She made straight for Thorne. "I wish I had known earlier you are awake."

"You'd asked not to be disturbed," Isabella reminded her.

Miss Gardinier opened her mouth to refute that, then thought a moment. "I had, hadn't I? And it would have been very disagreeable to have accidentally singed someone's eyebrows if I'd been suddenly interrupted. That was probably best."

Thorne decided he didn't want to know what sorts of experiments she had been doing.

"How do you feel?" Miss Gardinier took an oil lamp from the table and held it close to his face—perilously close to singeing *his* eyebrows—as she stared in his eyes. It was a terribly disconcerting feeling, but her expression was impassive and impersonal.

"My body feels healthy. My head is clear."

She thankfully set the oil lamp down, but then started looking in his mouth like a horse, so he couldn't answer further. She also insisted on yanking down the neck of his coat to peer down his naked back.

It was incredibly uncomfortable to have a woman view his body, and he was relieved when she at last stood up and put her hands on her hips. "You seem well. I would have been concerned if you had slept for longer than you did, but the sedative dosage on Phoebe's knife appears to have been just weak enough to incapacitate you without making you sleep for a week."

"A week?" He hoped she was only joking about that.

She now turned to Michael. "Mr. Coulton-Jones, I had not known you'd arrived, also." Her voice was faintly accusing. "I was not here last night when you arrived with Mr. Rosmont, so I was not able to examine you. One would think you were avoiding me."

Michael looked faintly guilty, so perhaps her accusation was not completely without merit.

"How do you feel?" she asked. "You also breathed in the pollen?"

He nodded, but the movement was jerky. He hesitated, then said, "I had been feeling a mild headache earlier."

"A headache?" She seemed suddenly alarmed. "Why hadn't you told me?"

His look was apologetic, but also pragmatic. "What could you have done for me?"

Mis Gardinier bit her lip.

Michael continued, "I had also been feeling slow ... sluggish. But after the fight, I felt I could run around the city of London and not feel tired."

Her eyes narrowed as she surveyed him. "Were you struck during the fight?"

Michael's eyes slid to Thorne for a moment, but quickly returned to Miss Gardinier. "I was not cut, but Thorne landed a facer or two. And I was punched in the throat." His hand went to his neck. "It feels a little stiff, but otherwise fine."

Miss Gardinier examined his face, his throat. "You have no bruises," she said slowly.

"Because of the Root?" Michael suggested.

"Perhaps. But Mr. Rosmont has no bruises, also. And you both breathed the pollen."

Thorne and Michael exchanged a glance.

"Did the pollen smell different from that in Jack's greenhouse?" Miss Gardinier asked.

"No …" Michael drew the word out. He was in thought for a minute, then he said, "But the scent of the plants was strong."

"Strong?" she asked.

"It felt as though the smell utterly filled my senses." He scrubbed at his forehead as if to rub the memory away. "I wanted more of the Goldensuit. It was easier to ignore while we were fighting, but afterward, it was hard to concentrate."

And afterward, Michael would have been busy trying to find a way to discreetly haul his friend's heavy body out of the building with only Miss Sauber for assistance. Thorne wondered how he had accomplished *that*.

Miss Gardinier was quiet and solemn, an expression uncharacteristic for her sunny personality. "This Goldensuit plant is dangerous, and the more I hear about it, the more convinced I am that it is deadly. But it also may be the means to keep you alive."

Michael shook his head. "I don't want the Root."

"I know, and I would not want to enslave you to the Root elixir or this plant. But I have been considering this." Her expression was earnest. "I cannot do experiments until I can get a sample of the Goldensuit plant, but I believe I may be able to concoct something—a tincture, maybe even a powder—that can keep you alive until I can find a way to wean you off of the Root."

Since waking, there had been a light missing in his friend's eyes, like an overcast day outside glass-green windows. But now a speckle of light shone through, a ray of hope.

"I will be completely honest with you," she continued. "Your strange attraction to the pollen's scent worries me, as does Mr. Rosmont's reaction when he breathed it in." She glanced at him, but there was no condemnation in her gaze, no horror or fear.

He hadn't realized that he'd been steeling himself for some form of all of those until he exhaled and felt his muscles relax. Because all that was in Miss Gardinier's eyes was concern tempered by clinical logic.

"I don't understand what happened," Thorne said. "I remember the events, but vaguely, as though I were completely foxed."

"Considering what Jack had said about the tainted batch of plants, perhaps your reaction was not surprising," Miss Gardinier said. "Even Jack does not have the control over his plants that he claims he does."

"It happened so quickly," Michael said. "Within minutes, although we were all breathing hard because of the fight."

"From what I could see when studying that tiny sample of the Root, I think there are particles in the plant that react to a person's blood, which is why it reacts so quickly," Miss Gardinier said. "When you both breathed it in, it was immediately taken into your bodies and then reacted with your blood. But either your blood is different from Mr. Rosmont, or it reacts differently because you were given the Root. When the pollen reacted with Mr. Rosmont's blood, it caused that unexpected reaction."

Thorne wasn't certain if he wanted to laugh or be disturbed that she spoke of his animalistic behavior as an "unexpected reaction."

"But this is all conjecture," Miss Gardinier added. "I cannot do more than that unless Phoebe can grow a Goldensuit plant." She eyed the uneaten soup in front of Thorne. "You should eat to regain your strength."

"That has grown cold. I'll fetch you more." Isabella took his bowl from him and followed Miss Gardinier out of the room.

"I've never liked working with civilians," Thorne said in a low voice, "but now I am ashamed of my prejudice. If not for Miss Gardinier and Miss Sauber, I don't know what would have become of me."

The side of Michael's mouth quirked upward. "I understand what you mean."

"I have not known many scientists, but the few I've met were all men. While they were interested in the science and in the thrill of discovery, they were also focused upon receiving the acknowledgment and acclaim of their peers. They wanted to be the first to discover something new and be recognized for it."

"Miss Gardinier and Miss Sauber are not like that," Michael said.

"I find I am especially grateful for them because they are not. They are more interested in helping us than in recreating the Root elixir."

Michael was staring sightlessly toward the darkened corner of the room. "Do you think she can do what she says?" he asked in a soft voice.

"She has studied the small sample Miss Sauber found. She seems to understand the Root better now." Thorne shook his head, feeling helpless about his friend's situation but not wanting to express negative thoughts. "I am hopeful she can save you."

Michael didn't reply, nor did his pensive expression shift.

"What's wrong?" Thorne's voice was hoarse. He wasn't used to speaking like this to Michael—talking about *feelings*, of all things—and yet the thought that his time with his friend might be cut short made him more bold with uncomfortable topics than he might have otherwise felt.

In a soft voice, Michael answered, "Lady Wynwood believes God will save me."

Thorne didn't know how to respond to that. He had been bitterly angry at God for the past several years. His upbringing by the cruel despot who was his father, his injury in the army that cut short a career that he had hoped would be his escape from his home, the infidelity of his wife, Timothy ... There had been too many turbulent emotions piled upon him by a "Heavenly Father." It had been too much, and he'd given in to the resentment. For a long time now he'd felt like a caged tiger, waiting for any opening to escape and ruin and tear and destroy. Only Isabella had been able to soothe him, and it was only her presence that kept him civilized.

Michael knew all this. His own thoughts on religion were not as extreme as Thorne's, but he had not been very pious.

Yet Thorne had noticed that he himself had begun to view God differently since meeting Lady Wynwood.

Nothing drastic. But it felt lately like the sharper edge of his bitterness had dulled. The acid in his chest was still there, but it had cooled from a rolling boil to a simmer.

People around him—Lady Wynwood's coachman, her niece—now pointed out to him the ways in which they believed God was working in their lives, and even in Thorne's life. He would normally only respond with derision, but there was a strength in Lady Wynwood, in Mr. Havner, in Miss Sauber, that made his sneering response seem childish and inappropriate.

And a small part of him had begun to think that to be watched over by God felt lightening, relieving, sustaining. And if that God could save his friend ...

Michael shook his head and simply said, "I don't want to get my hopes up."

Thorne could understand that kind of attitude. It was what he would have done in the same desperate situation.

And yet, in a desperate situation, Miss Sauber had quoted a Bible verse, and the words had stirred something in him that he couldn't quite remember. He didn't understand what exactly it made him feel, and he didn't know why he was feeling it. He didn't know what to make of it all.

He was brought out of his reverie when Michael looked at him. "You are all right?" Michael asked, his concern evident in his voice.

"You needn't worry about me," was his automatic response.

But he knew it wasn't true. The paroxysm of anger he'd felt in Maner's greenhouse, the barbarism that had coursed through him while he hadn't been in control of himself, had frightened him more than anything he'd faced on his missions for the Home Office.

He worried about *what he was becoming.*

Chapter Eleven

As soon as Laura entered the kitchen of Stapytton House, she heard the strident protests of an unfamiliar male voice, and guessed that was Maner. Sol must be questioning him at this moment, but from the tones of Maner's voice, it wasn't going well.

Phoebe and Keriah were seated at the kitchen table, drinking tea. The table had warped so badly that there was a slight hump in the surface, so it looked as though the teapot—pilfered from Laura's kitchen—was tilted.

The girls both smiled at Laura's entrance. Keriah's hair was a bit messy, and there was a distinct smoky smell coming from her person, with what looked like a slightly singed edge to her sleeve cuff. In contrast, she looked immaculate next to Phoebe, who sported a black eye from where Mr. Rosmont had hit her during his crazed rage last night.

"Here again, Aunt Laura? Your friends are going to think you're deliberately avoiding Hyde Park."

"I have never particularly enjoyed Hyde Park," Laura said scandalously. "I never saw the point of moving at a snail's pace in a carriage in order to be forced to speak to other people in carriages whom you would much rather avoid." She set her full basket on the table and began removing food. It seemed all she was doing these days was delivering snacks and foodstuffs to the team at this dilapidated manor, making her feel a bit like a catering service, but they appreciated the supplies since very little could be stored here.

"Did Mr. Ackett come with you?" Keriah asked, perhaps a bit too casually.

"I have left the hapless man instructing the servants in moving furniture in the area that used to be Wynwood's sitting room."

"Is he ... doing well?" Keriah asked.

Laura knew she was worried about his mind rather than his body. In many ways, perhaps Keriah, out of all of them, understood best what Mr. Ackett was struggling with. "He chafes at the necessity of sitting and directing the servants rather than moving things himself," she admitted. "So far, he has been remarkably creative in suggesting places where Wynwood might have secreted another hiding hole. While he hasn't found anything, he has approached the situation like a puzzle to solve, which keeps his mind from brooding over his injury."

Keriah seemed both relieved and yet still concerned, but she nodded.

"Has Mr. Rosmont awoken yet?" Laura asked.

"Oh, yes," Phoebe said, pausing in the act of peeking into a paper packet full of biscuits that Laura had just set down. "He woke only an hour or two ago."

"He is in perfect health," Keriah said. "Too perfect, for a man who was in a brawl. No injuries or bruises. Even the knife wound has healed."

"But how is he feeling?" Laura asked. After what Phoebe had told her about last night, she worried about his reaction to what he had done.

"He is quiet," Keriah said soberly. "And yet, he also seems rather tense and on edge."

"He has always been a little ... high-strung," Laura remarked.

"He's now a bit more antagonistic." Keriah frowned. "It concerns me because of what happened."

"Understandable." He had not quite become a Berserker, but he hadn't been in his right mind. He was not quite as strong as a man on the Root, but he had been stronger than normal. And they had nothing to help them understand how the pollen would affect him further. "And Mr. Coulton-Jones?"

Keriah looked even more grave. "He is also uninjured. But he also remarked that the pollen improved some symptoms of sickness he'd been feeling."

"Sickness?"

"Headaches, tiredness."

Phoebe had obviously already heard all this from Keriah, because she nodded. In contrast to her friend, she looked more cheerful. "Keriah thinks perhaps she can create something—not the Root, but something that will enable him to live without it. Something that will wean him from the Goldensuit completely."

Laura wanted to grasp that hope in her niece's voice, but also knew that to trust too firmly in it might only lead to heartache. "Let us hope so, my dear," was all she said. "Did you discover anything useful from the detritus left at the greenhouse in the gaming hell?"

"No. I had been hoping for seeds, perhaps, but there were only roots and dead leaves, just like at Jack's greenhouse. The French group were very thorough."

"How disappointing that French spies should have such a good work ethic," Laura remarked dryly.

Keriah giggled.

"I did discover something interesting, though," Phoebe said. "The plants at the gaming hell greenhouse were much more sickly than Jack's plants. From what I could see of the room, there weren't enough windows and skylights, so perhaps it was because there wasn't enough light. But from the dampness of the soil that had been dropped on the tables, I believe the plants may have been overwatered."

"So whoever cultivated those plants was not very knowledgeable?"

Phoebe nodded. "Which would not be Jack."

"Well, we had guessed it would not be his greenhouse."

"*You* guessed." Phoebe looked at Laura. "How did you know?"

"I didn't know for certain, but you said that the carpenter hadn't built Jack's skylights," Laura hedged. She turned to Keriah. "Phoebe said she found some blood on one of the tables. Did you look at it?"

"Oh, it was merely pig's blood," Keriah said. "I think someone—Maner, probably—may have been trying to make the Root to heal his ear. But from what we've heard, the Root doesn't regrow lost extremities. Oooh, is that preserves?" She eyed the jar Laura had just removed from the basket.

"Good gracious, no. I absolutely forbid you to eat this." She handed Phoebe the jar, which contained makeup. "Aya purchased this, and says it will completely cover that bruise."

"I would much prefer being here than going to balls and parties." But Phoebe accepted the jar.

"It is quite the most magnificent shiner I have ever seen," Keriah said seriously.

"Considering the cases your uncle must have treated, that is quite the compliment," Phoebe answered. She looked hesitantly at Laura. "I am very grateful for the powder, but I admit I am a bit surprised that you are so accepting of what I am doing that you would give me cosmetics."

Laura reached out to touch her niece's cheek—the unbruised one—and she only had to exert herself a little bit in order to smile at her. "I am still worried about you—I shall always be worried about you. But I also do not want to stand in the way of the decisions you have made and the direction you wish to go."

Phoebe's eyes shone like peridot, and her smile was just as brilliant.

Keriah sighed. "I do not suppose my mother would be as accepting."

"She might surprise us all. Your mother has been accepting of your chemistry, which can certainly be as dangerous as any situation Phoebe may walk into." Laura touched one of Keriah's errant curls, which had most certainly been singed recently. "Speaking of chemistry, a parcel arrived for you from one of Phoebe's botanist friends." She handed it to Keriah.

Keriah opened it to reveal various types of roots, each wrapped in paper. "Mandrake roots! And Nightshade ... but no Devil's Trumpet." She sighed.

"No complaining," Phoebe said. "You gave me quite a list to ask my friends to procure for you. You should be glad you received any at all."

"I shall begin at once to try to improve upon the sedative formula." Keriah jumped to her feet and headed into the stillroom next to the kitchen.

Laura removed the last bundle from the basket and handed it to Phoebe. "When you told me about the masks coming loose last night, I told Aya, and she improved the design so that they may be tied more securely."

"Wonderful!" Phoebe tied a mask around her face and looked to Laura.

"You look quite disreputable," she affirmed.

"Excellent. I shall give these extras to Mr. Rosmont and Mr. Coulton-Jones. Isabella left to attend to her mother this afternoon."

Laura followed Phoebe up the stairs, and they could hear Maner's whining voice.

Phoebe sighed. "Uncle Sol is not having an easy time of it."

"He is questioning Maner?"

"Actually, Mr. Coulton-Jones is questioning Maner since he

saw his face. Uncle Sol wished to remain anonymous. But Uncle Sol is writing questions down and passing them to Mr. Coulton-Jones to ask."

"Maner is being difficult?"

"From what I heard before I left, it appeared to me that Maner is close-lipped about giving any information for which he was not paid. It's become a habit for him. But Uncle Sol is becoming quite vexed."

"He was already in a rather foul mood," Laura said. "He stopped in to speak to me this morning after you'd left, and before he arrived here. He spoke to Mr. Farrimond at the Ramparts but discovered nothing. The man pretended ignorance of all."

"That is what Maner is doing, also."

They approached what had been the master bedroom of Stapytton House, but bypassed the door and instead headed toward the dressing room next to it. Phoebe put her finger to her lips as she opened the door, and they entered.

Mr. Rosmont was pacing in the small confines, which was unfortunately only a handful of steps from one broken-down wardrobe against one wall to the water-stained chest of drawers against the other. His face was aggravated, and Laura understood why when she suddenly heard Maner's voice, loud and clear.

The connecting door to the master bedroom was opened, and in front of the open doorway had been placed a standing screen. Sol stood behind the screen and stared at it, which confused her until she realized there must be a peephole cut into it. He glanced back at them when he heard the dressing room door close softly, and nodded to Laura.

From beyond the screen came Maner's protests. "You can ask as many times as you like, but the answer won't change."

"Why were you at the greenhouse?" Mr. Coulton-Jones's voice sounded weary, with the kind of sing-song cadence that indicated he had asked the question many times already.

"I was there by accident," Maner said in slow, biting tones.

Laura walked up behind Sol and softly touched his shoulder. He glanced down at her, his face close, and she could smell his unique musk that reminded her of ivy, but she also caught the faint scent of woodsmoke and green grass from his coat. He must have been out walking at some point today.

His expression was flat and tight, and she could tell his patience was nearing its breaking point. He had indeed been peering through a peephole in the screen, just a narrow slit cut into the fabric. The screen was quite thick, and looked to have been hastily painted with swaths of dark gray to make it opaque.

She tilted her head toward the screen with a questioning look, and he nodded, stepping back so she could take his place to watch the proceedings. She had to tilt her head up slightly to see into the peephole, which was a little too high for her.

The master bedroom was devoid of any furniture except for a chair, a small bedside table placed about ten feet away, with a small lamp on top of it. The light was necessary since all but one of the windows had been boarded up by the owner, with newer boards where Sol must have reinforced weaker ones. The light from outside spread across the dingy, mold-stained ceiling, and with the lamp, illuminated the man sitting in the chair.

Maner was a painfully thin figure, wearing a coat too short for his long arms so that his thin wrists stuck out from the ends. He wore dark black boots with the laces untied at the top, and the boots open like a cup to catch the sticks that were his legs.

At the moment, he was sitting in a chair and had been secured with a rope around his chest, pinning his arms to the sides, but his legs were not bound. His face was a motley of bruises, mostly radiating from his swollen left eye and left ear— or rather, from the bandage over the remains of his left ear.

Keriah, likely, had dressed it with a clean one, but his brown hair had not been washed and it stood up in tufts on his head, stiff with blood.

Mr. Coulton-Jones stood in front of Maner and to one side, so as not to block the view from the screen. "I didn't ask you how you got to be there, I asked why you went to Hendey's." He had adopted a coarse accent, and she realized it was likely what he'd used when he'd been in disguise and met Maner earlier.

"I went based on a tip about the French group," Maner said. "I didn't know there was a greenhouse there, I swear it."

Interesting.

"I'm the victim here," Maner continued loudly. "I'm injured."

"We dressed your wounds," Mr. Coulton-Jones replied in a deceptively sympathetic voice. "How did the French group know about the greenhouse?"

"How should I know? What are you doing to track them? You should be trying to find them rather than questioning me like a criminal. If Jack finds the Frenchies, I'm a dead man."

Sol reached next to her to rap softly on the wooden frame of the screen. Mr. Coulton-Jones glanced over his shoulder at the screen, then walked toward them.

Laura retreated back into the dressing room, followed by Sol and Mr. Coulton-Jones, who closed the door behind him. As soon as he did, Mr. Rosmont burst out, "I'll go in and make him talk."

Keriah had been correct—he was unusually warlike. His frantic pacing from earlier was simply indicative of something deeper, something destructive.

"He'll hear you," Mr. Coulton-Jones hissed at him.

"Who cares if he hears me?" Mr. Rosmont snapped. "We should toss him out and let Jack find him."

"He's likely to go straight to Jack and sell him information about the tall man and woman healer who accompanied the twins to his bolthole under the church," Sol replied sternly, his voice sharp and heavy like an axe.

"He won't if I break a few fingers," Mr. Rosmont growled.

He moved toward the closed door as though he would do just that, but Mr. Coulton-Jones swiftly set himself in front of his friend. Mr. Rosmont tried to slide around him, forcing Mr. Coulton-Jones to grab him. Mr. Rosmont's muscles bunched and the tendons stood out on his neck as he glared at him, but Mr. Coulton-Jones held fast, almost effortlessly. The Root made him much stronger, even though Mr. Rosmont's belligerent attitude, slightly taller height, and greater muscle mass gave him a physical edge.

"Michael, you're just his lapdog," Mr. Rosmont sneered, indicating Sol.

The skin around Mr. Coulton-Jones's eyes grew taut, as did the lines alongside his mouth, but he said nothing.

"It's the Goldensuit speaking," Phoebe said desperately. "His anger is botanically induced."

"What do you know?" Mr. Rosmont snapped at her.

Mr. Coulton-Jones's voice was like the crack of a whip. "Watch how you speak, to her and to everyone else."

Mr. Rosmont attempted to break out of Mr. Coulton-Jones's grip, once, twice, but found he could not.

Laura stepped forward, skewering Mr. Rosmont's eyes with her own. "Calm yourself," she barked. "You are not an animal."

Her words seemed to shake his mind free from whatever haze had gripped him. He visibly relaxed, although there was still tension across his shoulders and in his jaw. He shook himself away from Mr. Coulton-Jones, who released him.

There were a few long moments of strained silence in the dressing room. The only sounds were the drafts that whistled into the small space from cracks in the floor and the walls.

Mr. Rosmont finally stood and leaned against the frame of the wardrobe—the broken wardrobe door was hanging open—and Mr. Coulton-Jones seemed to deflate slightly as he leaned back against the dresser. Sol remained standing near the corner, his frustration radiating from him like heat from a stove.

"Has it been like that this entire time?" Phoebe asked the men.

Sol nodded.

"Maner was clearly lying when he said he didn't know it was a greenhouse," Laura said. She'd seen the ticks in his face. "And simply from what Phoebe observed about it, the greenhouse is certainly Maner's, not Jack's."

"And if it's Maner's greenhouse, it's unlikely he told the French group about it," Phoebe said.

Mr. Coulton-Jones nodded. "He also would not have told me about it when I found him under the church, because then I'd have no reason to pursue the French group for him."

"However, he wasn't lying when he said he went to Hendey's in response to a tip about the French group," Laura said.

Sol straightened at her words. "You're certain?"

"I had a clear view of him," Laura said. "I saw every expression and movement of his body."

"Uncle Sol," Phoebe said, "maybe Aunt Laura could question Maner?"

Everyone seemed to stare at Laura for a few heartbeats. Then Sol slapped his thigh and said, "That's an excellent idea."

"It is?" Laura's head was spinning at the fact she'd gone from caterer to interrogator in the space of a few minutes.

"We could never lie to you, Aunt Laura," Phoebe said. "Maner doesn't stand a chance."

Sol unearthed a pencil from his pocket and there was a scramble to find scraps of paper upon which Laura would write her questions. They resorted to pulling pieces off the peeling wallpaper. They also found a light, thin piece of wood upon which she could write as she stood behind the screen.

They opened the door connecting the dressing room to the bedroom where Maner sat. He very loudly complained, "A bit drafty in here, you know."

Mr. Coulton-Jones ignored him as he stepped out into view and took her first question, scrawled on a scrap of paper. He stood only an arm's length from the edge of the screen so that he could reach for her next question, and she positioned herself at the viewing slit to see Maner's reaction.

She had decided upon questions that only required a yes or no answer, since Maner was clearly reluctant to speak, and in order to conceal her identity, she could not question him directly. She hoped that despite his unwillingness to cooperate, she would be able to tell which key words spoken made him uncomfortable.

"Did you nick a plant from Jack's greenhouse?" Mr. Coulton-Jones asked.

Maner didn't answer, and did his best to remain impassive, but a tell-tale twitch in his left jaw muscle indicated that yes, he had. Laura nodded to Sol, who stood slightly behind her and to the side, also hidden by the screen. Mr. Coulton-Jones was close enough to her that he could also see her nod.

As they suspected, Maner had been trying to grow the Goldensuit, and he knew that Jack would surely kill him if he knew.

While Keriah had conjectured that Maner had been hoping to make the Root in order to heal his ear, Laura also remembered Maner's truth about going to his greenhouse in response to a tip about the French group. They needed to understand what exactly had made him risk exposing himself. She quickly wrote another question on a piece of paper and handed it to Mr. Coulton-Jones, who reached behind the screen to take it from her.

His eyebrows rose at the question, but he asked it quickly. "Does a Miss Eades know about the greenhouse?"

Laura had remembered that the carpenter who made the skylights in Maner's greenhouse had been contracted by a "Miss

Eades." She suspected the answer but wanted to ask it anyway.

Maner attempted to look away while pressing his lips together, but there was a tightening of the lines alongside his mouth. She nodded to Sol, who also looked surprised at the direction her question had taken. She wrote another question.

"Was Miss Eades at the greenhouse when you got there last night?"

Maner again refused to speak, but his body spoke for him. No.

"Were you expecting Miss Eades to be there when you got to the greenhouse last night?"

No, but ... There was a hint of frustration in Maner's face, perhaps from the probing questions, but Laura suspected it had to do with Miss Eades. He had not expected her to be there, but ... She handed Mr. Coulton-Jones another question.

"Was there a chance she could have been there?"

Yes. There was also the faintest hardness in his eyes. Was it a fear of betrayal?

"Were you expecting the Frenchies to be there?"

The answer was unclear. Perhaps he had expected it, perhaps he had not known. Then she connected the dots.

"Was there a chance the Frenchies would have been there?"

Yes.

"Was there a chance Miss Eades told the French group about your greenhouse?"

Yes.

Sol's face was a mask of surprise and confusion as he stared at her. Mr. Coulton-Jones deliberately kept his expression neutral, but he quickly looked to her for the next question.

"Did you go to the greenhouse last night to see if Miss Eades told the French group about your plants?"

Yes.

It made sense. He had needed to know who had betrayed him to the French group in the first place. If it had been Miss Eades, she would have told the French group about his greenhouse, and the plants would probably have already been missing.

"Did Miss Eades betray you to the Frenchies?"

No. There was perhaps a hint of relief in Maner's expression. He had not wanted her to be the one who had betrayed him.

It was likely because Sinah Eades knew too many of his secrets.

"Do you know who betrayed you to the Frenchies?"

No.

"Do you know how the Frenchies found your greenhouse?"

No.

Maner finally cracked. "How are you figuring this out?" he shouted. "Who's behind that screen?"

"See, Maner? It's useless trying to lie to us," Mr. Coulton-Jones said, almost in a bored tone. "Why don't you just answer the questions?"

Maner sighed and hung his head. Then in a tight voice he said, "I didn't tell you about my plants because I didn't want you to get your hands on them. If you took them, you'd have no reason to help me."

Laura nodded to Mr. Coulton-Jones, indicating he was telling the truth.

Mr. Coulton-Jones turned back to Maner and nodded. "Makes sense."

"I'm being honest, here. I went to the greenhouse to find out if the Frenchies already knew about it. And if they hadn't, then I could still trust Sinah."

"But they showed up. Can you still trust her?"

"If she'd betrayed me, they would have taken my plants already, before they attacked Jack's greenhouse. Who would you be afraid of, me or Jack?"

"So how'd they found out about your greenhouse?"

Maner sighed gustily, his face openly showing his vexation. "No idea. No one should've known except Sinah." He shot Mr.

Coulton-Jones a narrow glare. "How'd you find it?"

"Wasn't easy," he answered, perhaps as a sop to Maner's pride. "Tell us all about this French group—all the juicy things you thought you'd keep to yourself."

Maner began to protest, but Mr. Coulton-Jones cut him off. "If you cooperate, we won't tell Jack about the fact you stole his Goldensuit and was trying to grow it for yourself, and that you were trying to make the Root."

"I wasn't trying to make the Root!"

"So you were using pig's blood as fertilizer?" Mr. Coulton-Jones asked.

Maner ground his teeth together and turned his head, looking away. "I didn't have a chance of being able to make it, anyway. I ain't no apothecary, and the plants never grew all that well, the few that survived."

Laura thought of a question and made a quick movement of her hand behind the screen. Mr. Coulton-Jones thankfully noticed and waited for her to write her question, then asked Maner, "Did anyone else know the plants weren't growing well?"

He seemed confused by the question. "No." Then he understood why she'd asked the question. "So anyone who did find out about my greenhouse wouldn't have known, either. They'd assume my plants were growing as well as Jack's."

"Did you know anything about growing them?"

"No, but ..." Maner's eyes slid to the side. "I grew marigolds. I figured they wouldn't be all that different."

From behind Laura came a barely muffled snort of laughter. Probably from Phoebe.

Maner's head snapped back to Mr. Coulton-Jones with suspicion in his eyes. "I'm still in danger. Whoever told the Frenchies about me might have told Jack about me giving the location of his greenhouse to them."

"We won't throw you back out onto the streets for Jack to find you," Mr. Coulton-Jones promised. "But how much we can help you will depend on how much you help us."

Maner gave a loud, gusty sigh, tilted his head back to look at the stained ceiling. "Fine, fine," he said with every appearance of reluctance, but Laura could tell he wasn't as begrudging as he pretended to be. He knew he hadn't much choice in the matter.

"You must have some idea of how the Frenchies knew about your greenhouse," Mr. Coulton-Jones said. "Would they have tailed you from the bolthole under the church?"

Maner gave a harsh laugh. "They're not the sort of people to tail anyone. They would have grabbed me and *made* me tell them where it was. In case you haven't noticed, they're not squeamish in the least."

Mr. Coulton-Jones ignored his sarcasm. "Did they say anything to you when they showed up at the greenhouse?"

"Hardly. Just started thrashing me."

Laura felt a tug at the back of her sleeve and turned to find Phoebe passing her a note she'd scrawled on a piece of paper she'd torn from the walls. *Find out about the Goldensuit.* Good idea.

She signaled to Mr. Coulton-Jones and handed him Phoebe's note.

He nodded and turned to Maner. "How'd Jack get the Goldensuit plant?"

Maner shook his head. "Don't know. And as far as I can tell, no one knows. And this is coming from me. I spent a lot of money to try to find out."

"What do you know about it?"

Maner shot Mr. Coulton-Jones a sharp look. "Why do you need to know? I don't give information out for free."

Mr. Coulton-Jones returned Maner's look with one so frosty that Laura thought the temperature in the already chilly room dropped to wintertime levels. "You need our help, Maner, and there's no guarantee we're going to be able to stop this group, much less get ourselves a plant. We don't work for free, either."

Maner gave a disgusted grimace. "Fine, fine. I'll have you know there isn't much information on the plant, since so few people have seen it."

"And you didn't want to risk asking an actual botanist to look at your plants?"

Maner gave him a look that seemed to say, *Do I look like a halfwit?* "From the people who heard Jack talk about it, it's not native to England or even Europe. Some people say he must've found it in Russia or Asia, but from what I can tell, Jack's never been out of England."

"How would he have gotten a plant like that? If anyone sold it, they would be rich and there would be Root elixirs across Europe."

"That's the big mystery. No one knows." But then there was a subtle shift in his face. Laura scribbled a note to Mr. Coulton-Jones: *Ask him what he suspects about how Jack acquired it.*

Mr. Coulton-Jones repeated the question to Maner, who looked a little guilty at being caught out, and answered resentfully. "He might've stolen it. I spoke to a gardener—who is now dead, by the way, like I soon will be—"

"You already made that clear, Maner," Mr. Coulton-Jones said impatiently.

Maner huffed. "The gardener said he saw Jack looking over pages of notes, but the notebook was old and falling apart. And the handwriting wasn't Jack's."

"How'd he know it wasn't Jack's?" Mr. Coulton-Jones demanded.

"Have you seen his handwriting?"

Mr. Coulton-Jones's face remained impassive, but Laura caught a slight tightening of the lines of his eyebrow. Yes, he had seen it.

Maner continued, "He writes thin and neat, like he's writing slowly. The notes were messy as spit."

Laura felt another tug on her dress sleeve, and Phoebe passed another note, which she passed to Mr. Coulton-Jones.

"Where's Jack's other greenhouse?"

Maner expressed genuine surprise. "I don't know anything about another greenhouse. And out of anyone in London, I'd know, wouldn't I?"

"Why'd you assume the one at the boarding house was his only one?" Mr. Coulton-Jones asked.

"'Cause Jack spent all his time at that greenhouse, almost every day. In fact, the rumor going 'round was that he was getting irritated because he was unhappy with the batch of Goldensuit he was growing."

"The Frenchies didn't ask about another greenhouse?"

"No, they only asked about the one. But I wouldn't have told them about a second one even if I knew about it. Which I didn't," he insisted loudly in response to Mr. Coulton-Jones's skeptical expression.

Laura nodded to Mr. Coulton-Jones to indicate that, yes, Maner was telling the truth about that.

"Any ideas where the French group is hiding out?"

"No." Maner looked just as frustrated as Mr. Coulton-Jones.

"How about the men you hire to keep an ear open for information?"

"Don't know which of them to trust, now don't I?" Maner replied bitterly. Then his eyes fell as he thought, and he said hesitantly, "Maybe I could point you toward how you can find them, but you have to *promise me*," he said earnestly. "Promise me, swear on your life, that you'll make sure Jack doesn't know about my plants, or that I was talking to you."

"I promise you," Mr. Coulton-Jones said.

Maner sighed and hung his head. "I didn't know if Sinah was the one who told the Frenchies about me knowing where Jack's greenhouse was, or if she'd told them about my greenhouse. I had to find out, you know? That's why I went to Hendey's, to find out."

Mr. Coulton-Jones nodded, but said nothing.

Maner continued, "I don't know who among my people told them that I knew about Jack's greenhouse. If it wasn't Sinah, it might have been one of my other men, but I don't know how they'd have found out. And now I don't know who to trust. So I had to find out if Sinah had betrayed me. It didn't look like she did. Otherwise the plants would have been gone already."

Mr. Coulton-Jones sighed. "The French group, Maner," he reminded him.

Maner looked up, and his eyes seemed to be pleading. "She might be able to find out, but no guarantees."

"I understand."

Maner nodded, and seemed to come to a decision. "Send a message to Sinah Eades."

Laura closed her eyes tight. She should have known it would come to that.

A touch on her shoulder made her open her eyes, and she saw Sol looking worriedly at her. She had forgotten he was there.

"Who's she?" Mr. Coulton-Jones asked Maner.

"She finds people," Maner said. "She and I have been friends for a long time. We work together sometimes."

"Can she find the French group?"

"If anyone can, she will. I don't think she betrayed me, but ... you understand the risks, don't you?"

"Will she be willing? Finding people like them isn't a safe job."

"I'll make sure she'll help you. Just let me write a message."

Mr. Coulton-Jones looked toward Sol, who nodded. To Maner, Mr. Coulton-Jones said, "Fine."

"And tell them ..." Maner swallowed, then stared at the screen as if he could see Laura there. "Tell the twins I'm sorry I'm asking them to talk to her."

Chapter Twelve

Michael didn't know what Lady Wynwood had said to her twin servants, but the young boy and girl now walked the streets of Jem Town with faces set like flint.

She had likely not ordered them to help him, but had instead given them a choice. And yet they had chosen to help, just as they had chosen to help Michael when he had been given the Root. He wondered if their faces had looked like this when they had gone after him in the dark streets, following the crazed monster to try to stop him from harming others.

It looked as though this task were paining them, but they had steeled themselves against it. It reminded Michael of when he'd broken a bone in his calf when he was a child, and he'd had to prepare himself for what he knew would be excruciating pain when the local doctor set it.

Michael didn't like walking into something when he knew very little about the situation. Maner's message to the twins had concerned him, and Thorne had grown thunderous with rage, although Michael couldn't quite discern who his target was. He suspected some of Thorne's anger was directed inward, even if he didn't realize it yet. Isabella had told him that Thorne's relationship with his son remained unchanged. His friend may not have interacted with children at all except for the forced cooperation with Lady Wynwood's young charges. It had perhaps drawn out memories of Timothy, and his parentage.

Calvin looked particularly stoic, so Michael directed his question more at Clara. She was dressed as a boy again, and looked so like her brother that he had to look closely to tell the difference between them, despite the afternoon sun warming the stones under their feet and reflecting golden against the buildings around them.

"Who is this person we are going to see?"

He had thought his question would make the twins upset, but he didn't expect the storm that flashed in Calvin's eyes. Clara paled slightly, but she answered in a soft voice. "She finds people."

"Anyone?"

Clara nodded. "Anyone in London. No guarantees if they're not in London, but she can sometimes find their trail out to the countryside." The way she said it sounded like something she'd repeated many times, like a shop clerk to customers.

"So she's like Maner?"

"No, not like Maner. She collects information, but she often works with him."

"Oh."

"They're friends," Calvin suddenly said, but his voice sounded hard.

"We don't know if she'll be there, but The Wicker Basket is where you can talk to her or leave a note if you want to hire her," Clara said.

Both children fell silent, and Michael sensed they didn't have anything else to say about her.

He, Thorne, Calvin, and Clara turned down a narrow, twisted street that had a faded name painted on a building on the corner: Rabbit Lane. The street was a little cleaner than others in Jem Town, although since it was so narrow, there wasn't that much of Rabbit Lane to sweep. Buildings rose high above them, but they had not been well-built and looked crooked, leaning to either one side or the other. Or perhaps it only seemed that way because the street wound its way around each building, which seemed to stick out or recess away from its neighbors according to an incomprehensible plan. Yet despite that, the windows and doors showed signs of careful repair, warped wooden panels in walls had been filled in with wood and plaster and covered with whitewash that was recent enough that it had only gone gray with the soot from the air.

It was as they approached a busy tavern that he suddenly smelled it—grass and rabbit droppings. In one of the buildings, someone was breeding rabbits, perhaps in a basement. The scent of rabbit droppings was not strong, as though it was frequently cleaned out, and it was overpowered by the strong scent of dried grass and hay.

And then the smell was overtaken by the savory aroma of meat pie, coming from the tavern, The Wicker Basket. Light and noise filtered from the open window into the street, but it was the sound of talk and laughter rather than raucous drinking. As they passed The Wicker Basket, a woman opened the heavy wooden door and exited, a basket over her arm and the stronger scent of meat pies wafting from it.

"They have good rabbit pies," Clara murmured as they walked past.

The twins led the two men past a couple more houses, then they turned right into a narrow alley that ran between two buildings. They climbed over a mound of something foul-smelling that Michael had to fight to not breathe in. Thorne also looked green at the noxious odor.

He wondered if Thorne's sense of smell had grown stronger from breathing in the pollen at Maner's greenhouse. During their walk through Jem Town, Thorne had been fidgety, turning toward every sharp sound. He did not appear nervous, but he walked like a man looking for any excuse to start a brawl.

Preferably with two or three opponents.

They turned right again onto another narrow alleyway, this one a dead end against the wall of a building. Michael realized it was the tavern, which had extended out into the track behind it. However, when he turned to see the other end of the alleyway, it again dead-ended against another building a couple houses further down that had also built an encroaching extension.

Thorne also noticed that there was only one way out of this area, and the muscles of his neck and shoulders visibly tightened.

The twins walked with assuredness down the dark track to a small door set into the side of The Wicker Basket. They picked up a rock near the side of the door and banged hard on it, six times. Then they waited.

As Michael stood a few feet away, with Thorne lounging casually on the other side of the door, the scent of grass and hay was strong again, as was the undercurrent of rabbit droppings. He occasionally smelled the rabbit pies, but only in random gusts of scent, since the back of The Wicker Basket had no windows, only the single door.

The various smells were so strong that he almost missed it. The realization came to him slowly that he'd been breathing in deeply for several minutes now, and the reason why hit him in a rush—Goldensuit.

It was the grass and hay—likely the rabbits' food and bedding—that had masked it. But now that he was aware, he could clearly smell the thread of that familiar, slightly floral scent, a green smell that somehow seemed wetter and thicker than the dried grass.

"Do you smell it?" he shot in a low voice to Thorne.

Thorne looked startled by the question for a moment, then sniffed. It took him longer to recognize it, but his eyebrows rose. "Yes. I think so. It's like the greenhouse." He breathed deep, then seemed to stop himself with a heave of effort. "It's making me ..." His jaw clenched, as did his fists.

Michael pointed farther down the alley. "Stand over there. It might be fainter."

Thorne obeyed with alacrity, betraying his fear. Michael knew his friend probably didn't like how the smell made him feel as though he were not in control of himself. He knew this because he felt the same.

The wooden door opened, and a paunchy man appeared. Sweat glistened against his nearly-bald head and stained the armpits and neck of his tunic, over which he wore a dirty apron. His eyes alighted first on the twins, and a wide grin broke across his round face. "Lemon cake and treacle bun! It's been a while." Then his eyes slid to Michael and Thorne, and immediately grew suspicious. "'Ere now, who's this? I won't stand for it if you're using these children."

Michael felt faintly guilty since he *was* using these children, but Clara immediately told him, "Sonny, they're all right. They hired us."

Sonny's eyebrows rose. "Are you two taking jobs now? I thought you were working for that rich lady."

"We are, but ..." Clara looked at her brother. "... We're worried about Maner."

A strange sour scent came from Sonny's direction. It seemed familiar to Michael, although not in the strange familiar way the Goldensuit smelled. This was like a scent he knew he'd smelled several times before, but he couldn't place it.

Sonny frowned at Michael and Thorne, then at the twins. "Did you hear about Maner? He disappeared. They say he was taken by some dangerous-looking people. You shouldn't get involved in that."

"But it's Maner." Calvin's voice was stubborn.

"Is Sinah here?" Clara asked.

Sonny shook his head, and even from where he stood, Michael

could see the fear in his eyes. He leaned down to speak softly to the twins, and Michael slid closer to overhear.

"Some Frenchies came by asking for Sinah," Sonny said. "And they didn't ask politely."

"What happened?" Calvin demanded. His voice had risen.

"I told them she wasn't here, naturally," Sonny said. "They almost didn't take no for an answer."

Michael interrupted to ask, "Did they leave a message?"

Sonny frowned at him again, but Clara reached out to tug at his apron. "Did they?" she asked.

He gusted a sigh. "No. But I told Sinah, and she bolted. Haven't seen her since."

It was the sigh that did it, wafting greasy air toward Michael over the heads of the twins. The sweet scent of French perfume came riding on the moving air, a distinct thread over onions and ale.

The Goldensuit he smelled outside the door had likely been from the Frenchmen, who'd been in contact with the plants. But the cook wouldn't have had the smell of French perfume unless he had taken something from the Frenchmen.

Michael rushed forward, gently shoving the twins to the side in order to grab at the man's shirtfront. He dragged him outside the building and then slammed him back hard against the wall.

"What are you—?!" Thorne said behind him.

Sonny was startled for a few moments, which allowed Michael to search his pockets. Then when he realized what he was doing, he began to struggle. However, while his arms were strong from mixing and chopping, they were no match for Michael's Root-enhanced strength. He slammed a hand against Sonny's thick, grease-coated throat and held him back against the wall of the building as he searched the pocket of the apron.

The coin pouch was small, but it reeked of French perfume.

"What did you say to the Frenchmen?" Michael demanded through gritted teeth.

Sonny looked frantically toward the twins. "I told you, I didn't tell them anything about Sinah. She wasn't here when they came, and I told her as soon as she showed up. She left right away."

"Where did she go?" Clara asked, her voice tight and frightened.

"I don't know, lemon cake, I swear it."

Michael shook the bag of coins. "You didn't get these coins for telling the Frenchmen nothing."

"That's from something else."

That sour smell wafted from Sonny again, and Michael realized that now, on the Root, he could clearly smell the man's lies. His hand tightened around the cook's throat. "Don't lie to me."

"I didn't know!" Sonny said, his voice cracking in panic. "I didn't know they were gonna take Maner."

Michael's suspicions had been right. These coins were what the Frenchmen gave to the cook in exchange for the information about Maner. This was the man who had betrayed him.

"Think real carefully before you next open your trap," Michael growled. "What exactly did those Frenchies say, and what exactly did you tell them?"

"They were offering a lot of money to find out where Jack's greenhouse was," Sonny said in a high voice, "and I guessed Maner would know because he had Sinah look for that one gardener who had worked for Jack before."

Maner had mentioned the gardener, who had seen Jack looking through the old notebook with handwriting not his own. The gardener who was now dead.

But the Frenchmen would have given Sonny the money for that several days ago. The coins wouldn't still be in his apron pocket.

"If you didn't tell them about Sinah," Michael said, "what did they pay you for today?"

"It wasn't today," Sonny said. "It was yesterday. Maner escaped and the Frenchies came back asking about him. I told them that Maner often went to Hendey's."

That was how they'd found Maner's greenhouse. If they had breathed the pollen and become like Thorne, whose sense of smell had become enhanced and sensitive to the Goldensuit, they would have smelled the plant as soon as they drew near to the building and then followed it to the attic greenhouse.

"Then they came back today asking about Sinah?" Thorne asked. His voice was low and growling, and Michael looked sharply at him.

Thorne's eyes were wide, his face tightly pulled back over his snarling teeth. The smell of the Goldensuit—and perhaps Sonny's betrayal—had caused his rage to rise more to the surface.

"Everyone knows she and Maner are friends," Sonny said. "They probably think she knows where Maner went."

But their search for Maner didn't make sense. They already had Jack's plants and Maner's plants. Maner would be unlikely to go running to Jack, because then he'd have to confess about giving them the information about his greenhouse.

Then Michael realized that the French group didn't know that he had found Maner's earring. They still thought Jack had found the earring in his greenhouse and now would be after Maner. In his rage over his stolen plants, he would comb London to find Maner, and once he did, Maner would tell him all about the French group that had captured him.

They had intended for Jack to do that, because they had expected to be long gone by then—except that the smugglers who ferried them over from France were now dead, and those who might be hired to take them were all lying low because of the murder. They were stuck in England for a few more days, so they couldn't have Jack finding Maner too soon. They were likely planning to kill Maner themselves, but they had to find him first.

"What else did you tell them?" Thorne roared.

"Nothing, nothing," Sonny sobbed.

Michael released him and kept a wary eye on Thorne, who had walked toward Sonny, his shoulders hunched, his hands clenched.

"Stop." Michael stood between Thorne and Sonny, his hand out toward his friend as though trying to soothe a wild beast. Beyond Thorne's figure, he could see the twins standing frozen like mice unwilling to move when a hawk was nearby. But their gazes were not afraid of Thorne—they seemed tense at the confrontation that might occur between Thorne and Sonny.

Michael's voice, or his stance, or both shook Thorne from his focus on the cook, who was sagging against the wall, trembling. He glanced up at Michael, eyes still wild but also with a touch of panic, and then turned and stalked away.

Sonny seemed relieved, but Michael wasn't. He hadn't expected to encounter the Goldensuit while out on this mission, and he was concerned because he couldn't afford to worry about Thorne going out of control like he did in Maner's greenhouse. He didn't have Miss Sauber and her sedative knives with him, and he didn't know if he could wrestle Thorne when he became strengthened by both the Goldensuit pollen and his own rage.

He motioned to the twins and they left Sonny, following Thorne back down the alley and returning to the street. But when they had gotten several yards away from The Wicker Basket, Michael motioned to the two children and leaned close. "Are you carrying sedative knives?"

The two nodded.

Michael breathed a sigh of relief. "If he begins to act strangely, be ready to dose him." He hesitated, then added, "If *I* begin to act strangely, dose me right away."

"What happened back there?" Clara whispered.

"Did ..." He couldn't say her name. "... your employer tell you about what happened last night?"

They nodded.

Good, that made the explanation easier. "We can smell the plant, and if it's strong, it might affect us."

The twins became perhaps a little pale, but nodded firmly.

Upon reaching Rabbit Lane, Thorne turned right rather than back the way they had come. When Michael reached the end of the alley and stepped out onto the lane, he understood why.

He hadn't smelled it when passing the tavern, but here, further down the street, he could clearly smell the Goldensuit. The Frenchmen had come from this way—perhaps had entered the alley from this direction, then left the same way.

And it had been recent.

"Stay alert," he instructed the twins, and followed after Thorne.

The street was not crowded, and they walked quickly to where it met with another. Thorne had stopped at the corner and was peering around the edge of a building toward the right. Michael caught up to him, and he stepped back so he could also look around the corner.

The large man and the slender, scarred man from last night were in the distance, walking down the street away from him. They were searching the buildings on the right side of the street.

Michael ducked back out of sight. "What are they looking for?" he whispered.

The twins had also peeked around the corner and it was Clara who answered. "Sinah sometimes meets clients in the front room of a boarding house down that way."

"Sonny must have told them," Thorne said in a low, tight voice. "He didn't tell us everything."

Clara shook her head. "I don't think Sonny knows. Sinah wanted to keep it secret from him, because he gives her a free room above The Wicker Basket in exchange for a cut of her jobs. She wouldn't want him to know she had another place she used."

"What do you want to do?" Thorne asked Michael.

His mind raced. Despite his misgivings about Thorne, he couldn't let this opportunity slip away. "I have a plan."

Chapter Thirteen

Thorne turned onto the street whose name he did not know, keeping his head down and his hands in his pockets. The disreputable hat he'd chosen for his disguise as a common man wasn't very warm and only covered the tops of his ears, so his shiver in the wind was real. As the sun started to set, darkness came early in this part of London because of the tall buildings, and the temperature dropped sharply.

While he didn't look up at the people on the sparsely populated street, he threw covert glances ahead of him. Just a few more yards. His timing had to be perfect.

He stepped around an elderly couple ambling along so that he was in full view of the two Frenchmen a few buildings down the street. He lifted his head idly, as though by accident, and then swiveled his gaze toward them.

They were already looking at him, and he knew immediately that they'd recognized him from Maner's greenhouse last night.

He paused between one step and the other, then smoothly turned to walk back the way he'd come. He increased his pace, but was still walking, not running. He wound around two men who had stopped to talk in the middle of the street, and nearly tripped over an old woman sagged against a doorway.

He allowed himself a brief glance behind him before he turned around the corner of a building. The two men were following, although their gazes were on the people and places around them, not on Thorne.

He counted to himself while the men drew closer to the corner. He couldn't get too far ahead of them, and this new road had even fewer pedestrians to slow him down.

When he had judged the men were about to turn onto his street, he broke into a run. There weren't many people to weave around, and he didn't waste time looking behind him. He knew they'd be hurrying after him. After all, just like a dog will pursue anything that runs away from it, the Frenchmen wouldn't be able to resist Thorne, alone, trying to escape them.

He made sure to slow down with large dramatic movements as he reached the alleyway, so that they would be sure to spot him turning, then ducked to the right.

Clara and Calvin had chosen the alley, which was another dead end. This one hadn't been blocked by a building, but by a huge heap of trash and junk that had been dumped at the end, with smaller heaps near the opening of the alley. Thorne skirted around some broken chairs and the remains of a rotting crate, then circled around a heap of food scraps that had been thrown at the base of an upended broken cart, which leaned against the wall of the boarding house that lined one side of the alley.

And then he waited. He was barely breathing heavily, and his body thrummed with strength and anticipation. He'd been wound up for hours, ever since he awoke, and he relished in the chance to put his fist in someone's nose. He felt as though only physical exertion and pain could make him feel calm ever again.

He heard footsteps a second or two before he saw the two men skid to a halt at the opening to the alley. He wasn't surprised to see them, but he hesitated at the look in their eyes.

Wide. Wild. Twitching and trembling.

Just like how Thorne felt.

A part of him understood that this was wrong, that there was something very wrong with them. But the more primal side of him didn't care, and simply wanted to pound them into the ground.

The two men didn't approach slowly, they ran through the trash in the alley, jumping over smaller mounds and skirting larger ones, aiming for Thorne like two wolves that had sighted prey. The larger man was in front, which suited Thorne just fine.

As the two Frenchmen ran past the upended cart, Michael rose from where he'd been hiding on top of it and dropped down on the latter pursuer, the slender man. The two went down, rolling in rotting vegetables.

The large Frenchman glanced back at the sound, and that's when Thorne stepped in.

His first blow went to the man's exposed jaw, but he must have seen the attack out of the corner of his eye because he tilted his head aside and Thorne's fist partially slid off of his ear, lightening the blow.

The man didn't hesitate but jabbed out at Thorne, and he had to lean back and step aside to avoid it.

The man had a smell that reached his senses, over the reek of the rubbish and the smoke of chimneys—a smell like a flower, but not a flower, more green and grassy. The scent was very faint but somehow heady, like a whiff of alcohol from a rich, peaty scotch.

They faced each other, watching for an opening. Thorne threw a short left jab, but the man attacked with a cross that looked like his arm extended three feet further. Thorne bucked backward to avoid it, then immediately hurled a roundhouse punch, but his opponent ducked.

It was similar to the fight with this same man in Maner's greenhouse. He had been able to see Thorne's motions, predict the blow he was about to throw, and react quickly enough to avoid or counter. This man—and probably his companion—were trained fighters, skillful and experienced.

And brutal.

They circled another second or two, then they both threw right punches at each other at the same time. Thorne ducked backward and only felt the graze of the man's knuckles against his cheek, but his own punch also missed. Thorne quickly swung his left fist, but the man dodged neatly and struck out with a curving right blow that knocked into Thorne's temple.

He staggered, but righted himself quickly and backed away, giving himself time for the stars to clear his vision.

No, not stars. He was seeing red flames that matched the fire stoking inside him. He stared at the man's face, wide with a nose broken twice, and desired only to pummel it into the ground.

A distant part of his mind heard the sound of wood crashing and splintering. Something about that should concern him, but he couldn't remember. He couldn't take the time to remember.

The man feinted another left jab but then swung his right fist. Thorne backed up, enough to narrowly avoid the right punch, but not enough for the man to be out of Thorne's reach. He countered with a left cross that connected with the man's jaw even as his opponent was throwing his own left cross. The left fist lost speed midway in the swing as the man fell to the ground, stunned.

Thorne didn't hesitate. He fell on the man, beating at the back of his head, then on his jaw as he slumped onto the side of his face. He felt bone crack, felt warm drops of blood fly upward into his face. His breath came quickly, with exertion and ... *excitement.*

"Stop!"

He dimly recognized the voice.

"Stop!"

Michael. His friend. Why was he telling him to stop? He needed to pulverize this man's face into just bones and blood.

"Stop or I kill her!" The woman's voice shot through his head like a bullet, jerking him out of the blood haze.

He looked up. The cart, which had been leaning against the wall, had fallen to the ground. Michael had been hiding on top of that cart, and he'd dropped onto the slender man from above.

But he hadn't been the only one hiding on the cart. He had been with ...

Clara stood several feet away. Her knees were dirty—she must have fallen when the cart fell.

Standing behind her was a woman. At first she looked like an old woman, but then he recognized the dirty gray wig, the clothing that seemed to be nothing but rags, which covered limbs that were a little too clean to match.

He stared into the woman's eyes and recognized her from Maner's greenhouse. Unlike the two Frenchmen, her gaze was calm and cool rather than wild. Thorne was downwind from her, and while he could smell the Goldensuit on the man he'd been fighting, there was none of that scent coming from her.

The woman's hand clenched and Clara winced, and only then did Thorne realize that she held Clara's neck.

"Let's talk, shall we?" she purred.

Thorne could only watch helplessly as Clara scrabbled at the hand around her neck. But she was only reaching with one hand —her other slid toward the waistband of the boy's breeches she wore.

Except that Brigitte noticed. She tightened her hand around Clara's neck even as she grabbed at the girl's wrist, which was only inches away from her waistband. Clara cried out in pain.

Brigitte released the wrist to fumble at her waist and remove the knife stashed there in a leather holster, that had been hidden by her loose shirt. She tossed it away, and it clanged against the stone ground.

"Hurt her," Thorne growled, "and I'll finish him." He kicked at the man at his feet, who was groaning and moving his limbs, trying to rise.

"You will not." Brigitte had only the faintest of French accents. If Thorne hadn't been listening to it, he might not have noticed. "Because I think you care about this girl much more than I care about Henri."

There was a slight movement to Thorne's right, and he saw Calvin peering over the top of the mound of trash where he'd been hiding. He had a throwing knife in his hand, which matched one sticking out of the calf of the slender Frenchman at Michael's feet. But he wouldn't throw them when Brigitte, short and close to Clara in height, was right behind his sister.

"Luc, Henri," Brigitte ordered.

Henri slowly lumbered to his feet. His left eye, which had been exposed to Thorne's flying fists, was swollen shut and covered with blood from a cut on his forehead, the same blood smeared on Thorne's knuckles. The look he gave Thorne from his right eye was bright and vengeful, even in the midst of his pain.

An answering fire rose in his gut, but he had to hold back because of Clara.

And then there was a slight movement behind Brigitte, so subtle that it might have been a piece of trash falling from a mound.

"Hey." Thorne shoved roughly at Henri's shoulder to get his attention back on himself, and away from Brigitte. 'What did you say?"

"I said nothing," Henri said in French, then proceeded to curse Thorne's mother, dog, reproductive capability, and intelligence with colorful euphemisms.

Thorne kept his gaze averted from Brigitte. He couldn't give away ...

Brigitte's cry of pain brought Henri's gaze back to his boss. Isabella had snuck up behind the Frenchwoman and slashed at the arm holding Clara. Brigitte had released the girl and was clenching her arm, blood smeared across her hand, as Clara darted away.

Isabella slashed at Brigitte again, but her knife-fighting skills were only adequate at best. A much better fighter, Brigitte easily avoided the blade, then moved in swiftly to punch at Isabella's exposed chin. Isabella fell backward, her body both stiff and limp at the same time as the blow dazed her.

Brigitte called to her men and ran. The two Frenchmen raced after her, leaving them alone in the alleyway.

Calvin went to his sister while Michael and Thorne ran to Isabella's form on the ground, but she was already moving sluggishly and sitting up. "That woman was so fast," she mumbled.

"She's well-trained," Michael said.

"You did a good job sneaking up on her," Thorne said.

"Is the girl—?"

"She's fine." Thorne nodded in Clara's direction, where Calvin stood protectively next to her as she rubbed her sore throat.

Isabella slapped her hands against the ground in a rare show of temper. "I've never before failed to see someone in disguise. Until now."

"I didn't see her at all," Thorne said.

"You passed her when you were running away from the two Frenchmen." Isabella reached out and Michael helped her to her feet. "She's even better than I am," she admitted sullenly.

Thorne was feeling sullen and frustrated himself. He had had the best of the large Frenchman, and from what he'd seen, Michael had also felled the other one, with the help of one of the twins' thrown knives. If they'd been able to get one or both of them back to Stapytton House, they could have discovered where the French group was keeping the Goldensuit plants.

He walked to Clara. "Are you injured?"

She shook her head, but looked down. "I'm sorry, sir. When I threw a knife, she saw me and pushed the cart over so she could get to me."

"It wasn't your fault," he said firmly. He didn't know why he was so intent on reassuring her, why he wanted to lift the cloud over her expression. He had never been good with children, but he had somehow grown close to these two.

Michael and Isabella walked up to join them. "Where would Sinah go?"

The twins glanced at each other. "Only one place," Calvin said.

Surprisingly, the ruined church wasn't far from the alley. They kept watch to make sure no one saw them enter the empty lot, then Isabella did something that made her melt invisibly in the shadows while the rest of them headed to the wall of the church.

Michael opened the hidden door. They tried to be quiet, but it seemed to roar in the melancholy pall that hung over the crumbled stones and spiky weeds.

Michael entered first. Calvin at first opened his mouth as if to protest, hesitated, then let him go. Thorne brought up the rear and closed the hidden door even as Michael headed down the stairs. He smelled smoke, and guessed someone had just blown out a candle.

"Sinah Eades?" Michael called softly. His footsteps stopped— he must have reached the bottom of the stairs. "Maner sent us —"

There was a thud and a man's grunt. Thorne tensed and started forward, only to plow into Clara, who still stood in front of him. He grabbed at her and managed to snag her arm before she fell down the stone steps.

Then Clara's voice sounded in the silence. "Mama, it's us."

Mama?

For some reason, Thorne suddenly couldn't hear anything beyond the roar of his heartbeat. It was as if the darkness had become a shroud that thickened and stopped the sound from reaching his ears.

How had he not guessed? He had assumed the twins were orphans, for some reason, perhaps because the cook from The Wicker Basket and even Maner were very paternal toward them, as though they had no one else for family except the ones in the community who had taken on that role.

But their mother was alive. And yet, why did the twins respond as they did to her name? What kind of mother was she?

Even as the thought formed in his mind, the guilt pressed on his chest like a stone weight.

There was the sound of fumbling in the dark, then light slowly seeped through the half-open door ahead of them. All Thorne could see was Michael's feet where he lay in the doorway, but then they shifted as he slowly rose to his hands and knees.

The twins continued down the narrow stairs just as Michael stood, rubbing the back of his neck where he'd apparently been hit, and Thorne finally pushed his way into the small room at the bottom.

A nondescript woman stood there, dark lanky hair, big dark eyes. Her nose had been broken twice. She would never have been beautiful, but there was a luminous quality to her face that made her difficult to forget. However, she kept her head down, hair covering the sides of her face, and because of her trick in manipulating the rest of her body, it would have been easy to not look in her direction if he passed her on the street.

There was a softness to her cheeks and her jaw, and yet a hardness to her shoulders and arms, a stiffness to her trunk. The tendons stood out on the backs of her hands, and yet she moved them with an elegance that would not have been out of place in a drawing room. Thorne realized that her distinctive feature was that she was a mass of contradictions.

The gaze she shot him and Michael was fierce and cold, a dagger in the dark. And yet when she looked upon the twins, her fear so suffused her face that it looked as though she was suffocating in it.

Calvin and Clara also had mixed emotions as they stared at her. Longing. Nervousness. But they said nothing, neither did they move closer to her.

"We have a message from Maner," Michael said, passing her a note that Maner had scribbled. "He couldn't trust any of his men right now because he didn't know who had betrayed him to the French."

"It was Sonny." Her voice was low, with a smoothness and yet a bite like aged brandy. She didn't look at the children, and regarded him with wariness.

"We know that now." Michael sighed as he stretched his neck.

"Sorry," she said, not sounding apologetic at all. She scanned the note, her brow furrowing. "I don't understand this note. Typical Maner," she groused. "What exactly does he want?" She didn't ask where he was, or how he was doing.

"A French spy named Brigitte and her three men stole some of Jack's plants," Michael said. "They'll be leaving England as soon as soon as they can threaten the right smuggler to take them."

"She shouldn't have to threaten a smuggler to take her," Sinah said.

"None of them want anything to do with the French because the ones who brought her here are now dead," Michael said.

"Oh. Then I guess she will need to threaten someone." She sounded unconcerned. "Maner needs me to find her?"

"Yes, before she can leave."

"Where can I reach you?"

Michael hesitated, then said, "I'll remain here. You have to come back here, don't you?"

She shook her head. "Too many people in here. The neighbors

will hear if you talk."

"I'll take the twins back to their employer," Thorne said sharply.

She still didn't look at them, just nodded to Michael. "If that's it, I'll get to work." She turned toward the door, but stopped and glared at Thorne, who still stood in the way. He took a step to the side.

"H-how are you, Mama?" Clara asked in a small voice.

Sinah still didn't look at her children. Her mouth worked as though she started to say something, then changed her mind, then started to say something else, then stopped. Finally, she said in a harsh voice, "Don't call me that. I'm not your mama anymore."

The twins' faces looked as though someone had stabbed them with knives through the heart. Perhaps they felt that they had been.

Thorne's rage flared so fast he felt like a torch. He took a step toward her, but Michael's bulk was suddenly in his way, pushing him back. His friend's eyes were wide and white, his breathing hard and fast. He didn't realize Michael had gripped his arms until he looked down to see hands, white-knuckled, as they held him back.

Sinah had jerked like a startled deer at Thorne's advance and Michael's response, but otherwise she was strangely unaffected, her gaze cold and dead.

So was her voice as she said, "Wait a few minutes before you leave." She exited the room and closed the door behind her.

They heard her soft steps climbing the stairs. The twins stared speechlessly at the closed door, and then they fumbled to grab each others' hands and squeeze tightly.

The sight of their clasped hands turned his anger in a different direction. What kind of parent deliberately hurt her children like that?

A parent like him.

There was that weight on his chest again. It pushed his anger out of him, like pushing water from a sponge. Even though his anger at her still smoldered, he knew he was a hypocrite.

He walked up to the children and grasped them gently by the shoulders. They were both trembling, and it was as if he could feel their pain soaking into his body through his hands.

Finally Thorne said in a soft voice, "Let's go."

Chapter Fourteen

Laura knew the twins had willingly agreed to go to speak to their mother. But after they left her house accompanying Mr. Coulton-Jones, Mr. Rosmont, and Lady Aymer, she still felt a deep, aching worry about them. She decided to return to Stapytton House.

Only Sol, Keriah, and Phoebe were there. None of them expected her to return, since she had long ago promised to attend a soiree tonight at the home of her mother's cousin. But she couldn't return to society at this moment, not after seeing the faces of Calvin and Clara as she had explained what Maner had told them.

The children had wanted to help. They had been upset, apprehensive, and struggling to hide their desire to see her, but they had volunteered to go with Mr. Coulton-Jones to see Sinah.

Right after Laura had bought them at the illegal slave auction, she had tried to discover what had happened to them. She knew Maner was Sinah's friend, and even went to him one night a few weeks after the twins came into her household. But he only gave her lies, even when she offered to pay him for the information she sought. She didn't know how to force him to tell her the truth, and she had left frustrated.

But Maner had seen the twins since then. Laura saw the

difference in his attitude toward them when she questioned him.

She would not leave frustrated today.

Maner was still in the master bedroom, still tied up. Sol had deliberately left him there since there wasn't any other room in the dilapidated manor that had a working lock on the door. He had also left the key with the others for the house, on a shelf in the kitchen.

She unlocked the door and entered the room. The afternoon sun streamed through the one window not boarded up, and the small table had been moved next to Maner's chair, holding some pieces of chicken and a wedge of bread, as well as a mug of tea still steaming. His arms were freed, but Sol had somehow found metal shackles that bound his ankle to his chair. The lamp had been removed.

He looked up at her as she entered, but his face didn't display much surprise. "I knew you were involved," he said.

"I don't know what's happening right now," she said coolly. It wasn't a lie, since she didn't know exactly what Mr. Coulton-Jones's team was doing at the moment. "The twins were upset, Maner." It wasn't hard to make it sound accusatory, since that's what she was feeling.

His eyes dropped to his plate, but he said nothing.

"I found out where you were being kept," she said. "I wanted to speak to you."

"About what?" Then he looked at her face and seemed to guess. His eyes shifted toward the closed door to the hallway, and the connecting door to the dressing room.

"There's no one else listening." She stopped a few feet away from him. Because of his shackled ankle, she was a bit more secure that he wouldn't attack her, but she still wanted enough space between them to avoid him if he tried anything.

He seemed to understand that, also, but he gave her a wry smile. "I won't do nothing to you."

"You'll forgive me for not believing you."

"You're watching over the twins. That should be enough reason to believe I wouldn't do anything."

"You care about them." She steeled herself, then asked the question, "Are you their father?"

He barked a laugh. "No." Then his face sobered, and a wistfulness came into his expression, but he repeated, "No."

"Today, you sent them to their mother, Maner."

He frowned at his teacup. "I told them I was sorry."

Laura took a deep breath. "There is one thing I want to ask you. I asked you this before, but will you answer me today?"

His half-smile was sly. "For free?"

"For the twins' sake."

He grew somber, and seemed to be thinking. Finally he said, "For them, I'll answer you."

"Why did Sinah sell them?"

The words were bluntly spoken, and the truth, and yet they hung with such ugliness in the stale air of the room that even Laura had to look away for a moment.

Maner licked his lips. "The Senhora didn't tell you?"

"She said she didn't know," Laura answered.

Maner paused to consider that. "She might not have."

He seemed reluctant to speak more, so Laura said, "I know Sinah sold her children to that auction. What I don't know is why."

"If I tell you, I don't want them to know." His voice was harsh, as were his eyes as he looked up at her.

"I won't tell them."

He nodded, but almost as if to himself. Then he took a deep breath and began to speak. "Sinah was hired for a big job by Jem Falan, used to run a gang in Southwark. Jem needed her to find a con man, James Ruell, who managed to become personal secretary for a very wealthy merchant in Falan's employ. Ruell stole a fortune from the merchant—essentially Falan's money— and then went into hiding. Around the same time, Sinah got involved with this man named Abraham Welley. She's always had terrible taste in men, but this guy treated her right. I'd never seen her happy and carefree before she met him."

"You and Sinah were never in a relationship?" Laura asked.

"Naw." Maner tried to look unconcerned, but she suspected he wouldn't have rejected Sinah if she'd expressed interest in him. "She's more like a sister to me. Nags me like one, too." A smile cracked the corner of his mouth, then disappeared just as quickly. "But maybe I wasn't even that, because … I failed her. You see, I met this guy once, thought he was a nice chap. You'd think with everything I know—" He tapped his forehead harder than necessary with his finger. "—that I'd at least know things that would protect myself or the people close to me. But I didn't even realize who this guy was."

"What do you mean?"

"He was working for Shepherd Willie. Gang leader and rival with Sinah's employer. Abraham Welley was Shepherd Willie's cousin, and he had just arrived in London from somewhere up north. Shepherd Willie sent Welley to get involved with Sinah to keep tabs on her job for Jem Falan."

Laura then understood. "To find James Ruell first."

Maner nodded with a bitter expression. "She drifted away from me for a little while after meeting Welley, but I saw her a few weeks after. She was so relaxed and content." There was a tremor in his voice as he said the word. "She said he was everything she wanted in a husband, that he'd even hinted at getting married."

Laura remembered that sweet, frothy feeling in the months when Wynwood had been courting her, when his lying face seemed to glow with love for her. That love was like the finest champagne, filling her with joy. She felt so alive when she was with him.

And she remembered the first time he hit her, only a week after they married. Her hopes shattered like a cannonball destroying a stone castle wall. She could predict what had happened next to Sinah Eades.

"She found Ruell—she's good at her profession—and she accidentally gave Welley a clue about where he was. While she was giving the information to Falan, Shepherd Willie was capturing Ruell and stealing all his money."

Laura could almost hear the thunderous crumbling of stones that would have been Sinah's heart.

"Falan beat her and almost killed her when he found out." Maner swallowed as he remembered. "I had to take her to Lady Nola, and even Nola hadn't been sure she could save her. And while she was recovering, Falan went and ruined her reputation. When she finally could work, she couldn't find any clients. And then she found out she had a bun in the oven. Two, actually."

Laura knew that especially in areas like Jem Town and the Long Glades, pregnancy didn't always bring joy to the mother. But considering how Sinah had been hurt and betrayed, how must she have felt about those two lives inside her, Welley's seed? "Did she find Welley?"

"A'course," Maner said. "That's what she does. But she couldn't get revenge on him, because he's Shepherd Willie's cousin. They'd kill her if she killed Welley."

Deprived of the object of her wrath, how had she felt about the twins?

Maner continued, "I helped her find a place in the country to have the kids. The twins were small, so we said they were a year younger so Welley wouldn't know they were his. You have to understand." Maner's face seemed to plead with Laura. "Sinah's not a motherly person. She don't like babies in general."

"She hated them," Laura guessed, speaking in a low voice. She had to remember that her own situation was markedly different from Sinah. While she couldn't imagine hating her own children, she could understand that someone of Sinah's personality would have looked at Calvin and Clara and only seen the man who had betrayed her and caused her to lose everything. "I'm surprised she kept them."

Maner glanced to the side, and faint color rose to his cheeks. "I convinced her to keep them."

Laura suddenly suspected that Maner loved children. It had been in the way he'd spoken about them.

He quickly added, "I use children a lot for my work, and the twins are smart. They matured right quick, although I think it was partly because Sinah seemed to like them better when they acted more like adults. She started working for me, and I helped her get back on her feet, repair her reputation, find clients again."

"You trained them, didn't you?"

A smile flitted across his lips. "I train a lot of children who work for me. They also started working for Sinah when they got old enough, but she was demanding and critical—too much, I thought, but they still did their best to please her. Did they tell you how they learned to throw knives?"

Laura shook her head.

"One night, Sinah was attacked by purse snatchers. When she fought back, they beat her pretty badly. The twins wanted to help protect her, so they asked me to teach them to fight." He scratched his cheek. "They've always been small, so I taught them to throw knives, since I figured they'd best be able to protect their mama from a distance. They were skilled at it, but it shouldn't have surprised me, considering their father."

"He's good a throwing knives?"

"The best. Since he came to London, he'd been gaining a reputation as being able to pin a man's ear to a door with a throwing knife. So when the twins told Sinah, she had a screaming fit, and they didn't know why. I had to calm her down, and eventually she came around to it, since they were useful for her job. They're easily overlooked, you see."

There was a flash of emotion across his face, and Laura asked,

"What did she make them do?"

The emotion flashed again, stronger this time. "Most of the time she had them stand by to protect her but once in a while, she had them hit men with poisoned knives to slow them down ... or kill them. They didn't like it, but they did it because it was their mama asking them."

Laura exhaled and closed her eyes briefly.

"I tried to stop her, tried to make her keep it to a minimum," Maner said quickly. "And she didn't like seeing them throw knives since it reminded her of Welley, so it wasn't too often. I hired them instead so she wouldn't use them that way."

"Is that why she sold them?"

"No." Maner gave a long, heavy sigh. "Their father was still in London, working for Shepherd Willie. He happened to see them throwing knives while on a job for me and they interested him. He found out they were Sinah's kids." He grabbed his head with both hands and grimaced. "I was never so glad we'd lied about their ages. Never thought Welley would notice them."

"What did he do to them?" Her voice had risen in pitch.

"Nothing bad," Maner quickly reassured her. "A few weeks later, he happened upon them practicing in an alley and he gave them some pointers. They met with him for tips every so often. He told them not to tell their mother, but she found out." Maner sighed again. "I tried reasoning with her, but she's not reasonable when it comes to Welley. She kept insisting the twins had betrayed her. I tried reminding her that it wasn't the twins' fault because they didn't know Welley was their father, but she didn't listen. Started whaling on the kids even more than normal."

Laura's hands clenched into fists.

"I only wanted to get them out of the situation." Maner's voice had become pleading. "Sinah couldn't work, she was so angry all the time. The kids were always bruised. So when I heard from a merchant that he needed children to work as servants for English families in India, I told her about it and arranged it for her."

"So the twins thought they were going to India?"

"Sinah was too afraid to tell them she was sending them so far away, so she arranged for the merchant to take them from their home one day. The twins never knew their mama knew about it. But before he sailed, he heard about an opportunity to sell the twins in an auction set up by one of the more vile brothels, and that several people were interested in them."

"How could you have not known that about the merchant, Maner?" she demanded.

"He didn't have the best reputation," Maner admitted, "but he hadn't been connected to that brothel's slave auction before, either. I thought them going to India was a good situation for the twins. And once I heard about the brothel, I tried to buy the twins, but the merchant wanted to make more money through the auction. Sinah and I looked all over London for them, but we couldn't find them. We had only two days, while the brothel was setting up interested bidders."

Laura had to swallow around the bitter bile in her throat. "I'm surprised Sinah cared," she said harshly.

"Sure, Sinah hated the twins, but maybe for the first time, she felt guilt. I could tell, even when she gave me a tongue-lashing over everything that was happening." He now looked directly at Laura. "That's why I went to the Senhora and asked her to tell you about the sale."

Her throat tightened, but she said nothing.

"I knew you'd have the blunt to buy them instead of any of the clients." Maner gave a humorless laugh. "First time I actually paid for a favor myself. But it was the only way I could think of to save them."

"What did Sinah think about it?"

"She was grateful the kids would be in better hands than any of the brothel's clients, but ... also relieved the twins weren't her problem no more."

Well, he was being brutally honest. "Maner, knowing all this about Sinah, why did you send the twins to ask her for help? From what you've said, she wouldn't care if she put her children in danger."

Maner chewed on his lip a moment before answering. "Sinah always said that she wouldn't care even if the children knew she'd tried to sell them, but I think that she actually does care. She hates them, but there's a part of her that don't want to hate them."

Laura felt she could understand that. "Is she a danger to them?"

"No," Maner said quickly. "She'd be satisfied if she didn't see them."

He was telling the truth. "Are *you* a danger to them?"

Maner's face was a multitude of emotions—regret, self-loathing, tenderness. "Milady, I'm a terrible man, and I've done terrible things, but those two are the closest thing to family I ever had. I won't hurt them."

Again, he was telling the truth. "I'm trying to decide if I should keep the twins far away from you and Sinah, Maner."

Maner's face became desperate. "I saved their lives once, and now I need their help. Otherwise either Jack or the Frenchies will kill me."

It was true that he had saved them, even though that decision, made years ago, showed a weakness in himself that would surely destroy his reputation if anyone knew about it.

"But please don't tell the twins about their mother," Maner said.

"Why keep it from them? It would make the twins indebted to you," Laura said carefully.

He shook his head. "It'll hurt them," he said in a broken voice.

She realized that he cared too much about Calvin and Clara

to want to do that to them. "I won't tell them," she finally said. "I'll let them decide whether to help you or not."

He nodded, and he seemed sad. "I understand."

Laura turned and left the room.

Chapter Fifteen

Thorne found himself at a loss. The twins were surprisingly stubborn about not wanting to go back to Lady Wynwood's home, since Michael was waiting at the church for their mother to return with the information about where the French group was holed up. They insisted they wanted to help as they had in rescuing Mr. Ackett from the stable.

Isabella had entered the church after seeing Sinah leave, and it was she who convinced the twins to accompany herself and Thorne back to Mayfair. They did so with reluctance, hanging their heads as the four of them caught first a vegetable cart, then a hackney back to Park Street.

Dressed as they were, they all entered the house via the servants' entrance, where the cook made a loud fuss upon seeing the bruises on Clara's neck.

Thorne felt a stab of guilt at the sight, also. He had not caused those bruises, but he had been there when Clara had been put in danger. He somehow felt he had not done enough to protect her. After all, she was a child and he was the adult.

Isabella seemed to read his mind, because as they watched the servants bustle around Clara in the kitchen—while the cook also piled food in front of Calvin at the table—she said to him, "The fault does not lie with you. It lies with me."

He frowned at her, but she had long ago become accustomed

to his glowers and did not react with the slightest bit of fear.

"It was my duty to watch for anyone who may have followed you," she said. "I missed Brigitte though she was directly under my nose."

"Even if you had identified her, you could not have stopped her because you are not a fighter," Thorne said. "I am."

"You seemed rather occupied at the time, if I recall."

He grimaced. "I should have dealt with him faster."

"There," she said, as though she had accomplished something grand. "You have confessed your regret and so have I. Now we may turn our focus on what is ahead."

And like that, he realized she had tricked him into expressing what had been bothering him during the entire journey back here. The telling had made him feel a little bit better.

She smiled at him, as brilliant as a sunset over the ocean. An answering smile shone inside him, although he only showed it by quirking the sides of his mouth at her. He had not been able to fully smile in a long, long time.

Lady Wynwood had joined them in the kitchen, likely drawn to the noise. Thorne reflected that everyone in this household positively doted upon the twins. It was a wonder they were not spoiled rotten.

But then he remembered their mother, and understood why.

Isabella noticed his darkening mood, and gave him a sharp pinch in the arm.

"Ow!"

"Whiner," she replied.

Lady Wynwood approached them, her eyes strangely haunted as she asked, "Did you find her?"

Thorne realized that she'd known Sinah Eades was the twins' mother. It was also why she'd been able to focus on the name of the woman who had ordered the skylights in Maner's greenhouse. Now he knew why she'd been so apprehensive and reluctant to let Calvin and Clara accompany them, although she'd left the decision up to the two children.

"Yes," he answered. "We left Michael to await her reply."

She nodded, almost as though the news were unwelcome.

Isabella asked, "Where are Phoebe and Keriah?"

"They are at the stillroom," Lady Wynwood replied, meaning Stapytton House. She had not told her servants about the mansion where the two women were working except for Mr. Havner, the coachman, who drove her there and back. "I have just left them."

"We will need both of them," Thorne said. Two weeks ago he would not have admitted to wanting the help of civilians at all, and he marveled at how quickly his mindset had changed.

"Phoebe will need to help secure the plants that will be there," Isabella told her, "and Keriah may be needed for any ... injuries."

While there may very well be wounds for her to bandage, they all—but him especially—had to be aware of the possibility of effects from the pollen, despite the masks they would wear.

"We will sneak out," Isabella continued. "The twins insisted they were needed."

"Absolutely not," Lady Wynwood said quickly. "Not when the plants are poisonous. Shall you need Mr. Havner?"

Thorne shook his head. "I rented space in mews nearby your home and stored there an old cart and horse that I brought from my country estate. We shall walk there and head out of the city."

"I beg you to remind Phoebe about the altered masks I gave to her today," was all Lady Wynwood said to them before turning back to the servants gathered around the table.

As Thorne and Isabella left the ruckus in the kitchen, he caught sight of the twins being plied with scones and cold meat pie and hot tea. They responded to the warmth of Lady Wynwood's household with wide smiles that made them look their ages, but there was a bleakness shadowed in their eyes that had not been there before today. Before they'd seen their mother.

Thorne wondered how long it would take for that bleakness to fade away again.

He guided the open carriage through the London streets, carefully weaving through late afternoon traffic before he was able to pick up the pace when they reached the countryside. The cart was not fast, since it was roughly made and had been used by his father's old groundsmaster, but it enabled himself and Isabella, looking for all the world like a nondescript working man and his son, to tool along without attracting notice.

The air had chilled quickly, but Isabella had unearthed a large man's coat that hung loosely over her shoulders, making her look even more like a child. She had remained silent while they had been surrounded by the noises of the town, but now she told him, "You cannot make this poor old horse go any faster by strangling those reins."

He looked down and realized his hands were clenched around the leather thongs. He relaxed them and felt warmth seep back into his hands under the leather gloves.

"Are you feeling any better?" she asked.

"I'm fine," he snapped.

She merely gave him a level look, and he grimaced.

"I'm sorry," he mumbled. "I still feel … agitated."

But rather than accepting his words, she studied his face. "No," she finally said, "I don't believe that is so."

He considered denying it, but this was Isabella, whom he had known since she was in pinafores. "You didn't see her, Bella."

"Sinah?"

"You didn't see how she treated her children."

"You have never been very comfortable around children." He could tell she was treading delicately over the subject.

"I never thought I'd known any mother worse than Drusilla, but I was wrong." He had spoken her name before realizing it.

"Sinah was completely cold and uncaring about them, as though they were strangers. No, as though they were her *enemies.*"

Isabella frowned as she considered his words. "What would make a mother behave thus toward her own children?"

"I don't—" He'd been about to say, *I don't know*, but then the guilt and hypocrisy of his words slammed into him as though he'd been crushed by a falling brick wall. What would make a parent behave thus toward their children? What would make a father treat his son the way Thorne had treated Timothy?

He had made all the excuses in his head—it was because of his father, because of Drusilla, because of his vengeful wrath directed at both of them, and Timothy had simply been caught up in the space between them.

But he had seen Sinah's freezing gaze directed at Calvin and Clara, and he knew he'd looked at his own son in the same way.

"I don't know why, but I feel … hostile toward her," he finally said. He didn't want to admit it. He had never been comfortable expressing emotions at all, and yet here he was feeling as though he'd uncovered an open wound.

"Thorne," Isabella said gently, "why would you be feeling anger toward Sinah?"

"I suppose I simply don't like how she treated her children."

"But why would you care how she treats them?"

"They're children." And yet Timothy was barely five years old. He shook his head, suddenly feeling like a great lion who had become confused and weak.

"Thorne," came the soft voice again, "are you truly angry at Sinah, or at yourself?"

He had no answer for her. He only knew that he was drowning in a turbulent sea of self-loathing, and he didn't know how to save himself.

Finally he said, "It doesn't matter which it is, because I can't control it, Bella."

He was helpless, which was not something he had felt often, even during the most harrowing missions in his years as an agent for the Crown.

There was suddenly a soft touch on his hand, and he looked down to see her small one resting on his fists, which were again clenched around the reins. She hadn't been wearing gloves, because of her disguise, but she had some ratty fingerless mittens, which were dark gray against the dirty paleness of her skin.

"I think it is helpful that you are being honest about it," she told him.

"It's easy to be honest with you," he said.

"It's why I trust you," was her simple answer.

They drove in silence a few minutes longer, then his reply came from his strangled throat, "You shouldn't. I don't feel like myself ... I don't know if I could stop ..."

"Thorne Rosmont, you have endured pain and abuse I will never know." Her voice was strong, as though she could bolster him up with her words alone.

Perhaps she could.

"This is different," he muttered.

"It is not," she said, "because you survived *him.*"

His breath caught.

"That is why I know you will survive this," she said. "You will not let me down. You will not let my brother down."

Her speaking it did not make it true, but her speaking it made him want to believe it was true.

"Would you ever abandon me?" she asked him.

"I've never abandoned—"

"Would you ever do it?"

"No, of course not."

"Then don't abandon me now." Her eyes were wide and dark. "Don't abandon Michael now. Don't give in and leave us alone, not when we need you."

When she phrased it that way, he realized he could never do that to her, to Michael. They had saved him as a child. He owed them and their family everything.

"I won't," he said.

But as they drove through the fading light of afternoon, the rage in his gut seethed and bubbled.

Chapter Sixteen

Michael couldn't seem to focus.

At first he tried to blame it on the carriage ride to the Long Glades, because he'd been pressed closely to Miss Sauber, who was once again dressed in boy's clothing. Even the fact that she walked and spoke like a boy couldn't erase her wildflower scent, which was noticeable when he was next to her.

The atmosphere in the unmarked carriage was tense, which also might be why he couldn't force himself to concentrate. While the twins had been left behind, Miss Sauber and Miss Gardinier had joined him, Thorne, and Isabella, as well as Mr. Drydale.

The coachman, Mr. Havner, was driving them to their destination, but he would not be remaining—Mr. Drydale had made that decision, because while the coachman was tough as nails, he was not a trained fighter, and the French spies were very skilled in hand-to-hand combat. But bringing Mr. Havner enabled them to take Lady Wynwood's carriage, and then the coachman would find a coaching inn to stable and guard the horses while waiting for them.

Michael was relieved, because it would be one less civilian for him to worry about.

But if he were completely honest with himself, he'd started feeling unnerved and distracted while he'd been hiding under the ruined church, waiting for Sinah Eades to return with the information she'd promised them. He shouldn't have been able to smell it, but he thought he caught a faint whiff of the Goldensuit from when Maner had been there, and that was enough to cause his heart to pound and his head to ache again.

It reminded him of Maner's greenhouse, of the smell of the plants. He wanted to smell it again. He didn't want to admit that he was looking forward to finding the French team's hideout because the plants would be there, and he would be near them again.

Even as he yearned for it, he was afraid. He feared the person he could become, growing dependent upon the plant, losing control of himself.

But he was also afraid of dying.

When he'd been forced to drink the Root, and he'd smelled it, and then tasted it, every part of him had been screaming in rejection of it. It was simply *unclean*. There had been something indescribably foul about it, something corrupted.

He remembered that sense of rottenness and it had been easy to insist he didn't want the Root, even to remain alive.

But after being in contact with the Goldensuit, the Root no longer seemed so terrible. Now, every piece of him wanted the Goldensuit as violently as he'd once shrank from it.

That strange desire fed his fear of death. It made for an odd mixture of emotions inside of him, unfamiliar and alien. He had faced death a handful of times on missions, and he had thought he'd been able to face it bravely, resolutely. It had not felt anything like this.

There was no one to whom he felt comfortable speaking about this. He glanced across the carriage at Isabella, also dressed as a boy. When she had heard that he might die without the Root, she had been distraught. She couldn't tell her mother, the one person she was closest to in the world, and Michael could tell that her anguish over him was eating away at her. It was in the look in her eyes as she caught his gaze and tried to smile reassuringly.

She always tried to reassure him, so that she wouldn't worry him. And now he was the one worrying her.

Mr. Drydale spoke softly in the darkness of the carriage. "We're almost there. Remember, our first task is to scout the buildings around the place to find a means to sneak inside and surprise them. We will have little chance of success if we simply rush inside, and I would prefer not to injure any other civilians there may be."

The carriage came to a halt, and Michael peered out at the darkness beyond. He exited the vehicle and the coachman leaned down to murmur to him, "I can't get closer or we'll attract too much attention."

Michael nodded, and glanced around. He saw the dark bulk of the orphanage that Sinah Eades had told them to look for. "I can find the building from here," he assured him.

Once everyone had exited the coach, with Miss Sauber slinging her cloth-wrapped bow over her back and Miss Gardinier carrying a large satchel, the coachman whipped up the horse and left them. Michael led them to the shadow of the orphanage, past its side entrance, and then into a narrow lane behind it. Turning right, they kept to the shadows as they crept past dilapidated buildings on either side.

This was a mean, squalid area, where few survived and those who did were cruel and feral. Finding a place to stay was equally difficult, but Sinah had said that the French group had arranged beforehand to stay with a pimp and his girls in an old glass factory. Ferbin ruled his women with a heavy hand, and few dared to cross him, much less invade his chosen building of refuge. It was the perfect place for foreigners to hide.

Sinah had also said that there were four them, not three. They'd managed to threaten a smuggler to take them across the Channel tomorrow night, so Mr. Drydale's team had to capture them tonight.

There were no taverns or eateries or brothels along this road, and it seemed abnormally quiet compared to other brighter, louder streets only a stone's throw away. But the buildings weren't empty—darkness was a heavy cloak over the windows and doorways, but Michael sometimes caught the faint gleam of watchful, wary eyes. However, there were no pedestrians, and no one loitering outside. The people here reminded him of cockroaches, all taking refuge in deep shadows rather than exposing themselves.

He counted doorways as they crept along, but they found the factory easily. It was the only building on the street that had glass windows on the ground floor. Brigitte had probably deliberately found a place that had sunlight for the plants they'd steal.

However, there were no places for her to leave an outside guard, which would have been too noticeable on the quiet, deserted street. Even the buildings across the way had shuttered windows, so Michael suspected there were no eyes to witness them sneaking around.

There were also no alleyways alongside these buildings, which were built directly next to each other. He looked back to Mr. Drydale, who frowned as he studied the area. In a low voice, he ordered Michael, Isabella and Thorne to check the house on one side of the building, while the rest would investigate the house on the other side.

Michael followed Thorne and Isabella into the neighboring building. It was empty, but then Thorne's footstep caused a floorboard to creak.

The three of them froze. The creak wasn't very loud, especially considering the heavy silence of the neighborhood, but to Michael it sounded deafening. He strained his heightened hearing for any shouts of alarm, but there was nothing. He and Thorne finally both let out a breath and continued further into the building, all three of them moving slower and more carefully.

It had once been a workshop, perhaps, but a huge hole gaped through both the upper floor and the roof beyond, although the cloudy sky was simply a patch of black. Michael looked for a staircase, thinking they might be able to climb onto the roof, but Thorne instead headed deeper into the back. Michael didn't know what his friend was searching for as he led the way.

They traversed narrow, dark passages until they came to a long room empty of any furniture. In the far corner Thorne found a hole in the floor leading to the basement, and cautiously lowered himself down. Michael motioned for Isabella to stay, and then he followed.

The basement smelled hideously of mold and rotting things, and a thin layer of slimy water covered the floor. After Michael dropped down, Isabella passed him a small shielded lantern that she'd brought and lit for him.

Thorne had already made his way to the wall that was shared by the basement of the glass factory, and he laid his hand against it. Michael came up behind him.

"What are you doing?" he whispered.

"I had an idea," Thorne whispered back. "When I was running from Jack's men, I escaped by going through the wall of one building into the next because the wood had been damaged."

Michael now understood what he was hoping to find. He joined him in feeling the walls of the basement.

While the lower half of the wall was stone, the upper part was merely wood, and they found a section where the boards had rotted away, leaving a narrow opening. They carefully tugged at the remaining boards, which crumbled away under only a light pressure, leaving an opening large enough for a man to climb through into the next building.

Michael held up the lantern to reveal a similar basement, but while their current basement was empty, the other was crammed with deteriorating furniture. The sound of scuttling rats seemed to thunder as the rodents scrambled along the top surfaces of the furniture.

Michael returned to the basement opening and called up through it to Isabella. "Get the others. We found a way through."

He brought the lantern back to Thorne and was dismayed to find that he'd already squeezed through the opening into the next building. He couldn't very well chew out his friend for his recklessness, and in the faint light from the lantern, Thorne wouldn't see an admonishing glare. He'd probably planned it that way on purpose.

Thorne took the lantern and searched around the cluttered space, but he soon returned. "No one is here."

"I hear something," Michael whispered.

Thorne paused, head cocked. "Yes. Raised voices." He pointed above his head.

"They're arguing."

Movement sounded behind him. He took the lantern back from Thorne so he could meet the others at the basement opening. He set down the lantern and motioned for Mr. Drydale, but it was Miss Sauber who dropped down first. As he caught her, his body tightened, and her arms around his shoulders felt almost like an embrace.

Then she stepped away, and Miss Gardinier dropped down next.

After everyone had entered the basement, Michael and Thorne climbed through to the basement of the glass factory, then began helping everyone through the small opening. Mr. Drydale climbed awkwardly through the waist-high hole, but Thorne simply reached out and grasped Isabella by the waist, hauling her through.

Miss Sauber was up next. Michael hesitated, and they looked

at each other in the darkness. Then she reached out her arms toward him.

Her waist was soft through the thin fabric of her shirt and coat, and when he pulled, she hopped up a little so he could pull her through the hole.

It was at that moment that they heard voices.

Like the other basement, this had only a hole leading up to the building above. Through that hole came a woman's voice, "What was that?"

Another woman answered her, a lower and more gravely sound. "What was what?"

"I heard a sound."

They had all frozen in place. Michael still held Miss Sauber halfway through the hole in the wall, her legs dangling in midair, her arms around his shoulders. Her breath sounded close to his ear, fast and soft.

Then her bow, wound with cloth and slung diagonally across her back, began to slide.

He caught it with one hand, stopping it before it could knock against the wood boards surrounding the hole, while spreading his palm and grabbing her more tightly around the waist with the other. He could feel her stomach muscles tighten.

"Probably a rat—"

"I hear them all the time. This was different."

Michael sensed rather than saw or heard Thorne shift in the darkness. The women were probably some of Ferbin's prostitutes. They didn't want to harm innocent civilians, but they would have to make sure the women didn't alert the French group sharing their living spaces.

"What are you going to do?" the other woman scoffed. "Want to go down there yourself?"

The first woman gave a sound of revulsion. "I guess not."

"Come, let's see if we can sneak in without Ferbin noticing."

"I hear Ferbin arguing with that French lady again ..."

Footsteps drew closer for a moment, then faded away.

He and Miss Sauber exhaled at the same time. They also turned to look at each other, and her eyes were uncomfortably close to his. He hurriedly turned away and continued carrying her through the hole into the basement.

Thankfully, pulling Miss Gardinier through the hole didn't ramp up his heartbeat in the slightest.

They gathered around the hole to the room above and Michael was about to help Thorne through the hole when he felt a firm hand on his arm.

"Throw me up," Isabella whispered. "And wait here. I'll scout ahead."

He knelt so she could place her foot in his cupped hands. He lifted her slowly out of the hole so she could gingerly peek her head out. She nodded to signal the room above them was empty, and Michael hefted her the rest of the way up. She disappeared from sight, moving so silently that Michael couldn't even hear her steps with his enhanced senses.

They waited in the darkness for what seemed like hours. It wasn't as pitch black here under the hole since faint light came from the hallway leading to the front of the house, likely from the rooms Ferbin and his girls were using.

Isabella's face appeared above them so swiftly and silently that it was as if she had suddenly manifested like a ghost. She sat on the edge, then Michael caught her as she dropped back down into the basement.

They huddled close around her as she whispered, "There's a storeroom above. Go left, and a hallway leads to one very large room in the front of the building. The room has only one doorway near the back and a door to the street near the front windows. Ferbin's girls are huddled in the back of the room. No fire in the grate and the only light is a lantern near the women. The plants are in the front on tables near the windows. Brigitte is arguing with Ferbin near the middle of the room. Three

Frenchmen near the plants, two pacing and one sitting on the floor against the wall."

Miss Sauber had unwrapped her bow and quiver, but at Mr. Drydale's questioning glance, she shook her head. "My aim won't be accurate with that little light, but I can try. I'll need to get closer, or else I'll waste the sedative arrowheads."

"We'll rush them from both front and back," Mr. Drydale said. "Peter and Paul from the front, Archer and I from the back." Thorne and Michael's code names were the apostles, while Miss Sauber's was more obvious. "From what you said about meeting them the other day, Brigitte isn't as affected by the pollen, so Archer, prioritize the men near the plants first."

"There's another way out of the building," Isabella said to Michael. "If you go right instead of left when you leave the storeroom above, there's a room with fire damage. Go to the wall at the back of the building, and there's a hole into the building behind us, but there are people inside who will see you as you exit. You will likely need to swing around the streets to the front again."

Thorne shook his head. "We'll go back through the neighboring building."

"Prince and Doctor, use that back exit to get the women out quickly once the fighting starts," Mr. Drydale said.

"Masks," Miss Sauber said.

But Isabella put hands on Michael and Thorne to stop them. "Put them on before you enter the house from the front door. If you walk out onto the street wearing them, you'll attract too much unwanted attention."

The rest attached the masks Lady Wynwood had given to them.

But after helping four of them up through the hole in the basement, the arguing voices suddenly grew louder and Michael could clearly hear the words.

"I don't want excuses," shouted a hoarse male voice. "I want to know when you're going to leave my house. You said it would only be for two days and it's been four."

"Soon, I told you," Brigitte said tightly. Michael suspected she didn't want to tell Ferbin their plans to leave tomorrow. "Why should it matter to you if we are paying you?"

"I agreed not to send my girls out while you were here. I can't keep them inside for longer. They'll start losing their regulars, and then I'll lose more money than you're paying me."

A man's voice with a thick French accent said belligerently, "We wouldn't have stayed in your miserable 'house' if we could have left sooner."

"Oy! You—" Ferbin growled.

A soft woman's voice pleaded with him, "Ferbin ..."

"Shut up!" The sound of a slap and a woman's cry.

"Jack must have killed the smugglers," said a different Frenchman, as though he'd made this argument several times already.

"Don't say his name!" Ferbin said.

"You English are all cowards," the Frenchman replied.

"How could Jack have killed them?" the first Frenchman retorted, with impatience barely suppressed in his voice. "If he had, he would be here demanding his plants back."

"Yes," a third Frenchman taunted. "Don't be stupid. Smugglers have other enemies."

The second Frenchman swore at him in French, and then came the crash of breaking wood. A moment later, Michael smelled the green, floral scent of Goldensuit.

His body responded instantly, drawing in deep breaths, his heart racing.

Thorne responded, also, beginning to pant even as his face began to contort with strong emotion. Then before Michael could stop him, he'd leaped up and through the hole in the basement ceiling.

Michael followed as quickly as he could, meeting the shocked eyes of Miss Sauber and the rest. They were in the remains of an old storeroom, its door long since broken or rotted away.

Thorne was gone.

"The fool!" Michael hissed, fumbling with his mask.

"Go after him," Mr. Drydale ordered. "We'll follow behind you."

He slipped out of the storeroom and headed toward the front room that Isabella had told them about. Faint light filtered from the narrow hallway, and the air seemed to have a yellow glow. It took him a moment to realize it was the Goldensuit pollen forming a fine mist all around him. He recalled the crashing sound—likely the table of plants being knocked down, spraying the pollen into the air.

Women's screams came from the front room. Thorne had started attacking the French group.

Prostitutes, most dressed in rags and painfully thin, came streaming out from the front room. Some of them didn't even notice him as they ran from the sounds of fighting, but one or two shrieked at the sight of him.

"Go!" he ordered them.

At the same time, he heard Isabella behind him, calling, "This way! Hurry!"

He reached the door to the front room and thought the last woman had run past him, but he immediately saw a group of them huddling against the far wall of the room, with Ferbin crammed fearfully behind the wall of bodies. Between them and the door was Thorne, fighting three of the Frenchmen.

All four men were unmasked, and all four had wild eyes that gleamed in the faint light from a lantern near the girls. Thorne's training was nowhere to be seen as he swung ferocious blows like a madman at his three opponents, but they landed more punches than he did.

He got in a lucky slug against a slender Frenchman with a scar across his forehead, who twisted and staggered toward the group of women. Their frightened cries rang out.

The largest Frenchman suddenly lowered his head and barreled toward Thorne, grabbing him by the torso and flinging them both down to the floor with a loud thud.

One of the women, nearly hysterical with fright, suddenly bolted toward the door where Michael stood.

The movement attracted the notice of the slender Frenchman, who was in the process of pushing himself to his feet. Michael saw his expression and started in surprise.

His face was a mask of rage, lips pulled back and teeth bared. His eyes were crazed and feral, and they latched onto the running prostitute like a rabid dog.

He launched himself at her, knocking her to the floor. Michael darted toward him, but he'd already smashed his fist into the woman's temple.

The other women screamed, punctuated by Ferbin's yells.

Michael pulled the scarred Frenchman from the woman, who lay completely still with blood smeared across her head, but then he saw a blur.

The third Frenchman had abandoned the fight with Thorne and dove toward the group of women. Rather than fists flying, he grabbed one woman's head and twisted, and she jerked and slid to the floor, limp.

More screams. The women tried to scramble away, but the fighting blocked their closest escape route, the back door.

The scarred Frenchman in Michael's grip slammed back at him with an elbow, and he fell to the floor. Then the man joined the other in attacking the women.

The two men were on a rampage, grabbing bodies, punching, twisting, kicking. Bones snapped. Blood sprayed.

Thorne was still grappling with the large Frenchman on the floor, both of them oblivious to the frenzied killing.

Michael launched himself at the two men, even as he wondered if he could stop them.

But if he didn't do something, they'd kill them all.

Chapter Seventeen

Phoebe tried to tell her body to move, but she stood frozen with shock in the doorway to the room as the two men continued killing the prostitutes. Ferbin was grabbing women and throwing them behind him as he tried to scramble away along the wall toward the front door.

Keriah didn't hesitate. She slipped past Phoebe and knelt in front of the woman on the floor, which the scarred Frenchman had first attacked.

The sight of her friend, unflappable in the midst of the chaos, jolted her out of her horror. She grabbed Uncle Sol, who was also entering the room. "Get to the front door and open it." Hopefully it would air the pollen out of the room so that they wouldn't be so affected by it.

The pollen was already influencing some of the women. Several fought back against the two Frenchmen with bestial expressions, biting and clawing.

Mr. Coulton-Jones tried to pull one of them off a woman he was beating, but the man's attention wouldn't be torn from the screaming prey in front of him.

Phoebe notched an arrow, but hesitated. There simply wasn't enough light to see, and Keriah had warned her that a shot of these sedative arrows at one of the prostitutes might kill them, because they were much smaller and lighter than the men. But she couldn't let the Frenchmen kill them.

She switched for an arrow without sedative, and fired.

It hit one Frenchman on the very edge of his shoulder, and he screamed.

Mr. Coulton-Jones quickly yanked at the shaft of the arrow, pulling sideways to drag the man off of the woman he'd grabbed by the arm. With a high-pitched cry of pain, the Frenchman moved away from his victim, but the shaft broke in Mr. Coulton-Jones's hand.

Phoebe saw Isabella had already slipped into the room, and she was helping some of the injured women to their feet and toward the door.

The Frenchman she'd shot had finally diverted his attention from the women and now attacked Mr. Coulton-Jones, but the last Frenchman was still grabbing at bodies, some alive and some already limp and heavy.

Phoebe dropped her bow and quiver, pulled a sedative knife from the leather sheath at the small of her back and ran forward.

The man's back was toward her, but he must have sensed she was attacking, because he turned and spotted her mere feet before she reached him. Instead of plunging the knife into his back, it bit deep into his arm and then ripped away.

He screamed and swung a backhanded fist at her, but she managed to bend away from him. She felt the air of the blow barely an inch in front of her nose. He'd had blood on his hands and warm drops were flung onto her cheeks, dotting her lips.

He was as mindless as a Berserker, but he was not as strong and fast as one. If he were, Phoebe would not have had a chance.

She ducked as he followed up with another swing from his other fist, flinging her knife blade up to slice his forearm. He jabbed at her and she dodged, but not enough—his fist hit her hard in the left shoulder. She felt a painful pop.

Stupid! She couldn't fire her bow now. But considering the lighting conditions, perhaps it was just as well.

His movements were already slowing because of the sedative, but he was still able to fight her. He aimed another punch and she brought her knife up. It solidly connected his other forearm, slicing into his muscle, but the power of the blow knocked the blade from her hand.

Then suddenly there was a shadow beside them. Keriah had darted in and stabbed a knife into his thigh up to the hilt.

He screamed again, this time dropping to one knee and grabbing at the knife hilt, but he was already swaying. After another few seconds, he dropped face-first into the floor.

Now that he was down, some of the women were able to stagger toward the door and safety. Isabella was helping them, when she suddenly stopped and stared, her mouth pulled into a sneer.

One prostitute was not dressed as poorly as the others, nor was she as thin. Isabella grabbed at her hair as she tried to scramble past.

The wig ripped from the head of the woman. Even in the faint light, her white-blonde hair seemed to shine like moonlight.

Brigitte.

Michael could tell that Thorne was becoming worse.

Michael's attention was captured by the Frenchman he was fighting, but he could hear animalistic snarling and shrieking from behind him. At first he had hoped it was the large Frenchman Thorne was fighting, but then it became obvious that there were two voices, both of them from minds that had degenerated into rage-fueled beasts.

Michael's opponent was still savage, as he had been when he'd fallen upon the helpless women and started ripping them apart. But rather than fighting in mindless frenzy, he utilized his fighting skill to block and dodge Michael's blows, making him more dangerous than if he'd simply been fighting in heedless anger.

Just when he was thanking God that the man hadn't thought to produce a knife, a blade skittered into view. He glanced over and saw that it must have come from the fight between Miss Sauber and the third Frenchman. Alarm shot through him until he saw Miss Gardinier stealthily sneaking up behind the Frenchman from the side, another knife in her hand.

But his inattention cost him. He didn't even see the blow that connected with his cheek, and his vision filled with black and white stars. He felt the ground hit his back, dimly registered the thud at the back of his head, but couldn't force his body to move.

He expected another blow, but none came. When he could finally see, he was staring at the Frenchman's snarling face as he crouched above him, but he was being held back by Mr. Drydale, who had curled both arms around the man's shoulders.

"Hurry!" Mr. Drydale shouted.

There was suddenly another crashing sound, and the boards under Michael's back jumped. Only a flying shadow warned him before Thorne appeared, crashing into Mr. Drydale, throwing all three men onto the ground.

Dazed, he tried to rise to his feet. He looked up and saw the large Frenchman amidst the wreck of the table that had stood before the window. It had already been broken previously by the Frenchmen's initial argument, but now the large man was covered with broken pots and Goldensuit plants. Thorne must have thrown him, although he couldn't imagine the strength it must have taken to toss such a huge man.

"Peter!" Isabella shouted. "You have to help him!"

He realized Thorne was on top of Mr. Drydale, choking him. The other Frenchman was sprawled on the ground next to him, still confused at being knocked down, but in a moment he'd return to attacking Michael. Or Thorne.

Michael staggered to his feet and kicked at the Frenchman's head. It wasn't enough to knock him out, but it stunned him enough that he could try to save Mr. Drydale from Thorne.

He grabbed at Thorne's shoulders, but his friend's arms were outstretched in front of him with his hands around Mr. Drydale's throat, shaking him so that his head knocked against the floor. He couldn't break Thorne's hold. He considered bodily knocking him aside, but worried that with his hands so firmly around the older man's neck, it might cause Thorne to simply twist it and kill him.

He tried curling his arms under Thorne's shoulders to break his hold. "Listen to me! I know you can hear me!"

Thorne didn't respond to his voice, simply growling and knocking Mr. Drydale against the floor another time. The man's face was dark red.

He didn't want to speak his name for the others in the room to hear, but he had to get through to him. He climbed onto Thorne's back, trying to pull his arms away, his mouth near his friend's ear. "Thorne," he panted. "Thorne, it's Michael."

He felt rather than saw Thorne's muscles slacken slightly.

"I know you're not too far gone," Michael said. "Come back to us. Don't leave us."

Thorne shook his head, like a confused animal, but then his hands loosened from around Mr. Drydale. The older man twisted away, coughing.

"Focus on my voice. Look at me." Michael turned his friend's body toward him.

Thorne's face slowly relaxed, the barbarous mask melting away. His eyes grew more aware and looked *at* Michael rather than into some distant threat.

But he was not calm. Michael felt the trembling of Thorne's muscles, tightly clenched and hard as rocks. His eyes still burned with fire and hatred. He was no longer mindless, but he was not in control.

Roaring sounded from two different directions. The two Frenchmen, who had been knocked down but not knocked out.

The slender one came lunging at them, and Michael jerked away before the man's fist could connect with his eye socket. Barely a half second later, the large Frenchman had stomped up to Thorne and fell upon him, pinning him to the ground.

Michael had been distracted by his worry over Thorne before, but not anymore. Michael bent backwards, out of the way of a roundhouse, but then immediately closed in, trapping the man's arm across his chest. He pulled his head back, then slammed his forehead hard into the man's nose.

The Frenchman jerked, stunned, and Michael followed with a sharp, accurate punch to the jaw that rendered him unconscious.

He turned back to Thorne to see him roll, flipping the huge man around so that he was now with his back to the ground. Both men were huffing from the exertion of grappling with each other, but Thorne was faster. He pounded the Frenchman in the face once, twice, three times. The large man finally grew limp, his head lolling to the side.

Thorne heaved, his breath coming hard and labored, and then his eyes rolled back in his head and he collapsed.

Michael wanted to check him, but he instead turned toward the sounds of knife blades ringing.

Miss Sauber and Miss Gardinier were fighting Brigitte. They moved with a coordination he had never seen before between two fighters, with Miss Sauber's height, strength, and speed engaging Brigitte the most while Miss Gardinier darted in to try to land a strike.

But while they were more skilled with knife-fighting than any proper young ladies had a right to be, they were badly outclassed.

Brigitte's fighting style was smooth and swift, and faster than either of the two young women. She twisted and spun, her dagger stabbing here and arcing there, as fast and unpredictable as rapids in a swollen river. She advanced on them, driving Miss Sauber back step by step.

But she was also focused only upon them, and not upon Michael.

He moved silently behind Brigitte, moving slowly. He watched her movements from the back, but he also watched Miss Sauber's and Miss Gardinier's eyes. If they flickered toward him, they might give him away to Brigitte, in which case he had to attack fast.

Miss Sauber's gaze didn't waver toward him in the slightest, but he noticed a slight shift in her fighting style, since she was engaging with Brigitte the most. She started attacking in faster flurries, even though she knew she had no hope of landing a hit, in order to keep Brigitte occupied in parrying her stabs and slashes.

It seemed to work, for Brigitte countered Miss Sauber's knife almost effortlessly. She did not notice when Miss Gardinier's eyes flickered toward Michael, then quickly away.

He had been moving toward the knife that had fallen earlier and distracted him in his fight with the Frenchman. It lay nearly hidden in the shadows, and he leaned down to pick it up.

He had to time it correctly, or he would waste the element of surprise that he had. But he also had to act quickly, before Brigitte realized her other two men were no longer fighting Michael and Thorne.

He waited until Brigitte's hand had cut across her body to block Miss Sauber's jabbing attack, then he darted forward and brought the hilt of the knife hard on the base of Brigitte's skull.

He landed a solid hit, and both Miss Sauber and Miss Gardinier jumped away from her at the same time. Brigitte stiffened for a second, wavering on her feet, then she slumped to the ground.

He stared for a moment, panting, the blood still coursing through his veins, waiting for another enemy to appear. Then he realized there were no more enemies standing.

They had won.

But his gaze was caught by the still forms of several prostitutes on the floor where the Frenchmen had attacked them. A few feet away lay Ferbin, his glassy eyes staring up at the ceiling, his throat ripped out.

Yes, they had won. But at what cost?

Chapter Eighteen

Maner woke slowly, and in great discomfort.

In fact, he could probably say he'd never felt worse in his life. His stomach twisted with nausea, his brain was pounding as if it was trying to knock its way out of his skull, and his mouth tasted like he'd eaten a rotting rat carcass.

And ... he was swaying.

He didn't particularly want to move, but a sudden wave of nausea made his stomach heave. His eyes flew open and he turned to the side so he wouldn't throw up in his mouth.

He upended the contents of his stomach in a bucket that had been strangely placed right next to his bed. Convenient, that.

He heard cloth flapping, and metal links clinking. Wordless calls from men somewhere above him.

He was in a bunk that had been nailed to a wooden wall. And then he realized the entire room was swaying.

Not swaying—*rocking*. He was in a boat.

The room was tinier than his closet, with just enough room for his bunk, another bunk above him, and a chair in the corner. There was a portmanteau on the chair.

He rolled himself out of the bunk and barely kept himself from planting his face on the floor. Just knowing where he was didn't make the nausea or the headache go away, but he appeared to be alone in this room.

He crawled to the chair and pulled the bag from it onto the floor, then sat and opened it.

Clothing. Plain but decent quality. At the bottom, a small leather sack of coins. And under the coins, a folded piece of paper.

Dear Mr. Hansen,

I beg you to forgive this method of ensuring your safety, but I assure you that it was all for the preservation of your life. While Brigitte and her crew were captured, we discovered a note in one man's pockets that gave the name of a shipping office which Sinah Eades informed us is one of the places you use to meet with clients. She did not recognize the handwriting and it was not that of Sonny, the cook whom we had originally thought had betrayed you to the French. With this new potential source of betrayal, we deemed it best to book you passage to the Colonies posthaste. If any of your men had been inclined to give away your places of business to the French, they would certainly have betrayed you to Jack, and he would have eventually discovered that you were to blame for the theft of his plants. We wish you only the best in your new life.

The note was unsigned.

He should probably be upset, but right now, it was his stomach that was too upset for him to feel much of anything except a desire to die.

He put the note back in the bag, and only then noticed a small parcel wrapped in brown paper and tied with twine. He opened it to reveal a small round lemon cake and three round treacle buns, still sticky with a sugar glaze.

The sight of them made some of the tension in his gut ease. And here he'd thought he was entirely selfish! He must not be so very evil if he had been worried about not only his own fate, but those whom he was leaving behind.

He looked down at the lemon cake and treacle buns.

And he smiled.

"You'll be all right," he told the pastries. "Yes, I think you'll be fine."

Michael's friend was suffering.

Even in sleep, Thorne's face twisted in pain. He shook and jerked, and at times it seemed he was trying to scream. His eyes moved rapidly under the closed lids, and his breath came in panicked gasps.

And all Michael could do was sit and watch.

One of Lady Wynwood's servants had brought him tea, but it had grown cold on the tray as he sat in a chair near Thorne's restless form. At some point he'd tugged off his boots and propped his feet up on the edge of the bed, uncaring about if anyone came into the guest bedroom and saw him being so uncouth.

He hadn't slept for much of the night, even though Lady Wynwood had urged him to take a few hours to rest in a nearby bedroom. So it didn't surprise him that he awoke from a doze to find light streaming through the cracks in the drapes over the windows. He blinked and stretched, and his internal clock guessed it was not early morning, but later. Perhaps even early afternoon.

He didn't know if it was his movement that did it, but Thorne suddenly snorted and his entire torso shot off the bed. He sat up, eyes wild and staring around at the room until he spied Michael.

He placed a firm hand on Thorne's shoulder and pushed him back down. "Be at ease. You're safe."

His skin was clammy, and throughout the night, Michael had used a cloth in a basin of water near the bed to wipe his brow, which would dot with sweat. But it wasn't the sweat of exertion

—there was a bitter scent to it that Michael knew he had never smelled before, and yet it was familiar to him. Familiar in the same way that the Goldensuit pollen had struck him the first time he smelled it.

Only he could smell it—Miss Gardinier had professed not to smell anything except the typical scents of an ill man in a sickroom.

Thorne lay there, his breath still coming a little too fast, his eyes darting across the ceiling above the bed as if examining something there that Michael couldn't see. He was surprised at the fear and horror in his friend's expression.

Gradually Thorne's breathing slowed, and he closed his eyes and swallowed. When he opened them again, the fright had receded and he was beginning to calm. But there was still anxiety in the way his hands plucked at the bedclothes, the way his muscles randomly twitched all over his shoulder, neck, and face.

"Where am I?" His voice was deep and hoarse.

"Lady Wynwood's townhouse. Are you thirsty?" Miss Gardinier had mentioned that he might wake suffering from thirst, due to the amount of sweating.

Thorne nodded. Michael helped him angle upward slightly so that he could sip from a glass of tepid water that Miss Gardinier had left for him. The movement seemed to exhaust him, and he collapsed back onto the bed with a groan, his breathing heavy again.

"How do you feel?" Michael wondered if his question was inane considering how weak Thorne appeared to be, but he asked anyway because Miss Gardinier would have wanted him to do so.

"Terrible," he croaked. But then his face seemed confused, as though he were searching for something. "But I no longer feel the rage." There was a hollowness in his eyes as he struggled to recall what had happened.

"What do you remember?"

He shook his head. "I can't remember what was real and what was the nightmares." He drew in a shaky breath. "I don't feel anger, but ... the dark thoughts linger in the back of my mind. I don't feel ... *safe*."

"You're fine," Michael insisted, his voice sounding feeble to his own ears.

But Thorne was shaking his head again. "I can't stay here ..." he muttered.

"No one knows you're here," Michael assured him. "We snuck you in through the servants' entrance in the back. Isabella told your servants that in a moment of drunken inspiration, you and I decided to travel north on a hunting trip." When they were younger, the two of them had done a few irrational and foolish things in moments of drunken inspiration, so his servants would only be mildly surprised by the news.

"You should have left me at Stapytton House," Thorne said stubbornly.

He was right, for the most part. His recovery should have been somewhere away from Lady Wynwood's servants. It was one of the reasons Mr. Drydale had leased the remote manor house—so that they would have a place of safety where they would not need to worry about their actions—or in his case, his condition—being observed.

But one of the primary reasons they had brought Thorne here had been because of Michael. They'd captured the Goldensuit plants from Ferbin's building and Miss Sauber now tended to them in the conservatory at Stapytton House.

Except that Michael could smell them. Everywhere he went inside the house, he could smell the sharp, herbal scent with the softer flowery edge.

He'd told Miss Gardinier, who had immediately requested they move Thorne somewhere else. But he couldn't tell his friend all that.

"Miss Gardinier wanted to keep an eye on you," Michael said. "She didn't know how long it would take before you felt better, and so she requested you be moved here. Which was just as well, since Dr. Shokes finally contacted her and she asked him to come see you."

"What did he say?" Thorne's eyes had closed and he sounded exhausted.

"You seem to be doing well."

Thorne turned his head to glare at Michael. "Are you bamming me?"

"Not at all."

"I feel as though I were regurgitated by a whale." Thorne sighed heavily.

"Dr. Shokes said the discomfort was normal."

"'Discomfort'?" Thorne gave a sharp, humorless bark of laughter. "I feel as though my body is trying to crawl its way out of my skin." He idly scratched at his arm.

"You awoke a few times," Michael said.

"I don't remember that."

"You were shouting and not lucid. Dr. Shokes believes your body is weaning itself from the Goldensuit pollen, but it seems to be causing you agitation."

Thorne frowned. "I'm not ..." Then he seemed to realize he was still scratching at his arm, and stopped.

"Dr. Shokes said it is not unheard of with men being weaned from laudanum. He and Miss Gardinier are concocting something to help ease your symptoms, which will probably taste disgusting," Michael said cheerfully.

Thorne shot him a sour look. "The French group?"

"Mr. Drydale took them to the Ramparts for questioning."

"They were all ..."

"Knocked around a little, but nothing a bandage couldn't heal," he assured his friend, forcing joviality into his voice but knowing it wouldn't make him feel any less guilty about his loss of control. "Maybe Miss Gardinier will also give them a nasty tasting tonic."

"One can only hope. And don your boots again. Your feet smell." Thorne's eyes closed and his voice slurred, but Michael wasn't entirely certain if he were truly that weary or if he simply wanted Michael to leave him alone.

He didn't like how helpless he felt, that he could only sit like a wart on a horse's rump while Thorne wrestled with demons he couldn't possibly understand.

After long minutes of silence, Thorne's breathing had slowed and grown deeper, and his face had relaxed.

Michael tugged his boots back on, then rose quietly to leave the room, but just before his hand touched the doorknob, a soft voice came from the bed.

"How did you know I wouldn't kill you?"

Michael hesitated.

Thorne continued, "You took a dangerous risk, Michael. How did you know your voice would reach me?"

He stared at the blank door for several long moments before confessing, "I knew because ... it's what happened to me."

For the past week, whenever he tried to sleep, he had horrible dreams about wandering around in the darkness and mist, plagued by madness as if it were a cloud of gnats biting at his head.

But just before waking, he remembered one other thing from that night under the influence of the Root. A face that glowed with lamplight. Her voice saying his name, although he didn't know if that were real or not.

"Michael."

He had been lost in swirling black clouds, blind and filled with rage. But Miss Sauber had brought him back to the dark London streets, if only for a moment, if only in that small space around where she stood. He had followed her, because a nameless understanding in his gut knew she was his salvation.

Thorne hadn't responded. When Michael turned toward the bed, his friend had fallen asleep, his mouth hanging open and the air whistling softly through his nose.

He let himself out of the room softly, then hesitated in the empty hallway.

He blinked and the next thing he knew, his steps had taken him to the ground floor of the townhouse, to a door near the back. He hadn't even realized he had been moving, but he somehow wasn't surprised that he'd come here, to this room he'd only seen once, a week ago.

When he'd awoken, Lady Wynwood had taken a few minutes and made sure she brought him outside this door, so he would know it was there. She had not made him go inside, although she seemed to be hopeful he would, of his own volition.

He did so now.

The chapel was tiny and plain. Two benches filled most of the space, and there was a small, simple wooden table near the front covered by a knitted lace altar cloth, a candle in a silver candlestick, and matches.

He waffled over whether he should light the candle. Then he realized he was acting as though he were afraid that the smoke smell would let someone know he had been here, and so he defiantly lit the taper. He would not be afraid of trivial things. Not now. What was the point?

He sat on the bench and stared at the candle, at first unsure what to do. The ponderous prayers of the local vicar near his country home somehow seemed out of place here, and in his situation.

The room was not completely silent. He could hear noises from below the floor, the banging of pots and muted voices. He was above the kitchens at the back of the house.

But rather than distracting him, the noises made him feel not so alone.

Or perhaps he wasn't alone because he was in a chapel. If

God intended to meet a man somewhere, it would be in a chapel, surely?

He turned his attention from the candle to the small window set high against one wall, and ran his hand against the smooth wood of the bench where he sat.

Despite the fight with the Frenchmen, his knuckles were unbruised. They weren't even swollen.

Overall, he was feeling quite well. In fact, if Miss Gardinier hadn't nagged him with probing, detailed questions about his health, he might not have noticed that he was feeling so strong and fit.

After Brigitte had fallen to the floor, he'd stood there looking around. He felt the strongest desire to rip his mask from his face, breathe deeply of the pollen still drifting in the air, although it was harder to see because the front door had been opened, airing out the room. His fingers twitched with the urge, and he had to clench his hands into fists.

He had the strangest sensation that the pollen would make him stronger, would make him powerful. And he felt a foreign desire threading up from his stomach, something he'd never wanted for himself before—a need to be the most powerful, to be dominant over all men.

Had Thorne felt that urge, too? Michael still didn't know why his friend had been overcome by his aggression while he had only grown more clear-headed, his blows becoming more precise as he fought. He supposed that they had both desired to defeat their foes, although in different ways.

He had not told Miss Gardinier about the strange feelings he'd experienced in those moments after the fight had ended. She would likely suspect he'd been kicked in the head or some such. After all, it was ridiculous that a plant would have the power to suggest thoughts that were not his own.

All he knew was that he'd smelled the Goldensuit pollen and felt a strange yearning for it. And with that plant, he'd also been given a second door—or maybe a partially opened window—where before he'd only had a single door, a single option, a single fate.

Miss Gardinier had admitted that it was possible the Goldensuit pollen could help him stave off the certain death he was facing without the Root. Now that Miss Sauber was growing the plants, she could experiment.

She had also asked him, in a quiet voice, "Would you like me to try to recreate the Root potion?"

He was ashamed that he had not been able to answer her immediately. But eventually he had shook his head and told her firmly, "No."

He still was of sound enough mind to know that he did not want to become a monster again.

And yet he was still in the same place, facing that death's door.

What had Lady Wynwood told him?

"I believe God will save you. However, I also hope you will settle in yourself how you feel about God and what you believe about death."

He had not answered her when she said that to him.

He had faced death before, on missions, but he had never actually thought about what he believed. His local vicar had told him what the church said about death, and so he supposed he believed that.

But the way Lady Wynwood had phrased that made him think that was not what she was referring to.

He did not feel particularly close to the Almighty. Even that name implied distance as well as respect.

And yet he remembered the stories of Jesus from his childhood. How had Christ felt when he was stumbling toward the cross? When He was staring certain death in the eye? Michael wondered if He felt as he did now. What had He thought of when deciding to die?

The Son of God, who loved me, and gave Himself for me.

He didn't know why he suddenly remembered that snippet of a verse. He hadn't read a Bible in a long time.

But it reminded him that Christ had gone willingly to the cross in order to die for the sins of everyone.

Even Michael.

He didn't feel like he deserved to be saved. But then he thought of the people in his life whom he did not want to leave —his mother, his sister ...

And a beautiful oval face with sea-foam green eyes.

He had not prayed in a long time. He felt rusty, and uncertain, but he bowed his head—and, perhaps more importantly, he felt as though he were bowing in his heart, also.

"I don't want to die," he whispered.

The empty chapel gave him no audible answer.

Chapter Nineteen

Thorne was surprised he was able to sleep, but he found himself slowly coming awake at the sound of a gentle knock at the door.

He somehow knew that knock. "Come," he said in a dry, raspy voice.

Isabella entered. She was dressed in a rich plum walking dress that somehow did not clash with her reddish-brown hair, and which made her eyes seem brighter and more clear green.

"You're a bit overdressed for a sickroom visit," he said to her. He was proud he sounded almost like his regular self.

She rolled her eyes at him. "Of all people, only you would concern yourself with my appearance when you're the one flat on your back. I have come from Hyde Park, because Lady Aymer must keep up appearances, unlike her brother who can disappear for a week at a time."

He blinked. Had it been a week—no, it must be more than a week—since Easter Sunday? Since Michael awoke?

"You look nice," he amended, his voice gruff.

The corner of her mouth pulled into that amused expression he knew so well, when she wasn't *quite* laughing outright at him, but she really was, inside.

She closed the bedroom door and sat in the chair Michael had been occupying near the bed. "Is there anything you need?"

"A slice of a roasted beef joint and a pint of ale."

She gave him a baleful look. "I doubt Miss Gardinier would agree to such a menu."

"This morning, she threatened me with a nasty concoction to supposedly relieve my headache. I couldn't even dispose of it in the chamber pot because she stood there to watch me drink it."

She widened her eyes and clasped her hands to the sides of her face. "Oh! The horror! It's as though you are being treated like a five-year-old."

He frowned at her, certain she had indirectly called him a big baby.

There was a scratch at the door, and a maid arrived with a tea tray.

"No ale?" he complained.

"The tea is for *me*," she corrected him. "I requested it before coming to see you." She nodded to the maid as she lay the tray on the table near the bed.

"For an invalid, I am being woefully neglected," Thorne noted.

"Did you really just make a joke? I am flabbergasted." Isabella smiled and dismissed the maid, who was trying very hard not to smile at their banter as she closed the door behind her.

"Brat," he called her, without rancor.

"Behave or I shall not give you any of these marvelous scones. Oh! They're still steaming hot."

"You are a gem among women."

"That's more like it."

She even buttered the scone for him while he struggled to sit up in bed. He would have snarled at her if she'd tried to help him, and she did not give the slightest indication she even considered doing so, but he did feel foolish that his weakened body had a difficult time of it.

"Tea?" she asked him when he had finally situated himself, panting at the effort.

"Yes, please," he said meekly, suddenly realizing that he did, indeed, want tea.

They ate in that comfortable silence they had between them, which he remembered from his childhood when she could soothe him simply by remaining quiet in the same room as him.

"The twins were worried about you," she said just as he had finished the last scone from the tray.

He slowed as he chewed, and then needed some tea to help him swallow.

"Calvin seems to have become prodigiously attached to you in a short time." She studiously did not look at him as she sipped her tea.

He didn't know how to respond to that. He rarely even suffered to be in the presence of children, something he and Isabella had argued about a few times.

But in remembering their arguments, it brought back to mind Sinah's hard expression as she refused to look at her children. And then he remembered the hurt on their faces as they stared at the door she had closed behind her.

"I'm glad they have Lady Wynwood," he said in a gruff voice.

"Are you?"

He found refuge in glaring at her. "Of course I am."

She was not offended. "I'm simply surprised. I didn't expect you to care for them so much."

He knew why she thought that. He could have said something specifically to provoke her, to fall back on the same arguments they always had, but now he did not want to distract her that way. It would be too hypocritical of him after he'd already confessed to her how it had bothered him to watch Sinah neglect her children.

But it had not been simply neglect. Sinah's words had been like hammer blows to her children's feelings.

And the worst part about it, the part that tied his stomach in knots, was that he hadn't considered how his own words had caused pain to his own son.

"I saw her treat her children that way," he said slowly, "and it made me feel guilty."

She studied him carefully, then finally said, "Rather than simply feeling guilty, why not go to see him?"

Even though the effects of the pollen were wearing off, he still had to turn away from her and clench his fist against the bedclothes. "I still feel too much anger at Drusilla, and it would only make me hurt Timothy more."

She sighed, a lonely and sad sound. "Seeing how Sinah hurt her children, can you not let your anger go?"

She had asked him this question several times before, and always he responded in indignation. But this time he did not feel that. However, his answer was still the same. "I'm not ready to do that."

Isabella did not respond in the way she'd always done, with frustration or disappointment. She sipped her tea, then set down the teacup in the saucer. "I spoke to Lady Wynwood this morning."

Thorne had certainly not expected her to change the subject, but he admitted he was a little relieved. "Oh?"

"I was never so surprised as when she asked how I was doing. Me! When she has so many other things to worry about."

"I should have worried more about you," he muttered.

She smiled and touched his hand briefly. "You've had other things on your mind. But it made me feel better to speak to her —to another woman—about what has been happening with Michael."

Perhaps it had been the heightened emotions the Goldensuit had dredged up inside of him, but he hadn't thought much about Michael's plight, or about how it would affect Isabella. "I ... I'm sorry ..."

"Oh, Thorne," she interrupted him. "You speaking to me about *feelings* is one of the last things I would have expected of you. Usually I would speak to my mother. Or Richard." There was a slight catch in her voice as she said his name. "So to speak to Lady Wynwood was quite welcome. She said that she wouldn't pretend to understand what I must be going through. It was ..." She paused, remembering the conversation. "It was difficult to say it. That my brother might die. That there was nothing I could do about it."

"He's my brother, too," he said before he could wonder that he was indulging in a rare confession of his heart. "I have always thought of him as my brother. And ..." His throat grew tight and he could not finish his sentence.

Isabella said it for him. "I do not want to lose him."

He swallowed, and the silence grew heavy.

"Lady Wynwood prayed with me," Isabella said softly. "And somehow, having her pray for me made me suddenly feel God's unexplainable peace. It was quite supernatural, and very welcome."

She was experiencing something he didn't understand, something he had previously chosen not to understand. But lately, Lady Wynwood and her household had brought to his mind a God he had thought he was done with.

Simply because Thorne turned his back on Him didn't mean He was done with Thorne, apparently. He wasn't sure how he felt about that.

Isabella now held his eyes, and her expression was pleading. "You breathed in that poisonous pollen. What if something happens to you? Thorne, will you leave things unsaid?"

And he realized she had not changed the subject, but was coming at it from a different direction.

He had always been so stubborn about his viewpoint when they had argued before. But now, after the change in his behavior and the parenting example of Sinah Eades, he was not so belligerent.

"Isabella," he said, "I will not say I am the same man I was a week ago. But you know I've gone on many missions for the Foreign Office—"

"You haven't gone on any since your father died."

He hadn't wanted to return to England, but he'd had to take up the responsibilities of his father's estate. "It's only been a year," he insisted. "And putting a man in those kinds of situations makes him know who he is. On several missions, I had to face my mortality, knowing I'd left many things unsaid. But I had no regrets then, and I have none now."

She seemed to deflate, but after a few moments, she nodded.

However, unlike other times, he now felt as if he'd run away from something important. The feeling nagged at him even as Isabella began chatting brightly about how Michael had bought a pretty silver bracelet for their mother as apology for the week he had gone "out of town" without telling her.

It was ridiculous for him to feel any differently than he had been. It would change nothing for him to visit Thornesby.

He knew, as Isabella didn't, that he had a very good reason not to see Timothy.

Isabella was certain something was the matter with Thorne.

Whenever she brought up Timothy, they would argue and that would be that. However, this time, while he said the same things, he did not sound as sure and certain as usual. In fact, when she turned the subject and spoke of her mother, he seemed rather distracted.

She did not know what to make of it. But as she had been praying for several years, she prayed that the Lord would help him to see that he was not alone, and that God had always been watching over him.

A knock sounded and without waiting for an answer, Michael opened the door. He met the eyes of his friend, then his sister, and grimaced slightly.

LADY WYNWOOD'S SPIES, VOL. 3: AGGRESSOR

Isabella glared at him. He had obviously been unaware she had arrived.

He took a few steps inside the room. "I just dropped by to say that I'm leaving."

"Back to the Albany?" Isabella's tone was acidic.

"Yes," he admitted reluctantly.

Isabella had opened her mouth to argue again that he should return to their family townhouse, when movement near the door made him turn.

Aya, Lady Wynwood's lady's maid, appeared and seemed rather flustered. "I beg your pardon for interrupting, but a man has arrived with an urgent message for Mr. Drydale, and he will not put it in anyone's hands but his. And my lady has left with Mr. Havner for ... the other house." Lady Wynwood had not told most of the servants about Stapytton House, but Aya apparently knew at least a little about it.

An urgent, secure message for Mr. Drydale likely indicated it was from the Ramparts. "Why would he be looking for Mr. Drydale here?" Isabella asked.

Aya tried very hard not to roll her eyes. "Mr. Drydale left word at his home that he could be reached at Lady's Wynwood's townhouse."

He likely expected that if anyone from the Ramparts were looking for him, Lady Wynwood would know where he was to be found.

Michael said to Aya, "I shall speak to this man." He hesitated, then added apologetically, "It might be best if there were no servants nearby."

Aya understood perfectly, and was not insulted. "Very good, sir. He is in the drawing room." The maid curtseyed and left.

Thorne struggled to rise. "I could—"

Isabella held a hand out to restrain him. "You are in no condition to meet visitors."

Michael looked to Isabella. "Thorne and I both came from the

Foreign Office, so I have not met any other agents from the Ramparts, except for you, Mr. Drydale, and his superior officer, Sir Derrick Bayberry. Will this man entrust the message to me?"

"He must," she said with more conviction than she felt. "We have seen the reports Mr. Drydale has been sending to his superiors. He has told the Ramparts we are working with him."

"Would he know *you*?" Thorne asked her.

"Depending on who it is, it is possible, but the odds are against it. Aside from our team, Mr. Drydale, and Sir Derrick, there are only three agents in the Ramparts who know my identity, and they would never reveal their knowledge even in the presence of other agents."

Michael and Thorne both frowned at her, but it was Michael who asked, "Why is your identity such a secret? There were a few women working for the Foreign Office. There are other women working for the Ramparts, surely?"

She thought briefly of the highly secretive missions she had undertaken within certain royal residences. "I cannot tell you."

He sighed, but didn't press her. "If I cannot convince this man to give the message to me, we shall have to ride to Stapytton House and bring Mr. Drydale back here."

"If the message is truly urgent," Thorne said, "the sender won't like that."

Isabella had to agree with him, but didn't say so as Michael nodded grimly.

"I shall go with you to listen to your conversation." She rose.

"Is that wise?" Thorne asked.

"I am a great deal more quiet than you," she told him tartly. "I shall not be discovered."

He gave her a grumpy look but otherwise didn't respond.

She followed Michael downstairs, but rather than accompanying him to the drawing room, she slipped into the library, which was next door. The hinges to the library door did not squeak, but she opened and shut the door carefully just as she heard, on the other side of the connecting door, her brother speaking to the visitor.

"I beg your pardon, sir, but Mr. Drydale is not here. I am Michael Coulton-Jones."

A man's voice replied, "I have a message that must be given to Mr. Drydale with all haste. You will take me to him."

Did she recognize that voice? Isabella wasn't certain. She wished the door between the library and drawing room were open so that she could see the man's face.

Despite the man's imperious tone, her brother answered with politeness. "I am unable to do so. His location at the moment is known only to his group and must be kept secret because of what it contains. However, I can deliver the message to him immediately."

"I will not give this sensitive information to someone of whom I know nothing."

There was a slight pause, then Michael said, "If you are working for the men you claim, you know exactly who I am."

"Your social status does not give you the ability to order about men on matters of great national importance." Isabella heard the sneer in the man's voice.

Michael's voice was tight as he replied, "You know the work I have done as a soldier, and the various superiors I have served within the government."

"Then you may not understand how *this* particular department works. We do not disobey specific orders. I suggest you follow the orders I am giving to you and take me to Mr. Drydale."

Why was he so insistent upon being taken to Mr. Drydale? Michael had already refused him and explained why. Any other man would have then requested—or, in this man's case, *demanded*—that Michael fetch Mr. Drydale so that he might give the message to him.

She could tell Michael was only barely keeping a rein on his temper as he said, "The only orders I follow are from Mr. Drydale and his superior officer. I will not give you his location."

"It is imperative that this message be delivered as quickly as possible. What is so important about his location that it must be hidden? There is no need for secrets among a team of men working toward the safety of the country."

She had heard enough of his voice to suspect she knew who he was. Sir Derrick may have had the foresight to designate that only certain agents could be dispatched to deliver messages to Mr. Drydale—because *she* was working for him. This man sounded like one of the three agents in the Ramparts whom she had worked with, Mr. Clay.

And if he was, then why would he say that about secrets when he knew very well that she was one of the secrets kept from others within the Ramparts? But she then realized that his talk of secrets may not encompass only Mr. Drydale's location—but perhaps also what was hidden there.

In which case, he was arguing because he had been ordered to accomplish his task at any cost. It would not have been Sir Derrick who ordered it, but she thought she knew who had given those orders.

Michael finally said, "I cannot take you to Mr. Drydale, but I can go and fetch him for you. However, if that is the case, it may be another two hours before he receives this message."

"That is unacceptable."

The message must be extremely urgent for the Ramparts to dispatch a man to deliver it personally, and yet *someone else* at the Ramparts had given Mr. Clay another objective that might prevent Mr. Drydale from receiving this information. Would the other senior officers in the Ramparts be so self-serving that they would work against fellow agents, disregarding their recommendations and increasing risk to others' lives?

What should she do?

Lord, I pray Thee, grant me wisdom.

She debated with herself for another moment, then without caring what Mr. Clay would think, she flung open the door connecting the library with the drawing room.

Mr. Clay was standing in the middle of the room, facing off against Michael, and he recognized her as she entered. He was not very tall, although Isabella was so short that most people seemed like giants to her. He still had that slightly arrogant swagger that he thought made him appear confident but only reminded Isabella of an insecure young boy. When he wasn't glowering, his face was pleasant, although strangely unremarkable, with dull brown hair in a modest rather than fashionable style, and clothes that were plain but finely made.

Although they did not entertain often, Isabella's mother was perhaps the most skilled hostess she knew. She could convey worlds with a look, a tone, a word. Isabella pictured her mother sailing into the drawing room in her place, and spoke as if she were Belle Coulton-Jones rather than the soft, sweet Lady Aymer she normally presented to the world.

"Mr. Clay, isn't it? I nearly didn't recognize you. I have not spoken to you since Lady Antingham's card party."

There had been no card party, but the name made him stiffen.

She continued, "I believe I was paired with Lord Antingham, and you were paired with Mr. Uppleby."

He stared hard at her, wondering why she was speaking their names.

"La, I had nearly forgotten that Sir Derrick Bayberry lent me five pounds so that I could play that night. I really should repay him. Do you think it would be in bad form for me to visit him today to speak to him and thank him for being so kind?"

She smiled at him with her mother's effortlessly polite and friendly smile, but her eyes as she stared at Mr. Clay's face were hard.

She hadn't thought his face could stiffen any further, but it did at the mention of Sir Derrick's name. As she had suspected, he had been ordered by someone other than Sir Derrick to find Mr. Drydale's location, and he was unsure what Sir Derrick's reaction would be if he were told that Mr. Clay had been the messenger.

He recovered quickly and gave a stiff bow. "I apologize, my lady, but I'm afraid I couldn't say. I am in the midst of delivering a message."

She held out her hand. "If you give me the note, I shall personally explain it to the sender."

He hesitated.

She felt sympathy for him, but he was not allowed to know the existence of Stapytton House. "If you do not, we shall all wait here for Mr. Drydale to return. However long that may take."

Mr. Clay frowned. "Your brother—"

"I do beg your pardon, but I had forgotten to tell him that all of the horses are lame." She held his eyes steadily, daring him to refute her.

He grimaced and handed her the note.

She curtseyed. "I bid you good day, Mr. Clay. I do believe I was mistaken, and at least one of the horses can carry him."

She left the room and Michael followed, closing the door behind him.

He tilted his head toward the drawing room. "Is he—?"

"One of the three."

"Ah."

She handed him the note. "I believe he was ordered to discover Mr. Drydale's location, and what is stored there."

He instantly understood. "There may be another agent outside, ready to follow me when I leave."

"Not if you do your job." She knew her brother was quite

skilled at losing someone trying to shadow him. "However, I believe he was sent here alone. Otherwise he would not have been so insistent about being taken to Mr. Drydale, rather than allowing you to go to ask him to return with you."

Despite the tense situation, he gave her a half-smile and leaned over to buss her cheek. "Thanks, Ugly."

"You owe me. Don't think I shall forget, Smelly."

She watched as he left her, holding the innocent white note. Such urgency that the Ramparts would send Mr. Clay, and such security that only Mr. Drydale could receive the note, only spoke of one thing.

Something terrible had happened.

Chapter Twenty

Phoebe looked out the conservatory windows at the gray skies, where dark storm clouds threatened, and shivered in unease.

Where had that come from? Up until a moment ago, she'd been awash with excitement. She loved growing her roses, but she especially loved the challenge that came with growing a particularly difficult strain. Now, she stared at the pots of Goldensuit plants in the conservatory at Stapytton House, and felt the same elation at a new challenge.

The plants were actually quite beautiful. The flowers looked like poppies, although with slightly thicker and elongated petals, and they had fine yellow pollen, which poppies did not possess.

Except for attending church, Phoebe had spent all of the past three days here at Stapytton House, returning to her aunt's house only to sleep. Keriah had remained by Mr. Rosmont's side for two days, but after Dr. Shokes saw her patient yesterday and declared he was as well as could be expected, she had come today to help Phoebe.

The conservatory had a grate in the corner, which had regulated the temperature for the orange trees that had been grown in the room by the original owner, and she checked it now to ensure it was not burning too hot.

She was startled by a muffled knock at the conservatory door. Uncle Sol called out, "Phoebe, could I ask for your help? I repaired the kitchen shutters and I need to reinstall them before the storm comes."

"Of course." She gathered up her notebook, then went through her procedure to exit the room.

She had never before grown any plants that were quite so deadly, and so she had taken some rather extreme precautions. She had draped a large swatch of heavy canvas to completely cover the doorway, and she had to shift it aside to open the door. There was a second swatch of canvas covering the door on the other side, and she moved that aside to enter the hallway, stripping off her gardening gloves and mask as she did so and dropping them into a basket for washing.

Uncle Sol was standing several yards away from the door as a precaution in the event some of the pollen wafted out. After seeing what had happened to Mr. Rosmont, and hearing how the pollen even affected Mr. Coulton-Jones's symptoms, none of them cared to take any chances. He nodded as he saw her and led the way downstairs to the kitchen.

Keriah was exiting the stillroom as they entered the kitchen. She gave them a questioning look.

"We're reinstalling the shutters." Uncle Sol pointed to the kitchen windows.

"Shall I help?"

"If you'd like."

Since Uncle Sol had not wanted Aunt Laura to tell her servants about Stapytton House—aside from the coachman, Mr. Havner, who drove her aunt to and from her townhouse—there was no one to do menial tasks aside from the team. Although he was their leader, Uncle Sol had not considered himself exempt from these duties, especially since he wanted to be here if Phoebe or Keriah were using the conservatory or stillroom.

It was perhaps a bit improper for him to be in the house with two unchaperoned young women, but he also had not wanted those young women to be at the country house alone. The sticklers of society would be up in arms at the additional impropriety of him in his shirtsleeves and vest, his cravat only loosely and messily tied, but he had not wanted to dirty his coat during the humble act of fixing the shutters.

Phoebe and Keriah donned their pelisses, but apparently Uncle Sol was still feeling warm because he exited the house without a coat or cloak. The kitchen shutters had been in terrible condition, but he'd spent the day fixing them. They lay atop two sawhorses outside the kitchen window.

The wind was starting to pick up, and the light had become much darker than normal for late afternoon. Phoebe donned some old gardening gloves Uncle Sol passed to her, and she helped him to hoist the shutters up and set them in the window.

"Miss Gardinier, pass me those thin pieces of wood," he said.

Keriah handed them to him so he could slip them in at the top and bottom, then all around to position the shutters with a narrow gap on all sides.

"You are staying at Laura's home to monitor Mr. Rosmont, are you not? How is he doing?"

He had asked Phoebe about Mr. Rosmont yesterday, but she had only briefly spoken to Keriah and wasn't able to give him a satisfactory answer. This was the first chance he had to talk to them today, despite the fact he drove them to Stapytton House this morning, because she and Keriah had not seen Uncle Sol much. Keriah helped Phoebe in the conservatory, then they looked at the plants under the microscope in the stillroom, then Phoebe took care of the plants while Keriah did her own chemical experiments. Phoebe lunched with Uncle Sol, but Keriah was in the middle of a procedure at the time and had eaten alone later in the afternoon.

Keriah handed him another piece of wood, scraping loose strands of hair that the rising wind blew into her eyes. "His shaking and fever passed quickly, and when Dr. Shokes saw him last night, he was already looking much better. I checked in on him this morning before coming here with Phoebe."

"And how is his, er ... mood?"

Keriah swallowed nervously, but her voice was cool and clinical as she answered, "His violent emotions appear to have calmed down considerably. I don't think there will be any sort of unexpected turn for the worse, but ..."

"We know too little about the Goldensuit," Phoebe said. She had to push a little harder as a gust of wind made the wooden shutters tremble slightly.

"I'm more concerned about Mr. Coulton-Jones," Keriah said.

"Oh?" Uncle Sol was marking the position of the pintle on the window casing so he could screw it into place.

"He mentioned that he felt strangely better after breathing the Goldensuit pollen."

Uncle Sol frowned, although he was working the screw-driver and didn't look at her. "Oh yes, now I remember. You told me about that after the fight at Maner's greenhouse."

"I need to do more experiments and understand the Goldensuit better," Keriah said, handing him another screw. "I want to try to find a means to save Mr. Coulton-Jones—without the Root. I'm counting on Phoebe."

"The plants are troublesome," Phoebe admitted, blowing out a frustrated breath. "I may have difficulties simply keeping them alive, much less enabling them to thrive."

Phoebe felt her lack of experience keenly, whereas before, she had never bemoaned the fact she was a mere amateur botanist. Now she needed all her skills of observation to try to ensure the Goldensuit grew well.

"I even asked Aunt Laura to send a servant to Sauber Hill to collect my books and notebooks," she said. She hoped she had not thought of it too late, and that it had not yet occurred to her father or Mrs. Lambert to have them destroyed out of spite. "But I'm not a trained botanist, Uncle Sol. Perhaps you should consider someone else …"

"I think your experience is better than a trained botanist," Keriah said. "Your insights compliment my experience as a chemist. Alone, neither of us would have progressed very far in understanding the Root or the Goldensuit."

"I must agree with Miss Gardinier," Uncle Sol said. He moved to screwing in the pintle on the top of the other side of the casement. "And I trust you both far more than I would trust any stranger whom my superiors would have tried to find."

Phoebe considered the events that led to them finding the Root and helping Uncle Sol. "Perhaps God placed us both in this situation, a chemist and a botanist who can work together."

"I simply do not understand your belief that a higher power orchestrated all of it," Keriah answered sharply.

Uncle Sol also looked a bit doubtful, but not as scoffing as Keriah.

But Phoebe couldn't shake her suspicion that it was all too coincidental not to be the hand of God.

"Phoebe, what have you discovered about the plants?" Uncle Sol asked.

Phoebe wondered if he changed the subject because it made him uncomfortable, or because Keriah was so obviously antagonistic. "There were three different types of plants at Jack's greenhouse," she said.

"Were you able to discern which ones were from Jack's greenhouse and which from Maner's?" Uncle Sol asked.

"Yes, it was very obvious. Maner's plants were very unhealthy, and he grew only one type. Jack had a lily and two Goldensuit plants that were subtly different."

"Were those the ones we looked at under my microscope?" Keriah asked.

"Yes, the differences between the two were more obvious. I believe that one of the Goldensuit plants is a hybrid that Jack created by cross-pollinating the original Goldensuit plant with the lily."

"Hybrid?" Uncle Sol looked utterly confused. "Cross ... what?"

"A hybrid is the plant that resulted when Jack cross-bred a lily and the original Goldensuit," Phoebe said.

"You mean, such as breeding a mule from a donkey and a horse?" Uncle Sol asked.

"Yes, exactly. The plants from Jack's greenhouse were mostly that hybrid plant, and Maner's plants were entirely hybrids. I believe that Jack used that hybrid plant to make his Root elixir."

"Why the lily plant?" Keriah asked, handing more screws to Uncle Sol so he could attach the lower pintles.

"I'm not certain," Phoebe said. "It's a robust species of lily, to be sure. Perhaps he also chose it because it happens to cross-pollinate with the Goldensuit more successfully than other plants."

"The plants all looked the same," Keriah said.

"They mostly do, although the hybrid leaves are a lighter green color. However, the roots of the original Goldensuit and the hybrids look nothing like each other. And the original Goldensuit plant had some dried stems that may have held flowers which were cut. So far, no new flowers have begun to come in, but it is still early, and the plants may need time to become acclimated to their new greenhouse."

"Then, did all that pollen come from those hybrids?" Uncle Sol asked.

"Yes. They have copious flowers. Also, I think I know why the Root elixir that Jack was making from his batch of hybrid plants was creating Berserkers."

He paused to glance at her. "You do? Septimus did mention that Jack had complained about men becoming Berserkers from an overdose of the Root, and also that some men became Berserkers with a single dose, whether their first or not."

Keriah nodded. "Nick became wild even though he had been taking the Root."

"I believe the reason is because the hybrid plants are very inconsistent," Phoebe said. "I looked at several samples of roots and leaves under the microscope and I drew what I saw in my notebook. While the leaves of different hybrid plants always looked similar, the roots looked vastly different from plant to plant."

"Is that not normal?" he asked.

"Not usually. Plants of the same species will usually look very much alike, even under the microscope. For example, from plant to plant, the roots and leaves of the original Goldensuit looked the same under the microscope, as I would have expected."

"So you think that those men became Berserkers because of the differences in the plants used in the elixir?" Uncle Sol asked.

"Yes," Phoebe said. "If a certain type of root cell caused men to become Berserkers, and enough of that type were in one vial of Root elixir, it might make the men Berserkers. If they overdosed on too much of that type of root cell, they would also become Berserkers." She glanced at Keriah for confirmation.

"That might explain it," Keriah said, sounding more excited. "What about the pollen?"

"Under the microscope, the pollen from the hybrids are consistent from plant to plant, but I haven't investigated it very much because of how potent it is. I did not wish an accidental exposure."

"That is understandable, and wise of you. Laura would have my head if you were harmed by that pollen." He grabbed one of the shutters. "Let us set these back on the sawhorses."

"Mr. Drydale, aren't the hinges a bit crooked?" Keriah frowned at the window, her head tilted to the side.

"What?" Uncle Sol leaned back and looked at the windows. "It looks fine to me."

The sounds of carriage wheels made Phoebe's heartbeat

quicken. She glanced at Uncle Sol. "Was anyone due to arrive today?"

His face had grown tense. "No."

Phoebe hurried to the corner of the house and peeked out through the screen of an overgrown rosebush. She breathed a sigh of relief at the sight of her aunt's unmarked carriage, driven by Mr. Havner, which had not stopped at the front, but was continuing around toward the back. "It is Aunt Laura," she told them.

Keriah headed toward the kitchen door. "I shall put the kettle on for tea."

Phoebe waited outside with Uncle Sol as the carriage came 'round the corner and parked under a tree. Strangely, when Mr. Havner opened the door for her aunt, he said something to her. Aunt Laura nodded and headed toward Phoebe and Uncle Sol.

"Have you become a handyman, Sol?" Aunt Laura asked in greeting.

"I have found it helps me to think." He smiled at her startled expression. "Why does that surprise you?"

"I told Aya the same thing when she caught me beating carpets."

"I rather think the act of beating something with a stick was more soothing for you," he replied.

She grinned. "You're likely correct." Her eyes drifted to the window, then her head tilted to the side. "Is that straight?"

"Of course," he replied, rather defensively.

"Yes, of course," she said with a smile, and hefted a basket under her arm. "But I have brought seed cakes. Why not leave the shutters to Mr. Havner?"

"I cannot pile more work upon your poor coachman."

"Oh, he offered as soon as he saw your, er, handiwork."

Phoebe glanced at the hinges on the window and thought that perhaps they *were* a bit off.

"Did he?" Uncle Sol's gaze strayed to the basket. "Well, in

that case ... Seed cakes, did you say?"

In the kitchen, they came upon Keriah just heating the kettle. "Tea should be ready soon."

"Is everything well?" Phoebe asked her aunt.

"Is Mr. Rosmont well?" Keriah asked.

Aunt Laura laid the basket on the warped table and unwrapped herself from her scarf and bonnet. "Mr. Rosmont is grousing about his bland supper."

Keriah gave a rather wicked smile. "Then he is perfectly fine."

"Are *you* all right?" Phoebe asked. Her aunt looked unusually apprehensive.

Aunt Laura hesitated, her eyes sliding to Keriah. "I beg your pardon, Keriah, but I must speak with Phoebe alone."

The words seemed to fall into Phoebe's stomach like little weights.

"Of course." Keriah made to exit the kitchen, but Aunt Laura stretched out a hand to forestall her.

"You needn't leave. We shall go down to the butler's pantry." She turned to Uncle Sol. "Sol, perhaps you will accompany us. I would like your opinion."

Before they left the kitchen, Aunt Laura said to Keriah, "Please be sure Mr. Havner has a strong cup of tea. And perhaps some of those seed cakes."

Phoebe wished she'd had tea to bring down with them, because the cellar was chilly. Uncle Sol lit a lamp that had been left on the massive table, and it filled the space with a soft, warm glow. Phoebe sat in a musty-smelling chair next to him.

Aunt Laura sat down rather forcefully. Finally, she turned to her niece, but Phoebe interrupted her.

"Aunt Laura, you look as though you are about to face a firing squad." In point of fact, Phoebe herself felt as though she were about to face a firing squad.

Aunt Laura blinked, then sighed. "Perhaps I was fearing something like that. Pray, remember not to shoot the messenger. I had a visit from my attorney this afternoon."

It took her a moment to remember why that should involve herself.

"Attorney?" Uncle Sol asked.

"Did Phoebe tell you about her father's reprehensible behavior?"

He scratched the back of his head. "Er ... well, Mr. Rosmont told me that Phoebe's father had had her mother's jewels cleaned for resetting, and about the forged documents transferring her dowry to him."

Well, he had been the one to give permission for Mr. Rosmont to help Phoebe into her father's safe. Naturally Mr. Rosmont would tell him what had happened.

"I asked my attorney to look into the matter," Aunt Laura said.

"Are you certain you wish me to know this?" Uncle Sol asked.

Aunt Laura looked questioningly at Phoebe, who answered, "I have no objection to telling you, Uncle Sol, and if Aunt Laura feels your advice would be welcome, then I will, too." Her voice came out a bit high and tight, but otherwise sounded normal.

"Mr. Cossman was very thorough in researching the law about this," Aunt Laura said. The lines between her brows told Phoebe what the attorney had said even before she spoke. "You tore the forged document you found in his safe box, but if he forged your signature once, he will likely do it again. There is also no means to prove he forged your signature—no court will accuse him of lying, especially since you are a woman, and your dowry would not have reverted to you until you were thirty years old."

"There is nothing I can do?" Her voice was small, and she found her breath coming in quick gasps. She had already suspected she was powerless to do anything to recover her dowry, but saying the words somehow made it seem more final, that her father was laughing at her inability to take back what belonged to her. She felt weak. She felt shackled.

She felt so *enraged* she thought she might go insane.

Aunt Laura reached over to clasp her hands, which had balled into fists. "I am so sorry, my darling."

"How can he do this?" she whispered, but her voice shook.

"He is a man," Uncle Sol said grimly, and the anger was apparent in his own voice.

She remembered speaking to Miss Tolberton, a victim of her own father.

"I am not his daughter, I am his pet."

She didn't realize she'd repeated the words aloud until her aunt squeezed her hand even more tightly. "You are no such thing. You do not *belong* to him."

"Does it matter?" she asked bitterly. "He still has the freedom to do whatever he likes to me."

"He may have stolen from you, but he will not do so again," her aunt said fiercely. "Mr. Cossman will ensure that."

"I will ask him to work with my own attorney," Uncle Sol said. "They will protect you from him."

"How can the law protect a daughter from her father?" Phoebe demanded. "No one will dare come between a man's rights." She leaped to her feet and paced to the far wall.

It was as she paced that she remembered Mr. Rosmont pacing in the dressing room. She remembered his rage.

She also remembered how ugly she looked when her aunt showed her face in the mirror, how bestial she had appeared. She took a few deep breaths, bottling the storm inside her.

This was not what God would want from her.

But how could God have put her in this situation?

Would God save her?

She returned to the table. Aunt Laura and Uncle Sol had not risen to their feet, but they both had sat up straighter and were looking at her with concern. She sat as composedly as she could, but they did not relax despite her efforts to assure them.

"There is one option," Uncle Sol said slowly. "You could force your father to release your dowry if you pretend to become engaged to Mr. Coulton-Jones or to Septimus."

An abrupt thrill shot through her body, a feeling that she'd sprouted wings. She couldn't breathe for a moment, as though her heart would beat itself out of her chest.

"Sol!" her aunt objected. "Pretend to be engaged? This is not a gothic novel."

Of course, Phoebe had heard the word "engagement" first, and the word "pretend" only later. A fake, temporary engagement. Mr. Coulton-Jones was not the most eligible bachelor in London, but he was far above her touch.

"It would not do, Uncle Sol." She was surprised that her voice came out low and calm. She felt far from calm.

"Why not?" he asked. "I believe that either young man would trust you enough to do so for you. I could speak to both of them for you, if you like."

He was only trying to be helpful, but her feelings had gone from soaring in the heights to plummeting to the depths in the space of a minute. The dissolution of a fake engagement to Mr. Coulton-Jones would hurt her emotionally more than she wanted to admit to anyone. She wasn't certain if she could smile and give the appearance of not being disappointed when it ended.

And certainly, Miss Phoebe Sauber had nothing that the eligible Mr. Coulton-Jones could possibly want.

Her aunt had grown pale, then red, then pale again as she looked at Phoebe, then Uncle Sol, then back to Phoebe. Finally she cleared her throat. "Sol, Phoebe is correct. It will not do, even if one of the young men would be willing. Her father would simply say Phoebe signed her dowry to him already and had misled the young man into thinking she still had it. He would produce another set of forged papers as proof."

Uncle Sol groaned and scrubbed a hand over his face. "You

are right. I'm afraid I am no expert on these types of social matters," he grumbled. "I thought it might force his hand. And ..." He gave Phoebe a half-smile. "I admit I would not mind if you engaged yourself to Septimus in truth, and we were connected more formally."

That half-smile both warmed her and made her heart crack a little. Because she hadn't considered Mr. Ackett in her thoughts. Because Uncle Sol had mentioned a desire for a real engagement for her. Because his affection for her was so apparent.

But a darker feeling had also surfaced in her heart. Because even a real engagement to Mr. Ackett—or Mr. Coulton-Jones, unlikely as that would be—would send her father over the moon.

Both young men were from ancient, respectable, wealthy families. Mr. Coulton-Jones was the heir apparent of his baronet uncle. Mr. Ackett was the third son of Viscount Ammler.

Phoebe knew with a certainty, deep in her soul, that she had no desire to do *anything* for her father's benefit. Especially a marriage that would please him.

Her aunt took her silence for sadness, or despair. She reached out to touch her hand. "You will always have a home with me," her aunt said. "And I have resources that Denholm does not. Your father will not be able to harm you again, if I have any say in the matter."

"If he thinks you are without protection, he would be wrong," Uncle Sol added. "You have called me 'uncle' since you were a girl, but that was no mere form of address. I am your family, also. I will not abandon you."

Their staunch support, their claiming of the bonds of connexion, were like fierce embraces around her aching heart. She could not smile, but she gave them both appreciative looks.

She recalled how Miss Tolberton had mentioned that she had nowhere to go. Phoebe tried to feel more grateful to her aunt, and less upset at her situation. So many other women in London suffered far more than she.

But the anger was still a smoldering heat inside of her.

There were gentle footsteps outside the room, then Keriah poked her head in. "Mr. Drydale, Mr. Havner asks if you would help him finish hanging the shutters."

"Of course." He stood, although he hesitated as he looked down at Phoebe. "I shall see if there is aught I can do to help you."

"Thank you, Uncle Sol."

But as he left, she couldn't help feeling that the situation was hopeless.

Her aunt perhaps read the emotions playing over her face, because she asked in a gentle voice, "Shall I pray for you?"

She nodded.

Her aunt prayed in a soft voice, asking the Lord to comfort Phoebe and guide the situation, praying for justice but also entrusting the future to God's hands.

Phoebe prayed with her, but her prayers felt hollow and empty, and her emotions remained heavy and turbulent. She still couldn't stand the thought of her father, and she admitted that she couldn't let it go. She almost didn't want to. Letting go of the injustice somehow felt as though she were countenancing her father's actions.

One question surfaced like a bubble that rose through murky waters before it broke:

Heavenly Father, why did You allow this to happen to me?

The question was filled with anguish and, yes, rage. She had tried so hard to be obedient, to truly love the Lord with her actions and not just her words or outward behavior.

And yet here she was, caught in a trap laid by others.

My God, my God, why hast thou forsaken me?

The words from her Bible appeared in her mind, like a candle suddenly flaring to life. Christ had said those words on the cross.

Christ understood her pain.

Tears began to burn in her eyes, drip down her face, drop from the end of her nose onto the table. Only minutes before, she'd felt that she had not the tears to quench the fire inside her, but now she wept, her feelings gushing out of her.

She didn't want to feel this pain. She simply wanted to feel at peace.

What will happen to me?

She heard no answer, either from her aunt, who was still praying aloud for her, or from the small voice that seemed to whisper from the depths of her soul.

She continued to cry. She continued to feel the pain that clenched at her heart.

Phoebe did not feel comforted, exactly. But strangely, she felt she and her aunt were not alone.

She didn't know how long they remained there, but eventually she had cried all the tears she had left in her. She had soaked her own handkerchief and her aunt's, and she mopped ineffectually at the drops on the table.

"We should return to town soon," her aunt said gently. "We mustn't be stuck here when the storm arrives."

Phoebe nodded and followed Aunt Laura back up the stairs to the kitchen.

But she jerked in surprise to find Mr. Coulton-Jones standing there. A sudden star of warmth radiated briefly in her chest.

Until she remembered that her face probably looked like an overripe tomato. Of *course* he would arrive here, unexpectedly, just as she'd finished crying. Thankfully the kitchen was a bit dim, due to the closed shutters over the windows, and the scrupulously polite man did not so much as hint that he noticed Phoebe's swollen nose and eyes.

She felt horribly embarrassed and awkward. He would not have known about Uncle Sol's suggestion for a false engagement, but the idea had blazed through Phoebe's mind like a shooting star, and seemed to be leaving a ghostly shadow in its wake.

He was dusty and looked to have ridden hard from town. The reason why was the note that Uncle Sol was reading with an aggravated expression that made his face mirror the storm clouds outside.

He crumpled the paper partway, his face embittered, then seemed to change his mind. He sighed wearily and smoothed the paper out onto the warped kitchen table.

Only at that moment did Phoebe realize the kitchen had grown silent. Mr. Havner and Keriah were also there, staring at Uncle Sol.

"Brigitte and her men are dead," Uncle Sol stated flatly.

Phoebe had difficulty understanding the words. They filtered through her mind without meaning.

"What?" Keriah exclaimed.

"How?" Aunt Laura demanded in a hard voice.

"Weren't they being held at the Ramparts?" Mr. Coulton-Jones asked.

Uncle Sol nodded tightly. "The Foreign Office heard about the arrest and insisted that they be the ones to hold and question them. I objected strongly but apparently ..." He gestured curtly toward the paper on the table. "... I was overruled."

Understanding dawned on Mr. Coulton-Jones's face. "They tried to move them," he guessed.

Uncle Sol nodded. "Brigitte and her men attacked the officers transporting them and nearly escaped, but they were killed before they could do so."

Mr. Coulton-Jones and Uncle Sol wore identical expressions of outrage. Aunt Laura pressed her hand to her mouth.

"So ... all that we went through ... was for no purpose?" Keriah asked.

No one answered her, and the silence in the kitchen nearly vibrated with tension.

But then a distance rumble of thunder broke the silence, and Aunt Laura said, "Sol, you must go to the Ramparts at once."

He seemed shaken from a daze, and he nodded to her.

"Mr. Drydale, take my horse," Mr. Coulton-Jones suggested. "I shall drive your carriage."

"We must leave also," Aunt Laura said, "before the storm arrives."

But they were already too late. The storm was already here.

Chapter Twenty-One

Laura had been home for only half an hour, and was about to dress for dinner, when Aya interrupted her with a strangely neutral expression on her face as she handed her a note.

Tonight at your convenience.

The note was unsigned, and had only that line, but she knew who had sent it.

"Please tell Phoebe and Keriah, and Mr. Rosmont—oh, and whomever else is still here—that I will not be dining here tonight." Laura was beginning to feel her house had turned into a hotel, but she wasn't very upset about it. The more people in her home, the more it contrasted with her years of isolation when Wynwood had been alive.

She hesitated as she thought of Phoebe. She didn't want to leave her niece in the precarious emotional state she was currently in, but she could not bring her with her.

Laura admitted she herself did not want to go to this meeting. The thought of what she would learn caused a twisting mass of worms in her stomach.

Aya silently helped her don a certain dark blue dress, plainly made with fabrics not as rich as her normal apparel, and accompanied by a dark blue, thick veil. Both had been made by Aya, so no dressmaker would be able to tattle about a strange costume commissioned by Lady Wynwood.

Aya had already informed Mr. Havner, who drew the unmarked carriage up to the back of the house, outside what had originally been the mews, but which she had converted into a laundry house. Because she had purchased the slightly shabby carriage specifically for this purpose, she rented a separate, larger space for her horses and carriages only a short distance away from her townhouse.

She and Aya settled themselves in the carriage. On the box, Calvin sat with Mr. Havner as his tiger. As a child, he would be both overlooked and underestimated, which was the best sort of protection for a gently born woman in the dangerous area of Rachey Street.

In the darkness of the coach, she tried to compose herself, but she pulled and played with her handkerchief until the lace edging began to tear off, and only belatedly did she realize her legs beneath her skirts were constantly moving, as if she expected to jump from the carriage at any moment. These visits did not normally cause this kind of anxiety in her, but this was one of the few times she needed information from the Senhora. Normally, when the Senhora's messages arrived, it proposed some mutually beneficial arrangement.

And dealing with the Senhora was not for the faint of heart.

But Laura had the feeling that the information she sought would not really benefit herself. In fact, she was certain it would cause her great pain.

"This will be difficult," she said aloud, her voice sounding muted in the interior of the carriage. "But the truth shall set me free."

"If the Son therefore shall make you free, ye shall be free indeed."

The Bible verses, on her lips and in her head, served to calm her as none of her rational arguments could.

She had made terrible mistakes in her life, especially during her years married to Wynwood. She must stop denying those mistakes and admit to them, so that God could help her to heal and move on. Being free of the guilt and sin would be worth the pain of facing the past.

And first, she must face the truth about Mrs. Jadis.

Aya reached out to hold her hand, her eyes dark and concerned, but she didn't speak.

Laura's nerves twanged and vibrated like discordant lute strings. She couldn't formulate a coherent prayer, so she prayed the only thing she could:

God, help me.

There was no answering bolt of power or magnificent angel choir. But she clung to the words she had read in her Bible that morning: *"If ye continue in my word, then are ye my disciples indeed."*

Christ was with her and would not leave her, even when she had to face the mistakes and secrets of the past.

Mr. Havner stopped the carriage a couple blocks away, because the Senhora preferred that Laura did not announce her coming and going by alighting on her front doorstep. No one could see behind her veil, she was dressed very plainly, and the carriage was also unmarked, but it could still be remarked upon when a veiled woman visited an establishment like Saffron House.

The street was darker than the streets near Laura's home—narrower, with the tall buildings blocking out the cloudy sky and blackened with soot, uncleaned for decades. The people on the street seemed to mirror the dark colors in their clothes—Laura's dark blue dress and matching pelisse were the brightest things on the street, since Aya was wearing brown and Calvin had donned a dirty set of livery that had once perhaps been moss green, a cast-off that Aya had discovered at a second-hand clothing shop.

The three set off as the carriage pulled away. Laura would send a note 'round to Mr. Havner when she was ready to depart, and he knew where to pick them up.

Laura walked firmly, with head held high and boots knocking solidly on the dirt caking the street. Aya followed closely, and Calvin strolled casually behind them, seemingly unconcerned, but Laura noticed his eyes following everything around them with heightened vigilance. It must be difficult for him because the darkness of the early evening cast everything in pitch-black shadows.

They walked exactly two and a half blocks, then turned up the steps of a townhouse, not quite as dingy as the surrounding buildings and obviously in better repair, and yet not ostentatious enough to stand out too much on the narrow street. Even before Laura's hand touched the knocker, the door was opened by the butler. He was a middle-aged man whose name she had not been told, but she had never seen a butler with such large muscles and thick neck. Yet he bowed correctly as they entered, and closed the door behind them with barely a sound.

"The Senhora?"

"Waiting for you upstairs, ma'am." The butler led the way up a flight of stairs at the other end of the narrow entryway, lined with a fine carpet runner. The wood on the banisters gleamed with oil, and while Laura did not recognize the artist of the small paintings on the walls, they were of good quality.

The house was elegant and mostly quiet, with the usual sounds of bustling servants. However, there was also the sound of a beautiful piece being played on a pianoforte somewhere behind a closed door, with a slight echoing quality that indicated it was in a large, echoing music room. All the doors they passed were closed, even the drawing room on the first floor.

On the second floor, the butler led them down a long, narrow hallway, dim because there were no windows, and knocked at a door at the end.

"Come," the woman's voice commanded, a rich, smoky with a faint accent.

The small room they entered, holding a desk and bookshelves in the far corner, suggested it served as an office. But the carpet was a rich burgundy color, matched by the curtains at the high, narrow windows, which Laura knew, from past visits during the daytime, let in what little light filtered down from between the high buildings on the street. Opulent sofas and chairs circled a low table on the near end of the room, and a woman rose from behind the desk and approached them, gesturing gracefully to the chairs.

Laura sat in the chair she usually chose, upholstered in hunter green, sitting opposite a chair in green and burgundy stripes that was placed almost like a throne in front of the table. She nodded to Calvin and Aya, although she mostly spoke to Calvin when she said, "I'm certain the Senhora's chef has something you can eat."

"But of course." The woman's dark eyes crinkled in a smile. "When I told her that the Blue Madam was coming tonight, Cook was most anxious to have your favorite date biscuits prepared in time."

Calvin's brown eyes lit up like topaz, and he and Aya followed the butler out of the room.

The Senhora always remained silent for a moment, studying Laura, before she spoke. The woman was petite, but when sitting, she seemed much taller and very imposing. Her black hair was a shade too dark and glossy to be natural, but it was styled with elegance and her face bore only discreet makeup that did not attempt to completely hide the lines across her forehead, at the corners of her eyes, and flanking her lips. She was older than how she appeared at first glance, but still very handsome, and dressed very modestly in a dark purple gown with a truly exceptional gold-threaded shawl twined around her arms.

The Senhora was about to speak when a scratch at the door sounded and a maid appeared with a laden tea tray. She seemed to change her mind about what she was about to say. "Have you been well?"

Laura hesitated, then answered, "I am in good health. Have you been well, Senhora?"

"Well enough. My troubles seem to multiply day by day, and I can resolve only so many before the day ends." The maid deposited the tray and left the room.

"What sorts of trouble?" At the Senhora's nod, Laura moved to pour for them both.

"Ah, one of my customers beat one of the girls last week, and she is feeling poorly still."

Laura's throat clenched. "How badly was she injured?"

The Senhora's dark eyes were serious and troubled. "Very badly, and the apothecary in this part of town is not very caring of his patients."

"I will send my own doctor to see her, if you like." Laura handed Senhora a cup of tea.

"I should like that. Thank you. But …" Her eyes regarded Laura with calculation. "Perhaps you can render me an additional assistance, in exchange for the information you desire from me."

Laura gave the Senhora a hard look. "What sort of assistance?"

"Nothing illegal." Laura could tell she was speaking the truth. "But it may be a risk to your reputation in high society."

Laura did not care about the good opinions of her gently-bred peers quite as much as her mother did, but she had no wish to be ostracized, either. Then again, with the scandalous things she and her niece had been doing in recent weeks, she supposed one more thing would hardly make a difference. "I did not explain much in my short note to you, and you did not indicate what you desired for payment. How do I know the information you have is valuable enough?"

The Senhora broke out into a throaty laugh. "Ever the businesswoman, even more than myself. One would never guess you resided in Park Street. Very well." She seemed to be watching Laura's reaction as she said, "In your note, you mentioned you needed information about Wynwood's last mistress."

Laura tried to nod, but she felt as though her body had turned to stone. The silence in the room was complete enough that the corner of the log that dropped into the ashes could be heard with a soft *hsssssh*.

There was the faintest spark in the Senhora's face that might have indicated sympathy. She said softly, "Those memories of your husband will not merely be unpleasant, but may be too repulsive for you to want to know."

She exhaled slowly, thinly, as if trying to breathe out the pain. The action suddenly reminded her of that excruciating night five years into her marriage, when she had lost the most important thing in her life, in agony that at the time had seemed unbearable. She had breathed like this, trying to retain her sanity, trying to hold on to something over which she had no control.

In comparison, this knowledge could not possibly be worse, and it gave her the strength to speak. "I have recently found an accessory that belonged to Wynwood, and it is disturbing enough that I must look into it. I was able to see the bill of receipt and found that Wynwood commissioned a pendant at the same time, with drawings describing how it had looked. I recognized the pendant, because I had seen it around the neck of Wynwood's mistress the day before ... the day before she died."

The Senhora's eyes flashed with compassion. "Yes, I heard about her death, and about your visit to her."

Laura nearly choked, but she should not be surprised. She

suspected that the Senhora's web of information was far wider than anyone could guess. In an even voice that did not completely betray her surprise, she said, "Did you? This was before we knew each other."

"She was quite well-known. Partly because of your husband, partly because of herself. I can tell you all I knew about her."

"And your price?"

The Senhora tried to hide it, but a hint of vulnerability crept into her eyes. She hesitated uncharacteristically, then finally said, "I wish for you to sponsor my daughter for a Season."

Laura's heart nearly pounded out of her chest, she was so shocked, but she strove with all her might to remain still. "I had not known you had a daughter."

"I have not told anyone. You are perhaps the only one in town who knows." She fiddled with the folds of her dress, an abnormal gesture. "I have not talked with her about this, because I wished to speak to you first."

The Senhora knew the magnitude of what she was asking. "*Who* would she be?" Laura asked carefully. She could not sponsor a young woman and announce to all society that she was the daughter of one of the most famous of brothel madams.

"She attended a respectable seminary at the age of thirteen, under her true name."

Laura's breath caught. "So she has met other young women of the *ton*."

"She did not form close connections," the Senhora admitted. "She wished to return to be with me." She did not appear to realize that a small smile had crept onto her face. She loved her daughter dearly, and yet would send her away to a marriage of wealth and comfort, but which would irrevocably isolate them from each other.

"A Season is expensive," Laura said.

The Senhora waved away the concern. "She will have an obscene dowry, and I shall pay for enough gowns and jewels to draw leagues of respectable men."

"Will she desire a marriage to a respectable man?"

The dark eyes hardened. "She will see the practicality of the decision."

Laura had the feeling that if this young woman didn't, her mother would ensure she understood it quite well.

She was not averse to the idea, especially since the young woman would be entering society under her real name. If she had even half of her mother's elegance, she would smoothly fit in with any of the other debutantes of the Season. And knowing the Senhora's power and ability to keep secrets, her daughter's true parentage was unlikely to come to light … but if it did, Laura would be ruined. She would not simply be *persona non grata* among the *ton*, but she would be completely isolated from all she once knew.

"As you said, it would indeed be a risk."

The Senhora's face grew steely. "I assure you, I will do all in my power to ensure nothing scandalous about her will become known. You know the strength of my promises."

"Yes."

The Senhora was intelligent and cautious. She rarely allowed her own girls to encounter risks, and they were never unprotected. She would certainly do all she could to protect her own daughter.

However, Laura could not let down her guard when bargaining with this woman. "I would need to speak with the young woman. How old is she?"

"She is twenty-four, but she is small, like myself. She appears seventeen or eighteen years old."

"This is a great favor you are asking me."

The Senhora's gaze was steady. "I am aware."

Laura turned to look into the fire. She knew of no one else who could tell her about Wynwood's deceased mistress. Even Sol had hit a brick wall in trying to find out about her. This was information they needed, which could lead them to Jack's mysterious group. Her reputation would be worthless if Napoleon swept across England with an army of Berserkers destroying everything ahead of them.

She nodded to the Senhora.

The petite woman held her hand out to Laura. "Come, we will shake upon it."

She clasped the lace-gloved hand and was not surprised by the wiry strength in her fingers. The Senhora held her eyes for a moment, then released her hand and leaned back in her chair.

In contrast, Laura steeled herself and sat up straighter. "Tell me about Wynwood's mistress."

The Senhora's eyes darkened, perhaps in compassion. "Her name was Mrs. Bianca Jadis, a widow. She was very intelligent, and she was not a common prostitute before she married. She was patronized by many wealthy men. I tried to recruit her, but she refused because she wanted more control over her gentlemen friends." Despite the rejection, the Senhora smiled faintly, as if reluctantly impressed by Mrs. Jadis's resolve.

It felt as though a vice were squeezing Laura's throat, slowly killing her as she asked about this woman. "When did her husband die?"

"That is a curious story. In your visits, have you ever encountered a vivid red-head? No? Her true name is Chastity, but we call her Chantelle. She knew Bianca before her marriage, and saw her again after many years, the week before she died. She came to work for me soon after that, and then a few months later, I met you. It is the only reason she mentioned Bianca to me at all. Since I was now interacting with my mysterious Blue Madam—" The Senhora nodded toward Laura. "—I asked her a great deal about Bianca. You understand, do you not?" The Senhora's voice softened.

Laura struggled to regain her composure. "Of course."

"When I read your note, I spoke to her again about Bianca. I will tell you what Chastity told me, in addition to what I have learned about Bianca from other sources. She apparently appeared in London about twenty-four years ago, when she was perhaps nineteen or twenty years old, although she always looked more mature. She always had a rather cold personality, although some men find that alluring and challenging." The Senhora smiled wryly. "She was Bianca Irvine then, or at least that was what she called herself to her patrons. She had several rich patrons before she became mistress to a wealthy merchant with lands in France. Chastity tells me that Bianca was excited to be traveling to France with her lover, but this was in 1789. A month after she left was the storming of the Bastille. No one heard from her again, and they assumed she died in France."

"She and her merchant did not escape?"

"Her lover returned to England, but he spoke indiscriminately to other prostitutes he hired, and you know how they can gossip. From what he mentioned, it seems that he had abandoned her in France."

Laura blanched. "He simply confessed to those women that he abandoned his mistress?"

The Senhora's eyes narrowed as she tilted her head. "I have told you often not to be surprised at how men will tell their mistress or a prostitute what they will not tell to family or friends. They will sometimes even conduct business at their mistress's home as a safe place."

Laura nodded. "I remember."

The Senhora continued, "Bianca had a younger sister named Zephyra, considerably younger than herself. She looked to be barely a child, but acted quite maturely, making some think she was older, though not yet out of the schoolroom. Bianca was protective of her sister, but Chastity said that it seemed more out of duty than love—the sisters' relationship was cool, like Bianca's relationship with everyone else in her life. After her older sister failed to return, Zephyra stayed with some of

Chastity's friends for a few months, and then she suddenly moved out without telling anyone where she was going. They hoped she might have gone back home to some family members who were willing to take her in, but they suspected she had found her own protector."

"Not yet out of the schoolroom ..." Laura could hear how faint her voice was.

The Senhora gave her a kind but world-weary look. "It is the way of things. Most women have few options when they have no family and no money."

"When did Bianca return to England?"

"No one is certain, but when she did reappear, she had married a man named Jadis. By that time, her younger sister was living with her, so I personally believe that her sister left Chastity's friends in order to move in with Bianca, who for some reason wished to keep her new status in life a secret. If that is the case, then the marriage was soon after she was abandoned in France. She was widowed before she became Wynwood's mistress. She took up with your husband two years before he died."

Laura gave a small nod. "What do you know about Mrs. Jadis's death?" She was afraid of what the Senhora would tell her, but she had to know.

A frown appeared between the Senhora's dark brows. "She supposedly killed herself by cutting her wrists in the bathtub, but Chastity tells me that was not what anyone who knew Bianca would have ever expected. Chastity spoke to her briefly only a few days before she died, and she was as confident and arrogant as always. They exchanged mere chit-chat, but Bianca seemed to have been anticipating some positive change in her life soon."

"Perhaps that fell through, and so she took her own life?"

"And yet this is the woman who managed to survive when her lover abandoned her in a country torn by revolution. I do not believe it."

Laura did not believe it, either.

"You need not tell me," the Senhora said softly, "but I would like to know why you visited her the day before she died."

Somehow, speaking about it with the Senhora, who was not as close to her as Sol, seemed easier. Or perhaps because she had already spoken about this before, and so the telling was not quite so much like a sword stabbed into her chest. "I confronted her about Wynwood—not because I was jealous of her relationship," Laura said hastily in response to Senhora's snort of disbelief. "But because I had heard that she was pregnant."

The Senhora's eyebrows shot upward, and her lips parted in genuine surprise. "I had not heard of the pregnancy at all."

"In hindsight, I am unsure if it was true, but at the time, I was ... crazed with frustration." She could clearly remember how she had felt that day, as she rode a carriage to Mrs. Jadis's townhouse. She had felt phantom pains, and wild impulses, and such ... rage. "I assaulted her, and the women with her had to pull me off of her."

Yes, she understood Phoebe's anger at her father. But Laura also remembered how her feelings had turned her into a monster.

The Senhora looked slightly confused. "But you cannot believe you were the cause of her death because of your argument?"

Laura hesitated before answering. "I did not wish to think that, but I felt a deep sense of guilt that she had died and killed her child as well."

"You do not know if she was pregnant," the Senhora said. "She was buried quickly by her sister, and then her sister disappeared."

"Disappeared? But ... Bianca was very wealthy. She had that townhouse ..."

The Senhora shook her head. "As far as I know, Zephyra is

not in London." She hesitated, and when she spoke, her voice was so low that Laura had to lean closer to hear her. "I believe she is in hiding, in fear for her life."

Laura felt chilled even in the warm room. "From whom?"

"There was a single whisper of a rumor about Bianca's death. I did not hear this from Chastity, but from another source. A rumor that Bianca had involved herself with a dangerous group of people."

Laura tried not to react. "What group?"

"So dangerous that no one spoke of it. I know very little about it."

Laura sharply inhaled. Because for an instant, fear flashed across the Senhora's face.

She made a decision at that moment. She had prepared a piece of paper, not certain if she would show this to the Senhora, but now she removed it from her reticule and placed it on the table. "Do you recognize this?"

The Senhora was already sitting perfectly upright in her chair, but she stiffened even more, if that were possible, and frowned fiercely. She quickly waved her hand over the five-stemmed flower symbol. "Put that away. Or better yet, put it in the fire."

Laura picked up the paper and dropped it on the glowing logs in the fireplace. "When I saw Bianca, she was wearing a pendant. I recognized the emblem upon it, which was why I attacked her—an ancient coat of arms for the Wynwood family. I have discovered recently that the pendant had *that symbol* hidden inside of it."

The Senhora looked grave. "It was ten years ago. You are certain it had the symbol?"

Laura nodded.

The woman suddenly seemed to shrink in her chair. When she spoke, it was in a low voice, almost as if she were speaking to herself. "You will find it difficult to break the wall of secrecy that surrounds that symbol, and it will bring you grave danger if you attempt it, so be very cautious."

The Senhora was not trying to be melodramatic, but her words were very forbidding compared to the relatively innocent-looking symbol. This strong woman was afraid of that symbol and wanted nothing to do with it.

"I understand ... but I must know about this."

The Senhora closed her eyes and sat in deep thought. "This has only been in the past two years, but the few men I have seen with that symbol all work for one man. I do not interact with him, but I hear whispers about him. He cares nothing for the government. He admires France not for the new constitution, but for the violence of the purge. He desires nothing but chaos."

The thought of it turned Laura's heart into a block of ice. She remembered reading the stories of the French riots years ago, and she saw an image of London burning, masses of people screaming and shouting, beating and killing.

With surprise, she also realized that she had the opportunity to prevent that chaos and violence. It was not simply her niece —and the *sparkling* she had not wanted to see in Phoebe—but Laura herself was willing to do what she could. Perhaps Sol and his sense of justice was rubbing off on her.

"Who is he?" Laura asked.

"His name is Jack Dix, and he was originally known as an herbalist with an extensive knowledge and inventory of poisons. However lately, he rules his own kingdom in the darkest streets of London."

"And he alone uses this symbol?"

"I have no proof, simply rumors, but I do not believe he alone uses this symbol. It is simply that those who work for him have been careless enough to allow the symbol to be seen by others. I believe this symbol is connected to a group of men who cloak themselves with anonymity. This man is simply one of them."

The Senhora's gaze upon Laura sharpened. "But now you tell me that Bianca had this symbol, *ten years ago.*"

She nodded.

The woman sighed. "This is information I wish I had not heard. And yet it would be foolish to hide away while there may be great change about to occur in London."

"What great change?" But Laura already knew the answer.

"Nothing I can say with certainty. Jack's movements have been rumored to involve men in the Foreign Office, but I do not know more than that."

Somehow these events seemed too weighty to belong here, in one of the most famous brothels in London.

"What was the name of Bianca's first protector? And her husband's full name?"

A faint smile appeared in the Senhora's eyes, as if she was pleased Laura had asked the question. "Her merchant lover was Mr. Field Emsley, and her husband was Mr. Carl Jadis."

"It would be nearly impossible to find information about a dead prostitute, but *they* were men who dealt with other men in the world, so there would be records of their possessions, their transactions."

"Yes, you are correct. Do you have an attorney who will act for you? Discreetly?"

Laura thought of Mr. Cossman. "Yes."

The Senhora bowed her head in a strangely ancient gesture of politeness. "I have told you all I know about very dangerous matters. I believe that is worth the price of my daughter's happiness."

If the Senhora's daughter was similar to her mother, Laura wasn't entirely certain if the young woman would be necessarily *happy* about a marriage to a man from her world, but she nodded. "Yes. I can sponsor her next Season."

"Good. In the meantime, I shall prepare. No one will know the world from which she comes."

The sudden thought of that knowledge being discovered made Laura feel a *frisson* of panic.

The Senhora caught Laura's stiffened expression. "Oh, look at you, your face is like plaster." Then she grabbed Laura's cheeks —something *no one* else did to her—and gently pulled them back and forth. "You are worried, but you must trust in how I treat my own girls. I will treat you and my daughter with even more care."

"Wewesh ma chwks." Laura's eyes were beginning to water.

The Senhora complied, and Laura glared at her, but the madam simply smiled at her.

"Why must you *always* do that when I come to see you?"

"You are simply too adorable." The Senhora spread her hands and looked innocent. "I never do so in front of anyone else."

Laura rubbed her stinging cheeks. "I shall take my leave." Her voice might have sounded a bit petulant.

The Senhora seemed to be biting back a smile as she took up a small bell that rested on the low table and gave a sharp ring.

Within a few minutes, a soft knock sounded at the door and the butler entered with Aya and Calvin in tow. Laura rose, but was surprised when the Senhora also rose to her feet and approached her servants.

The madam reached out and gently ran the back of her hand down Calvin's cheek. "She came to me recently," she said to the boy. "She asked about you both."

Calvin grew still, and his eyes darkened as he stared at the Senhora.

"She will never be a good mother." There was a trace of disappointment in the Senhora's voice. "But she is not a bad woman. Do you understand?"

He stood there expressionless for a long moment, then he curtly nodded.

"Good day, madam," Laura said and left the office, taking her servants with her.

Epilogue

When Maxham entered the room above the noisy tavern, he was surprised to see the doctor hovering near Jack, who sat at his dressing table. Jack looked highly annoyed, but he was trying to very carefully draw a ladybug over the scar on his cheek, and so couldn't respond as he might have otherwise to the man's presence.

"Ah, Mr. Maxham." The doctor greeted him with an unctuous smile. "How fortunate you just arrived. I received a message from Dr. Ward."

Maxham didn't know what irritated him the most—the fact Ward insisted upon calling himself a "doctor," or the fact that *this* doctor insisted on referring to him with the appellation.

"I didn't realize you were so close to Ward," Maxham said in an even voice. No, he realized, the most irritating part was that Ward was speaking with this scraping and bowing insect rather than directly with Maxham or Jack.

"Oh, you know, simply correspondence between two men in the medical profession."

Jack laughed so hard that he snorted. Then he ground his teeth and snarled at himself in the mirror. "I ruined my ladybug!" He picked up a rag and scrubbed so hard at his face that his scar began to bleed, the red streaking into the green and white makeup on the rest of his skin. It wasn't that difficult to make his scar bleed—he scratched at it so often that it was practically an open wound.

Maxham refused to ask the doctor what Ward had said in his letter, so he crossed to the other side of Jack's dressing table and dropped in a chair. "Does the fact that you're here mean that you finally finished the new Root formula?" he asked Jack as he set on his knee the drawing pad he'd brought with him. He flipped to a page and continued working on the picture he'd started, using a slate pencil to draw light, short lines.

"Ugh-hngh," Jack said, reapplying white makeup.

"Did you test it yet?"

"Of course," Jack snapped. "It works perfectly."

"As perfectly as the last batch?" the doctor asked in a snide voice.

Maxham gave the doctor a flat look, although he had been about to ask the same thing.

"It works very well now." Jack again picked up a narrow-tipped brush to draw on his face. "Nick was very helpful."

The calmness in his tone convinced Maxham that he had indeed figured out how to stabilize the Root elixir that had been causing problems. He worked on the drawing without speaking, knowing the doctor wouldn't be able to remain silent for long.

"Dr. Ward's letter was quite refreshing," the doctor finally said. "He has made progress."

"If he had," Jack drawled, dabbing red on his cheek, "he wouldn't still be at his laboratory."

Maxham glanced up in time to see the doctor's neck redden, but the man continued, "Oh, that reminds me. Dr. Ward asked me to ask both of you if you've found the notebooks yet."

The tip of Maxham's pencil snapped.

Jack gave the doctor a baleful look, what a cobra might give to a mouse. Then he continued dabbing at his face with the paintbrush. "Ward is too focused on those notebooks," he muttered irritably.

Maxham took out his pocket knife and sharpened his pencil.

"I take it the answer is no?"

Neither Jack nor Maxham bothered to answer him.

The doctor sighed. "Dr. Ward will be so disappointed."

"Then he can come to London and look himself, rather than tinkering uselessly in his little house," Jack said.

Facetiously, the doctor asked, "By the way, how are your hybrids coming along, Mr. Dix? Have you found the one you need yet?"

Maxham himself knew that Jack had wildly changeable moods, but even he was surprised by the naked fury in Jack's face as he suddenly shot to his feet, his eyes burning like coals as they glared at the doctor. His slack fingers dropped the paintbrush on the wooden floor.

Lately, the doctor had seemed to be pushing his luck when it came to Jack, which Maxham didn't quite understand or trust, but the man wasn't suicidal enough today to remain here when he'd put Jack in such a mood. He gave a stiff nod of his head and scampered out of the room.

Jack gave a gusty sigh, then dropped heavily back in his chair, making the front feet jump up an inch or two before settling back down on the floor. He reached down and picked up the paintbrush.

For several minutes, the only sound in the room was the muted voices coming from the barroom downstairs. Maxham finished sharpening his pencil, then moved his chair closer to the lamp on Jack's dressing table so he could better see his drawing.

"Zephyra probably has them," Jack muttered.

"The notebooks?" Maxham's pencil darkened a line on the page. "If she did, she wouldn't have stayed hidden. We'd have heard from her by now."

"We wouldn't have *heard* from her. Instead, she'd have

planted a knife in my back. Or your back. Or Ward's back. I think she must be a very strange girl because she didn't even particularly *like* her sister."

Maxham regarded him incredulously. "Are *you* really calling Zephyra 'very strange'?"

Jack gave Maxham a wide, toothy grin. Then he noticed the drawing pad, and jumped to his feet, running around the table to peer down at the page.

"Hmm ..." Jack tilted his head as he stared at the drawing. "You'll never have your work hung in the Royal Academy, but you're not bad."

"I have no such pretensions," Maxham replied.

Jack took one last look at the page before heading back to his seat. Over his shoulder, he told Maxham, "His eyes were farther apart."

Connect with Camy

I hope you enjoyed *Lady Wynwood's Spies, volume 3: Aggressor*! I honestly waffled a bit on the title for this one. Originally it was *Lady Wynwood's Spies, volume 3: Rage*, but that didn't match well with the subtitles for volumes 1 and 2, and so I eventually settled upon "Aggressor" because of the violence that Thorne must struggle against when he is exposed to the Goldensuit pollen.

As I'm writing this, *Lady Wynwood's Spies, volume 2: Berserker* just released, and I posted on my blog a recipe for the treacle buns that have appeared in both that book and also in this one (https://blog.camytang.com/2021/02/treacle-buns.html). If you enjoy cooking, I hope you give them a try!

The story continues in *Lady Wynwood's Spies, volume 4: Betrayer.*

If you haven't yet, I invite you to sign up for my email newsletter (https://bit.ly/lady-wynwood). After a few welcome emails, I send out newsletters about once a month with a sale on one of my books, a freebie, or news about when my latest release is available.

Camy

Made in the USA
Middletown, DE
30 January 2024